MURDER IN THE SECRET MAZE

After a whirlwind romance and a glorious wedding at the luxurious Hotel Santa Sofia, Tory Benning is ready to let down her hair, slip into her dancing shoes, and celebrate—until she discovers that her newly minted husband has vanished. The police suspect cold feet and second thoughts are behind Milo's disappearance, but Tory's certain he's met with foul play. And since she designed the plush resort, she knows every nook and cranny of the grounds and adjoining secret maze, and wastes no time delving into her search.

As clues begin to emerge that Milo may have taken his last breath in the maze, Tory steps up her sleuthing, even as she learns she's the prime suspect of a cop with a chip on his shoulder and is squarely in the sights of a menacing stalker. And when a second body is found on the grounds, Tory fears she's up against a killer determined to silence any and all who get in the way.

Not to be deterred, Tory forges ahead, navigating a case with more twists and turns than the maze itself, until the labyrinth of clues leads her to shocking revelations about her husband, her family, and the identity of a killer who's dead set on making her the next victim . . .

Title Page

MURDER in the Secret Maze

Judith Gonda

Judith Gonda Books

Copyright

Murder in the Secret Maze
Judith Gonda
Judith Gonda Books
are published by
Judith Gonda Books
www.judithgonda.com

Cover design and illustration by Dar Albert, Wicked Smart Designs

ISBN: 979-8-9941464-1-5

ACKNOWLEDGMENTS

Writing is a solitary activity but to get a book published takes a village.

First and foremost I want to thank my wonderful, encouraging family, who are my world: My husband, Victor Regnier, an architect, professor, and author himself, who has provided me insights into the design world of my main character, inspired me with his work ethic, supported my writing, literally and figuratively, and who serves as my best publicist. My two daughters, who never doubted me. My daughter Jennifer Regnier, a landscape architect, was an invaluable source of material about my main character's profession as well as being an unflagging cheerleader and an astute reader to keep my thirty-something protagonist real and authentic. My daughter Heather Regnier, a screenwriter phenom who always provides the best critical notes that hit the nail on the head, honest and straight shooting, yet always kind and super encouraging. Also, my son-in-law, Matt Dines, an entertainment industry development executive whose words of encouragement and upbeat attitude sustain me and lift my spirits. And to my late parents, John and Marge Gonda, who always instilled in me the belief that the sky's the limit if you put your mind to it. And finally, to my two little Pomeranian pumpkins, Izzy and Ollie, who "help" me write every day by keeping me company and making me take regular walking breaks.

I also have so much gratitude for having the best agent, Dawn Dowdle. From the moment I first spoke to her on the phone, her positive and enthusiastic attitude was contagious. Not to mention her excellent editing and advice. As if that wasn't enough good fortune, I was then lucky to get Bill Harris as my first editor. Bill epitomizes positivity, encouragement, and graciousness, and, like Dawn, is brimming with good advice and insightful editing. Icing on the cake was getting a talented cover artist, Dar Albert. And special thanks to Beyond the Page Publishing and Jessica Faust for championing writers.

Thanks also to the writing community, wow, what a generous and supportive group, especially my fellow BRLA authors, past and present. I want to thank all the helpful writers I've met online, mainly through Brenda Drake and her Pitch Wars events, who have offered advice, reviews, and encouragement. Thanks also go to Patrick McDonald at QueryTracker, who feeds and nurtures writers in the query trenches. I'm also grateful to all the great writers I've met through Sisters in Crime, Guppies, Mystery Writers of America, and International Thriller Writers, all so generous and eager to give advice. To all the agents and editors I've met along the way who gave encouragement. And a huge thank-you and big hugs to all the readers who buy my book (and leave reviews). I hope my book entertains you.

CONTENTS

About the Author

CHAPTER 1

Instagram Post @ToryBenning: MILO IS MISSING! #MissingPerson
#SantaSofia This is a photograph of my husband, Milo Spinelli. He went missing earlier today, Saturday, September 30. If you follow my account, you know today was our big day—Milo and I tied the knot at two this afternoon in a beautiful Hotel Santa Sofia ceremony surrounded by our family and friends. By three, Milo was missing. He never made it to the reception. Milo's 2017 red Fiat, CA plate ARCHTCT, is also missing. His colleagues at Chandler Architects have always known Milo to be responsible and reliable and are concerned by this uncharacteristic behavior, as am I. Anyone who knows Milo knows he would never leave his beloved cat, Otis, without making arrangements for its care. I'm asking your help to spread the word and hopefully someone will know where he is. Milo is six feet two, has a slim build, has short brown hair and eyes, and is clean-shaven with an olive complexion. He has dual American and Italian citizenship and speaks fluent Italian and English (with a British accent, since he was educated in England). His left earlobe has a tiny scar from a former piercing. He was last seen wearing a black tuxedo with a white shirt and black bow tie and black dress shoes. He also had a pale pink rosebud and succulent boutonniere pinned to his lapel. Thanks for your help. Tory.

I fought back tears as I stared at the photograph of Milo I'd just uploaded to Instagram. I'd taken it last night at the rehearsal dinner. He was beaming his million-dollar smile, dazzling pearly whites, and twinkling eyes. We'd both been giddy with joy.

I couldn't believe this was happening. My heart raced with the speed of a hummingbird's fluttering wings, so fast it was almost as if it wasn't beating at all. I shook my head, not wanting to accept the inevitable conclusion—my husband was gone. My head pulsated in dull throbs as I struggled to reconcile what I'd known to be true with the surreal turn of the last few hours. I sat numbly, as if I'd been hypnotized, as I reflected on the day's events.

My wedding day started out as planned. In other words, it was pretty near perfect. Nothing more remarkable than my somewhat-of-a-diva hairdresser Philip taking longer than expected to primp the female members of the wedding party, which numbered two, my BFF since elementary school, Ashley Payne, and myself.

"Splendid, my love! You're going to be the most beautiful bride ever." Philip darted around me like Tinker Bell, squirting what I hoped were the last bursts of hairspray to my long blonde curls he'd spent the last half hour artfully tousling. Today, Philip had pulled his shoulder-length hair into a man-bun, hence the Tink reference. His abundant hair wasn't limited to his shiny black mane. Black hair covered his arms and chest, escaping out of his rolled cuffs and unbuttoned shirtfront like the thick, dense growth of a Chia Pet.

My maid of honor, Ashley, hovered nearby. Both of us had spent the last two hours in the Hotel Santa Sofia bridal suite laughing and chatting. Preoccupied with working on our hair and makeup, Philip tuned in to and out of our conversation. When we moved into hour three, Ashley and I got anxious, conveyed through our eye rolls and eyebrow raises, both of us reluctant to trigger one of Philip's artistic hissy fits that would delay us even more.

Ashley raised her freshly manicured eyebrows, pointed to her elegant watch, and mouthed to me, "It's one forty-five."

I furrowed my brow and ever so slightly shook my head to warn her off pressuring Philip and making matters worse. Ashley flicked her head of bouncy black corkscrew curls that Philip had styled to perfection and cleared her throat a few times to try to catch his eye, but when Philip was in the zone, he was like a pointer scenting game, totally focused on its target prey, which, in this case, was my hair.

After a few minutes of purposely swishing her gown to get his attention without success, she finally blurted out, "Tory, the wedding planner needed you downstairs five minutes ago."

Philip's eyes flashed and he abruptly put his hands on his hips. "OMG, this is your wedding day. What is she thinking? I'm not going to cut corners on such a momentous occasion. That's simply ridiculous. What am I? A magician?"

Ashley and I exchanged nervous glances. I held my breath, expecting a rant.

But instead, a gurgling laugh escaped his lips. "Well then, I'd better hurry up. I don't want to ruin your big day." Although his enthusiasm was endearing, his smile only thinly veiled the message his steely eyes conveyed: don't mess with me.

Needless to say, Philip didn't like to be rushed. Normally, neither did I. But these weren't normal times. Two weeks ago my father, John Benning, had died in an accident. He'd fallen off the Santa Sofia pier and drowned. And just like that, my world changed forever. I was now an orphan. Granted, a thirty-three-year-old orphan, but an orphan nonetheless. Since then, I'd been numb. Which, truth be told, had its benefits when it came to the hectic swirl of wedding planning. I didn't think I could have even functioned had it not been for the love of my life, Milo Spinelli, the rising-star architect who'd stolen my heart four months earlier. Milo convinced me to go on with our wedding plans because that was what my father would have wanted. He was right. Nothing had ever daunted John Benning, head of Benning Brothers, the landscape design firm where I worked as a principal designer.

Milo and I met on a site visit for the Hotel Santa Sofia condominium project up the coast. I'd worn gardening clogs, not the usual fashion choice for a landscape architect. Even when meeting clients at dirt sites, I usually wore dressy boots or flats to project a professional image. But that day, since the other two proposals on the short list were also from award-winning firms, I'd decided to throw in some theatrics to make our presentation more memorable. Hence, the gardening clogs to represent the community garden we'd included in our design concept, a feature we hoped would mollify the anti-development activists by demonstrating our sensitivity to the needs of the surrounding neighborhood. I'd hoped our proactive move would impress the owners of Hotel Santa Sofia Properties. Even though we'd designed the gardens for their luxury resort, the Hotel Santa Sofia, three years earlier, I took nothing for granted.

The jury was still out on the status of our bid, but my clog stunt worked wonders for my love life, which, like Santa Sofia, had been experiencing an extended dry spell. Milo worked as the lead project architect for Chandler Architects International, the prime firm who'd invited Benning Brothers to be the subordinate consultant, a.k.a. the sub. Having an invitation to sub was always exciting, but having it extended by a renowned firm such as Chandler was like sprinkles on the cupcake.

We'd exchanged amusing emails and phone calls while putting together our proposal. Milo's low-key humor and penchant for puns made the proposal process so much fun I might have cyber-stalked him a bit to check his relationship status—for a friend. Maybe once, maybe ten times. Whatever. All I knew was, when I finally met him in person and gazed into those dark eyes, like pools of hot fudge, emphasis on the hot, I was a goner. He'd instantly swept me off my feet or, to be precise, my clogs. As I stepped forward on the rocky dirt and reached out to shake his hand, my foot slipped off my clog and I lost my balance. Before I hit the ground, Milo swept me into his strong arms. Our embrace was a perfect fit. Thereafter, we'd referred to our romance as love at first "site."

The following week we had our first real date and our relationship heated up quickly, again reflecting Santa Sofia's status, since wildfire season was upon us. We became inseparable after that. It felt like destiny. Neither of us had ever been happier, caught up in the vortex of a whirlwind romance. When my father died, it was Milo, once again, whose support broke my fall. He provided a strong shoulder to lean on and had gotten me through the past two weeks of utter shock and profound grief.

Philip grabbed another canister out of the twenty-odd ones he'd brought along and gave my hair a few quick bursts of glitter spray. More like pixie dust. Whatever it was, I had to admit Philip had worked his magic to transform me. I felt like a Disney princess. Yes, I had a master's degree in Landscape Architecture. And no, that didn't preclude my love of all things sparkly. What could I say? I was complex.

Gazing into the mirror opened a portal to thoughts of my father. He had been so looking forward to walking me down the aisle. My eyes got misty as I thought about how much I missed him on my wedding day. I still couldn't believe he was dead. How on earth did anyone fall off a pier and die, just like that, especially someone as athletic, fit, and sure-footed as my marathon-running father? Since all accidental deaths required an autopsy in Santa Barbara County, we were still waiting to hear the actual cause of death. Ashley, who had her own law practice, assured me that getting an autopsy performed would ultimately give me greater peace of mind. Knowledge helped with closure, she'd advised, and with any possible insurance or litigation issues that might arise.

"Perfection. *Now* you're done, Tory!" He removed the towel around my shoulders with a flourish and arched his eyebrow at Ashley.

Ashley waved her finger at him. "Hey, don't even start with me, Philip. I'm just the messenger."

Philip giggled with puppy-like enthusiasm and clapped his hands quickly. “You both look beautiful. Now, hurry!”

I scurried into the adjoining bedroom to quickly slip out of my white terry robe and into my wedding dress. Ashley fastened the last pearl button on the back of my lace gown as I stepped into my glittery Cinderella-like heels. She grabbed my hand and tried to pull me out the door, but Philip insisted on primping my layered tulle veil first.

Ashley tugged my arm. “Thanks, Philip. Girl looks gorgeous. Come on, Tory. You don’t want to be late for your own wedding.”

I turned around. “Thanks, Philip! Love you!”

“Love you, too, darling!” He blew me a kiss as Ashley yanked me down the hall.

I followed the blur of dusty rose chiffon, the pastel shade particularly flattering on Ashley’s light brown skin. Her gown rustled around her statuesque figure as she led the way through the carpeted hallway to the outside circular staircase, where we slowed to carefully navigate the narrow steps. We trotted around the stucco building and down a long outdoor corridor, the shady serenity broken every few yards by flashes of sunny brick courtyards and the sound of bubbling mosaic fountains. Taking care not to catch our gowns on the spiky succulents that overflowed from cement planters dotting the hardscape, we turned left down another arched walkway. A row of guest rooms, with carved wood doors, lined one wall. We turned where our path intersected a wider walkway and finally arrived at a shady portico with pink bougainvillea vines trailing up one side of its arch.

Hotel Santa Sofia’s Hidden Garden stretched in front of us. It had a special meaning to me because I’d designed it for the hotel’s recent renovation. Benning Brothers’ nursery division had planted the native, drought-resistant blooms I’d specified. When I first glimpsed my good-old-boy Uncle Bob, the other brother in Benning Brothers, who’d not only volunteered to walk me down the aisle but also agreed to grace his portly profile with a cummerbund, tears welled in my eyes. The last thing I needed were rivulets of mascara streaming down my cheeks. I tilted my head back slightly, took a deep breath, and told myself Philip would be crushed if I ruined all his hard work before I even made it to the altar.

I focused instead on the rows of white folding chairs on the lawn filled with our friends and family. With Pachelbel's "Canon" cued and my pink rose and succulent bouquet in hand, I glided along the white runner on my uncle's arm. At the other end of the garden, under an arbor adorned with white roses, ivy, and other greenery, stood Milo in his tuxedo, beaming at me. We recited our vows and exchanged rings, guests reached for their hankies, and we kissed and lost track of time and place for thirty seconds. Then, arm in arm, we marched down the aisle to the strains of Mendelssohn.

The ceremony had gone off as planned. We were hitched without a hitch. Even my Pomeranian, Iris, had behaved herself. We'd toyed with Iris being a ring bearer for about a minute. We put the kibosh on that genius idea once we realized unfamiliar settings triggered Iris's separation anxiety, manifested by obsessive barking, stemming from her past shelter days, and negated any obedience training she possessed, which wasn't much. To be honest, I was so attached to the little fluff ball that the thought of her not being there for my happy day triggered *my* separation anxiety. Our compromise was to let her observe from a front row seat in the warm but firm embrace of my neighbor, Katie Omstead.

Immediately after the ceremony, Simon, our chatty wedding photographer, steered the wedding party, which included Milo and me, Uncle Bob and Aunt Veronica, my cousin Sam, and Ashley, to a secluded garden alcove where we posed in various configurations. We were planning another celebration with Milo's whole family in Italy in a few months. After thirty minutes, Simon dismissed everyone except me, since we'd run out of time before the ceremony to take my individual poses. Normally, this change in plans would have stressed me out, but my father's death had put everything into perspective. So far I'd managed to compartmentalize my emotions for the day, focusing on love and not loss. I was grateful to have married my best friend. I was determined not to let an unexpected fifteen-minute delay bother me. My only concern as I skipped up the circular staircase to my suite afterward was that now I had less time to change into my dancing togs for the reception.

Soft strains of hip-hop music greeted me as I bustled into my room, where Philip stood over Ashley, lifting sections of her soft hair with a comb and wrapping them around a curling iron to refresh some of the curls. Ashley had changed into a silvery pink strapless minidress. She held court on a pale green damask love seat while sipping champagne from a crystal flute. She blew me a kiss. Another half-filled champagne glass sat on an end table.

Philip paused to hold up the bottle and offer me champagne. "Darling, the party has already started." A laugh gurgled from him before he resumed making Ashley even more beautiful.

"No thanks. Right now, I need to change."

I ran into the adjacent room. Off came my veil and gown and on came my frothy, snow-white chiffon reception dress with iridescent sequins. It felt good to feel less constricted in the shorter, flirtier dress. I went back to the other room, where Philip pounced on me with a comb and a triangular sponge. He flitted around me, still poking and pulling my hair and blotting my makeup as we all hurried back downstairs with a full minute to spare.

My phone vibrated with a text from Milo: *Taking Iris home because she's freaking out. See you in five.*

A tentative feeling of dread overcame me for a moment. Iris had seemed happy at the ceremony, sitting on my neighbor Katie's lap like a little princess. And why didn't Milo just bring Iris to me? She usually calmed down as soon as she saw me.

After considering the options for several seconds, I texted Milo back, *It's three. Where are you? We're waiting for you outside the ballroom. Just bring Iris with you.*

I turned to our stylish wedding planner, Helene, all dolled up in diamonds and a silver gray cocktail dress that matched her hair, and shrugged. Her personality was one part teddy bear, one part drill sergeant. Currently, she was a sad bear, with a furrowed brow and pursed lips.

I tried to reassure her with a confident lilt, "I'm sure he's on his way and will be here shortly."

She grinned quickly in response and then resumed her frown. After five minutes of phone checking had passed, Helene called Milo. When it went to voice mail, she left a message. "Helene here. Please call me back as soon as you get this. I need to know when you'll get here so I can plan accordingly. Thanks."

When she disconnected and our gazes met, I saw the expression of a doctor about to share bad news. She blinked her eyes slowly and looked downward.

I was still trying to figure out Milo's text about Iris. I looked at my phone as if doing so would make him text back. And then it hit me. What if he and Iris were in a car accident? It wasn't unusual for Milo to be late, but it was unusual for him to not respond to my text. He was a good driver, but Iris's separation anxiety caused her to lunge like a crazed hyena. I pictured her jumping in his face at an intersection.

The foyer was empty, except for Ashley, Helene, and me. And Philip, of course, who periodically swooped in with his sponge to blot my increasingly sweaty face, the first telltale sign of my visceral reaction that somewhere in my depths I sensed impending doom. Laughter and loud chatter escaped whenever a server opened the door leading to the Bella Mar ballroom, where we would be introduced as husband and wife for the first time. The cocktail reception scheduled after the ceremony had accomplished its mission of keeping the guests happy until they were fed.

The door to the ballroom swung open and my jaw dropped when my neighbor, Katie Omstead, strolled out with Iris on her bejeweled leash.

"Iris! Thank God!" I bent down as the little fur ball flew into my arms, nearly bowling me over with her kamikaze leap. "I've never been so glad to see you!"

Katie, elegant in black, threw back her head in laughter. "She's so happy to see her mama!" Strands of her neatly coiffed auburn updo fell softly around her face and her lightly freckled nose crinkled as she laughed. "Iris has been a very good girl."

"Where's Milo? He texted me he was taking Iris home because she was acting up."

The stunned look Katie gave me in response chilled me. Katie's eyelids fluttered and her mouth opened, clearly startled. "Excuse me? I haven't seen Milo since the ceremony. Iris has been with me the whole time. And like I said, she's been a very good girl."

Iris licked my hand relentlessly, as if to corroborate her story.

My mind started to spin out of control as I tried to process the disconnected information. Where could he be? Had he ditched me? It'd only been four months and he left? What else could have happened? Had he tripped and fallen somewhere? Had he taken ill? Was the text a lie? Was the text really from him? Was Katie mistaken? Was this a prank? What the hell was going on? I suddenly became obsessed with admiring the sparkle emanating from my engagement and wedding ring diamonds, scrutinizing their facets in the light, as if peering into a crystal ball, while I tried to make sense out of everything.

I checked my phone. Yep. He'd said he was taking Iris home. I showed it to Katie and Helene. "See? That's so odd. Why would he say that?"

Helene shook her head and Katie blinked quickly and shrugged. I was sure they were starting to draw the same conclusion as me.

Ten more minutes passed. Ashley and Philip were whispering to each other while I started to fidget with my rings more compulsively. *Where is Milo?* I texted him repeatedly, but he didn't respond. I called his phone and he didn't pick up. I looked at Ashley. She forced a faint smile, her dimples puckering her cheeks, but I saw panic in her hazel eyes. *Where the hell is he?*

When a full half hour had passed, Helene said we needed to make a decision about what to tell the hundred guests waiting to eat. With every passing minute, it looked like our rendezvous wasn't meant to be. I had a rock in my stomach as I considered the guests waiting next door with their champagne glasses poised to toast us. But just as the bubbly foam in their flutes disappeared into thin air, so had Milo. Our reception never took off. Milo, however, apparently had.

CHAPTER 2

I passed my phone with the draft of the Instagram post to Ashley. "Okay. How's this?"

We were back in the bridal suite huddled around a round glass table. I'd been editing the caption on the IG post for the last ten minutes. Philip had stayed downstairs with Helene to handle the guests in the aftermath of the realization that Milo was definitely gone. Where? No one knew. But gone he was.

Ashley studied the screen.

"Well? What do you think?" I leaned back in the peach-colored brocade side chair and crossed my legs, sniffling.

She looked up solemnly and handed my phone back. "Looks good to go."

"You don't think I'm overreacting? Should I wait a couple of hours?"

She rested her hand on my shoulder. "Definitely not. In missing person cases, the first couple of hours are critical. It's not like he had anywhere else to be. It was his own wedding, for God's sakes."

I took a deep breath and hit the "Share" button. I checked to make sure it showed up on my account. It had. And it had also posted to Facebook. It was real now.

"Okay, done. I'll post the link to Twitter later." I was hoping that the wider audience wouldn't be necessary.

"No. Do Twitter now too."

"Okay."

Ashley squeezed my shoulders. "Good. Now, let's go look for him. Where do you want to start?"

I thought for a minute. "I don't know. I guess retrace our

steps from the last time we saw him? Where we took the wedding photos."

Ashley, my biggest cheerleader throughout our shared history in grade school, high school, and college, where we were roommates, jumped up and high-fived me. "All right! We have a plan. Let's go back to where Simon took the wedding photos after the ceremony."

Stopping only to grab our purses, we hightailed it to the hotel garden area. We took the Secret Maze shortcut, a labyrinth of pathways bordered by ten-foot hedges. I'd designed it for the Hotel Santa Sofia's renovation, and it led from our wing to the Hidden Garden, an expanse of lawn surrounded by impatiens and begonia flower beds and azalea, camellia, gardenia, and night-blooming jasmine plants. We'd opted not to waste time changing out of our wedding outfits but now found ourselves regretting that decision, since we were shivering in our short flimsy dresses as the sun started to go down and the fog crept in from the ocean. Plodding through the twists and turns of the gravel and dirt path in heels hadn't turned out to be a fun choice, either.

Ashley held my arm lightly as I led the way. "You sure you know where you're going?"

"Are you kidding? I designed this baby. I could figure out the fastest route in my sleep."

"What about in the dark?"

"It's not dark yet. It's just the shade from the tall hedges. Calm down." But even as I spoke, the dimming light, like my bravado, began to fade, making it increasingly hard to see where I was going.

Ashley spoke quickly and verged on hysterical. "Okay. FYI, it's official—I think I'm claustrophobic. It's like a jungle in here. Who knows what type of wildlife is roaming around hungry—"

"Oh, stop!"

I didn't need any of her negative thoughts. I had enough of my own. But she had a point. It was kind of creepy in the maze and, though hardly a jungle, Santa Sofia was home to a diverse wildlife population, many nocturnal, including coyotes, raccoons, possums, skunks, and even mountain lions, but I didn't want to stoke Ashley's fear. The dense hedges were three feet wide and shut out the light and connection with the other pathways, making us effectively isolated from other humans, but not from any critter worth its salt, especially when recent wildfires had caused them to come into more populated areas in search of water, shelter, and food. Although we could hear voices when someone was on the other side, we couldn't see anything. For all I knew, an unseen predator might be silently stalking us on the other side of the thick hedges, waiting for the right moment to pounce through the dense foliage to seize their next meal, in other words, Ashley and me.

As it turned out, around the next bend we did come face-to-face with a predator, but he was of the human, creepy stalker variety. Standing before us reeking of garlic was Santa Sofia Police Department (SSPD) sergeant Ernesto Gomez, my old middle school classmate who'd been obsessed with me in seventh grade. According to several mutual acquaintances, he'd never really gotten over my rejection, nor any female rejection, for that matter, because he had zero empathy. It never occurred to him that the reason we all rejected him was that being stalked twenty-four seven by a mouth breather with the social skills of a turtle was intimidating to a thirteen-year-old girl. Ernie never perceived himself as the problem, as demonstrated by his badmouthing of any girl who'd rejected him. Nevertheless, career-wise his bravado had served him well and was put to good use intimidating criminals and impressing police department higher-ups since he was rising through the ranks quickly. Any time I ran into him he tried to hit on me, and when I would once again rebuff him, he'd resume a surly attitude. I stopped short and Ashley, on my heels, bumped into me.

Ernie leered at us expectantly. "Well, well, well. Look who we have here, the jilted bride."

He might just as well have said "Gotcha." I forced a weak smile. "Hi, Ernie."

"And her jilted bridesmaid." Ernie raised his bushy eyebrows up and down at Ashley.

I swung my arm back to keep Ashley from attacking him on the spot. "I only wish the explanation for Milo's disappearance was that simple. I'm worried something bad has happened to him."

Ernie had always reminded me of a cold fish, literally and figuratively. He had a cold-blooded, reptilian vibe going on. He had no chin to speak of, a feature his constantly gaping mouth only accentuated.

He gave me a lurid smile as his gaze roamed my body. "Yeah, I saw your Instagram post. That's why I'm here checking things out."

Ashley broke through my block. "The only thing I see you checking out is Tory." Under her breath she added, "Some things never change."

I'd always suspected Ernie had gone into law enforcement for the wrong reason, more for the power than for the nobler calling to protect and serve. Already our brief interaction had confirmed my worst fears. I believed in giving people the benefit of the doubt but, dude, my eyes were up here.

Ernie's smile faded. "Why do you think something bad has happened to your husband? Did he have any enemies?"

"None that I know of."

"Who would want to hurt your husband on his wedding day of all days?"

I shook my head. "That's just it. I don't know. He never mentioned any jealous ex-girlfriends."

He moved closer to me. "You know, I would never leave you on your wedding day."

Ashley stepped up. "Really? Are you trying to hit on her when her husband has just disappeared?"

Ernie furrowed his brow.

"Ernie's not hitting on me, are you, Ernie?" I tried to salvage his pride by denying the obvious only because I needed his cooperation.

He shook his head and glared at Ashley. "But you suspect foul play?"

Heartened by the thought he might actually be of help, I forced an ingratiating smile. "I do."

"Why exactly?"

"Because we had plans for our future together. We had reservations to fly to Italy to celebrate our marriage with his family. We'd lined up a realtor to sell his town house. We were looking ahead and we were in it for the long term together."

Ernie scratched his head. "Hmm. Would anyone profit from his death?" He scrutinized me with a mean squint. "What about a will? I'm assuming you're the main beneficiary."

Ashley moved in between Ernie and me. "What about it?"

Ernie threw her a sly smile. "I was wondering if he had one, and if he did, who benefited." He gave me the side-eye.

Ashley had helped both Milo and me with legal matters recently and, in fact, we'd both had wills drawn up and had designated each other as beneficiary.

Ashley stood up straighter. "Don't say another word, Tory. As her lawyer, I must insist you set up a formal interview if you want to ask my client any questions regarding her husband's disappearance. Come on, Tory. We have a real investigation to conduct."

Ernie sputtered for a few seconds. "I'll call you to set up an appointment. Make sure you don't leave town. I could always extradite you, you know."

Ashley tugged on my arm as she pushed by Ernie. Once we'd moved out of earshot, she stopped. "Okay, you lead the way. I have no idea where I'm going."

I took the lead. "I can't get over Ernie. Where does he think I'm going to go? Italy?"

"Well, you did mention you were planning on going there."

"Oh, yeah. You're right. Shoot! I need to cancel the tickets."

Great. As if I didn't already have enough to worry about, the last thing I needed was to have to deal with Ernie and his insinuations. Ernie's words echoed in my head. Even Ernie wouldn't have left me on my wedding day. What did that say about Milo? Had Milo had second thoughts? Was I an idiot for searching for someone who might have purposely left me? Or did he have an enemy he'd never told me about? If he did, what had Milo done for someone to hate him enough to possibly harm him? I shivered at the thought a dangerous person might be at large. For the next few minutes, Ashley and I marched onward through the maze in silence as I struggled to get my mental turmoil under control.

Ashley clung to my arm. "Are you positive you know how to get out of here? Wild animals pale by comparison to being lost in this maze with Ernie."

I chuckled. "I think Ernie's the one who should worry. You were fierce back there."

"Thanks."

"Don't worry about getting lost. We're good. I promise. Just keep your eyes open for anything out of the ordinary. Maybe Milo dropped something. I don't know what we're looking for really. Just be observant."

My gaze roamed the ground, straining to see something, anything, that would give me hope. I really wasn't hoping we'd find Milo on the ground. The whole host of morbid scenarios that conjured up made my knees wobbly just thinking about them. I started to tremble, nevertheless, and tried to convince myself it was the cooler temperatures of the late afternoon rather than my visceral reaction to the shock of Milo's disappearance. Probably both, but despite freezing and feeling like I'd been shot in the heart with a stun gun, my brain geared into overdrive.

Where the devil is Milo? And why did he lie about Iris? It was bad enough he was gone, but he knew how attached I was to her. Why would he give me the scare of my life and make me think they were both missing? That was just plain cruel, and so unlike him. Whatever the reason, I had a sinking feeling I couldn't deny. Not only figuratively, but literally. A stretch of the maze had turned into a quagmire. With each step, the heels of my Cinderella slippers sunk into the squishy dirt underneath the gravel pathway. I continued the rest of our journey on tiptoe as I silently swore at the hotel groundskeepers for over-irrigating during a drought.

The Secret Maze had three outlets: one that led to the wing of the hotel where the bridal suite was located, one that led to a small parking lot, and the one we now approached that led to the Hidden Garden, where we'd had our ceremony. The nomenclature of Secret Maze and Hidden Garden was a bit misleading, less a literal reference and more a branding attempt to conjure up the wonder of childhood adventures, since both were in plain sight for anyone who visited the hotel grounds.

Ashley stopped abruptly. "Wait a minute. Did Milo ever go into the Secret Maze? What's the point of trudging through here if he never went here?"

My thoughts flashed to the moment days before when I first introduced him to the maze. He'd marveled over every detail I pointed out. I'd shown him all the little cubbyholes carved into the dense hedges with platforms and feeders for birds and squirrels, inspired by Iris's crazy squirrel obsession. We hadn't encountered any squirrels, but Milo had spotted a tiny hummingbird nest the size of a walnut shell hidden in one of the recesses.

"Yeah, we took the maze shortcut to our suite this morning from the parking lot."

Ashley lowered her head and squinted at me. "Are you okay?"

"What?" I gave her a wistful smile. "Yeah, I'm fine. He thought it was cool."

"Good. I just wanted to make sure I wasn't out here freezing my butt off for nothing."

I laughed as I picked up my pace.

"Hey! Can you slow down? I'm having a hard time keeping up with you in this tight dress. Last thing I need is to lose *you*."

"We can't linger too long. We won't be able to see as well once the sun goes down."

When I stopped and turned around, she was tugging at her

dress.

"Can't you just hike it up while we're in the maze? It's not like anyone is going to see you." I suppressed a chuckle as I resumed leading the way.

"Ouch!" Ashley swore under her breath.

"Now what?"

"I just kicked something."

I spun around and looked at her feet with her pearly pink toenails peeking out of her sandals. I didn't see anything at first. I scanned my phone's flashlight around the area and gasped. "Oh. My. God. It's a phone." I bent down to pick up the muddy phone and became lightheaded as I stood up. The screen looked like someone had smashed it with a hammer.

Ashley caught her breath. "I swear my toe didn't do that."

"It's not that. It's an iPhone with a blue case. It's Milo's phone."

Ashley's eyes widened. "Are you sure?"

"How many people do you know who have a blue iPhone cover like this?"

Ashley gulped hard, registering her agreement. "I wonder how it got here?"

"I don't know. But dropping a phone would never cause this kind of damage. Look at it—it's destroyed. It doesn't make sense unless he was trying to hide something."

Ashley shook her head. "Hold up. You're jumping to conclusions. Ruining your own phone like that doesn't make sense. It could have gotten smashed in a fight. I bet someone else did it. Looks like they were real mad too."

Our gazes locked.

I took a deep breath. "Okay, so let's say Milo cut through the maze to go back to the hotel after Simon took our group shots and ran into someone who was enraged for some reason and they smashed his phone to smithereens, then what?"

We both exchanged a frightened look as we realized at the same moment where this was heading. And it wasn't good.

My voice quavered. "Why would someone smash his phone

so violently?"

Ashley shuddered. "Maybe they wanted to send a message."

"Like what?"

She nervously fidgeted with her dress and spoke hesitantly. "Um, I don't know. Maybe to warn us off trying to find Milo or—"

I grasped her arm and leaned in closer, trying to get her to speed it up. "Or what? Stop skirting the issue."

Her eyes flickered and the corners of her mouth rose and fell as we both realized my unintended pun.

"Okay." She inhaled slowly and then exhaled. "Or we'll end up like his phone."

I hated to admit it. But I had to agree.

CHAPTER 3

Ashley scoured the gravel-covered ground looking for more clues. I dropped Milo's iPhone into my shoulder bag and almost immediately my upper body tensed. I felt like I was carrying the emotional baggage equivalent of an anvil. I was positive it was Milo's phone—I could feel it in my gut, and my gut feelings usually served me well. The last time I trusted my gut was when I met Milo, and that wound up being the best relationship of my life. Now my gut feelings were telling me something bad had happened to him. After seeing the devastating damage someone's violent act had had on his phone, it wasn't a big stretch to imagine how that same violence might look if directed toward him. I quivered at the thought.

Ashley stretched and adjusted her dress. "These heels and dress are killing me." The sides of her mouth turned up, forcing a weak smile, but her eyes froze in mortification. She crouched down again, her head hung in awkward embarrassment. "Sorry. I wasn't thinking."

Clearly she was thinking about Milo possibly being dead or killed. And yet I was the one she accused of jumping to conclusions. "That's okay." I patted her shoulder. "But let's not go there quite yet. If something bad happened to him, it doesn't mean he's necessarily dead. Although, if the dude ran off with another woman, I might be tempted to kill him."

"Um, tell me how you really feel. But I agree with everything you just said. Our imaginations are in overdrive and we might be getting ahead of ourselves." Ashley laughed lightly. "That being said, I wonder if someone smashed the phone here or somewhere else. They could've flung it over the hedge from another pathway. What do you think?"

I chuckled. "So much for considering other possibilities. But good call. We should probably check out all the maze pathways to see if there are any clues there. The more I think about it, I don't think it was smashed to send a message as much as to destroy evidence."

Ashley straightened up and wiggled her dress into its proper position. "You mean his phone log and text messages?"

I nodded. "Yeah. I think the intent was to wipe out a record of who Milo had been talking to—especially right before he disappeared."

"Like a kidnapper?"

"Yes, maybe."

"So you think someone took him for a ransom?"

"Right now, that's my hope, given the other possibilities."

"But why didn't they take the whole phone with them and dispose of it somewhere else?"

"I don't know. I'm free-associating. Trying to consider all possibilities. If he was kidnapped, maybe his kidnapper stepped on it accidentally and got flustered and was afraid of being caught with Milo's phone on them."

Ashley pulled her face into a sad pout. She rearranged a few wayward curls of mine like a mama cat grooming her kitten before resuming her search for clues, cursing at her tight dress as she crouched down again.

"Look, Tory, over here!" She pointed to a big rock in the shallow gully at the foot of the hedge. Her voice was breathless with excitement. "I bet that's what someone used to smash the crap out of his phone."

The light gray rock was about the size of my open hand. I imagined it would be easy to grip and use to smash a phone. Or hit someone. It was big, smooth, and oval—and out of place in the maze. The only other rocks in the maze were the small ones in the pea gravel covering the pathways. I caught my breath when I realized why this larger rock looked so familiar. Rocks like this decorated the base of trees that bordered the Hidden

Garden. I knew because I was the one who'd specified them. Landscape architects favored them for trim and borders. Their smooth, clean look lent a Zen-like quality to gardens—the exact opposite of what it now represented, violence.

I inspected it without picking it up or touching it. "I don't think we should touch it because—"

"Fingerprints?"

"Exactly. I don't know whether it's possible to leave fingerprints on a rock, but I don't want to mess them up if you can."

Ashley stood upright. "I doubt it, but they might be able to get DNA evidence."

We both took pictures of it with our phones. I moved to the opposite side to take some shots from a different angle. When my flash went off and spotlit the rock, my heart sank.

I squeezed Ashley's wrist. "Please tell me that's not blood on the rock."

Ashley knelt down, using her phone's flashlight, and let out a whistle. "Holy crap. That's what it looks like." She grabbed my hand and stood up. When our gazes met, I saw fear in her eyes and she hugged me. She pulled back and held my gaze. "You need to file a missing person's report with the police as soon as possible and tell them about the smashed phone and bloodstained rock."

I nodded in sad agreement, hating the turn our search for Milo was taking.

"And by police, I mean someone who is smart and fair-minded, pretty much anyone other than Ernie."

I took a deep breath and forced myself to push on. "Okay. I'll call Adrian right now."

One of the benefits of living in a small town was you were likely to know someone, or someone who knows someone, in practically every city department, from the mayor's office to the police department. Adrian Ramirez was another old classmate of ours who was currently a police sergeant bucking for lieutenant. If there were a bell-shaped curve of decent stand-up guys, Adrian would fall on the right, above-average tail of the graph, whereas Ernie would find himself on the left-side tail at the lower end of the distribution. My rankings were based on years of observing their behavior and interacting with them from kindergarten through high school. Since Santa Sofia was a small town with slim pickings on many counts, Ashley and I had spent our four high school years chasing after the same few good guys. Adrian was one of those guys so, consequently, we'd both briefly dated him, and by "dated" I meant we hung out with him at the strip mall opposite our school. We'd ended up becoming good buddies with him but lost touch when we'd all graduated and moved on to college. Ashley had since lamented to me, during a particularly maudlin happy hour session, ironically, that she viewed Adrian as the one who'd gotten away.

The operator at SSPD took my name and number. I didn't give her much of a backstory other than I was an old friend of Adrian's and needed to talk to him ASAP regarding a missing person. She said he was on another call and she'd give him my message.

"Hopefully he'll call me back soon. In the meantime, let's continue our search. I don't think anyone will disturb the rock since it's tucked under the hedge in that little drainage ditch."

Ashley nodded. "For sure, Ernie won't notice it. Wouldn't even if he tripped over it."

I opened the Notes app on my phone and made a list of clues: Milo's smashed phone, rock used to smash phone, possible blood on rock. My hand quaked as I typed the last entry.

We continued on the maze path that led to the Hidden Garden. Ashley chattered away about another dress online she wanted to get for the upcoming firefighters benefit, which was being held at the Hidden Garden in a couple of weeks.

"The sequins are already coming off of this one. I'm leaving a trail." She chuckled and paused for what normally would've registered a giggle from me. "The one I saw online is made from a black stretchy material. Just in case I need to take a hike in a maze again."

"Let's keep our eyes on the ball, shall we? I can't even hear myself think with your constant banter." *Man, I sound mean and bossy.* When I spun around to look at her, her eyes were downcast. "God, I'm sorry, Ash. I didn't mean to come off so snippy. But we need to focus. I'm trying to reconstruct in my mind all of our movements today to see if I remember anything that seemed out of the ordinary."

Ashley kept her gaze averted. "Sorry. I was trying to lighten things up. I get super talkative when I'm stressed."

"You? Talkative?" I smiled sheepishly. "I'm the one who needs to apologize. I get super cranky when I'm nervous."

She was silent.

I mock glared at her. "Nothing? Really? Not even a 'You? Cranky?' Come on, Ash. I'm sorry. It's called fear."

She threw her arms around me and we hugged tightly.

"Forgiven. We're both in stress city right now. We've got to cut ourselves some slack and be kind to each other and ourselves. Deal?"

"Deal." I headed forward again. "Just a few more bends and we'll be at the Hidden Garden."

Moments later we emerged from the maze. Groundskeepers were stacking the folding chairs on gurneys, dismantling the arbor, and loading potted palms onto wheelbarrows. We traipsed over to the little alcove a short path away from the Hidden Garden, where Simon had taken our photographs and where I'd seen Milo last.

"There's nothing here to see except grass," Ashley said.

"Not quite." I rushed over to the trees around the perimeter. "See. The same rocks as the one in the maze. This is where whoever smashed the phone got the rock. They're identical."

"Wow. Good work, Sherlock."

I took some photos of the rocks. "What should we do now?"

Ashley scrunched up her face in concentration. "Well, we should check yours and Milo's place, but that's on the other side of town. And his office is downtown. How about we start here and drive around the neighborhood around the hotel first and look for his car."

"Good idea."

As we passed the groundskeepers stacking the chairs again, one of them, a weather-beaten sinewy man in a cap and a hooded jacket, quickly threw down a cigarette butt and stomped it out with his foot as soon as he'd made eye contact with me.

I smiled. "Hi there. How are you doing?"

His strength and ease of hauling and loading chairs made me think he was around forty. But as I got closer, his weathered face made him look at least a decade older. I guessed years of smoking and working outdoors without sunscreen had aged his face. The rest of the groundskeepers lifting chairs looked younger, so I assumed he was the supervisor.

He tipped his hat. "Howdy."

"You haven't seen anything unusual today, have you?"

He gave Ashley and me, in our frothy cocktail dresses, the once-over. "You referring to the missing bridegroom?"

I nodded.

"Yeah, heard about that. Weird as heck."

"Did you or any of your workers see anything odd?"

"I didn't see anything unusual, just the regular hotel employees and vendors. Hold on. I'll ask my men." He called to the three guys stacking chairs and rattled off a question in Spanish. Two shook their heads.

A third man I guessed to be in his late thirties stepped forward. "Hi, I'm Octavio. I heard men arguing in the maze after the ceremony."

I sucked in a breath. "You did? Wow. Did you see who they were or hear what they were saying?"

"No. I couldn't see them. They were real angry by the sound of it. I was walking through the maze to the patio cocktail party. One of the heavy potted palms on the patio needed to be moved. The vendor had already left, so they called me to move it. Potted palms are pretty but their wide fronds can get in the way if they aren't in the right position. They have to be arranged like this." He extended his arms to his sides. "Not like this." He extended one arm in front and one in back. "That way they don't poke people."

I nodded quickly, hoping he'd wrap up the Potted Palms 101 lecture and tell me more about what he'd heard.

Benning Brothers had supplied all of the plants for the wedding. Jed Barnes, our head nursery guy, should have checked on the palm placement. Jed was an excellent foreman and he usually was sensitive to plant placement at parties. But since he was also a wedding guest today, I figured once he started drinking, the only thing potted he'd been focused on was himself.

"Then what?"

Octavio's eyes glistened. "At first I heard two men arguing through the hedges. I couldn't see them because the hedge is thick. I heard one guy say 'Give it to me' or something like that. I didn't hear anything after that until one guy shouted 'Where is it?' The other guy told him to calm down."

He paused and stared at me.

I waited a good thirty seconds before prompting him again. "And then what happened?"

"Nothing."

"Nothing? You didn't hear anything else?"

"That's all I heard. I had to get to the patio for—"

"The potted palm. Right."

Ashley put her hand lightly on my arm. "Thank you so much, Octavio. Here's my card. I'm a lawyer. If you think of anything else, please give me a call."

She steered me back toward the maze.

I turned back to Octavio. "Thank you!" I tugged on Ashley's arm. "What's the rush?"

"As a wise woman once said to me, we have to keep our eye on the ball."

"Touché, but I *was* keeping my eye on the ball. He was probably a witness to Milo arguing with whoever smashed his phone."

"I know, but he's already told us everything he knows. He has my card if he thinks of anything else. That way we avoid another infomercial on potted palms and go look for Milo before the sun goes down. I call that a win-win."

"I guess you're right." Right now, the thought of sitting down anywhere had high appeal, but especially my Lexus with its heated seats. My reception outfit had turned into a torture chamber. My spaghetti strap dress gave me as much coverage as a Kleenex and my Cinderella slippers squeezed my toes like they were in a vise. "Okay. We can take the shortcut through the maze to the parking lot."

"Ugh! The maze again? This time I'm holding on to you the whole way."

My phone buzzed. "The caller ID says SSPD. I bet it's Ernie. But what if it's Adrian returning my call? What should I do?"

"Don't answer it. Let it go to voice mail. If it's Adrian I'm sure he'll leave a message and you can call him right back. Nothing good will come from talking to Ernie right now. Put off an interview as long as possible. I wouldn't put it past that little worm trying to pin Milo's disappearance on you as a murder just out of spite for rejecting him in seventh grade. It won't help once he finds out Milo's will names you as the primary beneficiary. He'll call that your motive."

"But that's absurd." My phone's voice mail icon indicated a new message. I put it on speaker as we listened to Ernie ask me to call him.

Ashley rolled her eyes. "Not to him it won't be. Like I said, nothing good will come from talking to him."

"I would never even think of hurting any living creature." Except spiders. If a spider ventured inside my house, game on.

"I know that, but perception is what counts. I could see him arguing that it seems like once you married Milo, you killed him but made it look like he left of his own volition."

"That seems counterintuitive. Why on earth would I do that?"

"Simple. To deflect attention from your insurance windfall."

"Let me get this straight. You think Ernie might say I killed

Milo for his insurance money but made it look like Milo skipped town? But then I wouldn't get the payout if he wasn't dead anyway. That makes no sense."

Ashley stared blankly. "True. But my point is he's going to use Milo's will against you somehow. Mark my words." She paused and a smile formed. "Honestly, I think he's still in love with you and just likes engaging with you. That and since you've rejected him multiple times, he's now in a position of authority over you and it's payback time."

I chuckled to myself. Ashley was a highly rated attorney, but she had a habit of letting her imagination run wild when she was stressed. "Okay. I don't know about that, but I'll keep dodging his calls if you think that's best for now."

Ashley grasped my upper arm. "Good girl."

After a series of meandering turns through the maze, we exited onto a brick sidewalk. We leaned against each other, balancing ourselves as we brushed the mud off our shoes. We followed the sidewalk to the small remote parking lot shrouded in tall hedges, where Milo and I had parked our cars earlier in the day. We'd checked the lot earlier before confirming his disappearance to our wedding guests.

What had won Benning Brothers the Hotel Santa Sofia renovation bid was our design concept for several small parking lots instead of one big one to preserve the resort's residential feel. I gazed at my ground cover choice, the carpet-like moss *Dichondra repens* peeping out between the brick pavers, and reflected on the irony of the tall hedges, back when the only feelings they'd evoked had been privacy and seclusion. Now the parking lot, like the Secret Maze, seemed almost sinister, its remote and isolated nature providing the perfect setting for a crime.

Dusk was hastening upon us, and the motion-detector parking lot lights flipped on as we proceeded to my car. My black Lexus SUV was now the only car in the otherwise empty lot.

I turned to Ashley. "I was so flustered when we rushed here earlier and discovered his car was gone. We need to make sure we didn't miss any clues."

I stood in the space where Milo's car had been parked next to mine and walked around, hunched over like a camel, searching for what, I didn't know. "Aha!" I pointed to what looked to be a fresh muddy footprint on the bricks near where the driver's side of Milo's car would have been. I aimed my camera phone and took a few shots. "Look. A footprint with treads, like a boot or athletic shoe. Milo was wearing his dress pumps, so this isn't his footprint, unless he changed into a different pair of shoes." It was someone else's footprint. I was sure of it. But whose?

Ashley muttered "uh-huh" and wandered off, pacing around the perimeter of the lot and scanning the ground. She turned back periodically to look where Milo had been parked. "Tory, come here. This strip of ground cover looks like something dug it up recently. Where cars have driven over the ground cover, it's flattened. This is different."

I examined the top of the sod. Something had ripped it out and exposed the mud underneath it. The remains of little leaf parts dotted the brick.

"Hmm. Looks like tire marks, but they're too narrow for a car tire." My gaze roamed the area nearby. "Look. There are more of them. The same marks on the sod." They formed a trail that led from the maze entrance to where Milo's car had been parked.

Ashley took out her phone and snapped some shots. "Yeah. Maybe a bike?"

"Maybe. It looks kind of wide for a bike, though, unless it was an old-school bike."

"Okay. We've got a footprint that isn't his and someone on a bike. Both point to another person. So, either Milo drove his car or someone else did."

Lightheadedness overcame me as reality seeped in. I tuned out for a moment, floating in an emotional limbo, wishing I could press a reset button to the morning again. My mind drifted back to a couple of months earlier, before my father had died and when Milo was still my fiancé, when my life had been near perfect. But now? No father. No husband. What was next?

Ashley continued on her manic quest to inspect every square inch of the lot while I leaned against my car, praying I didn't lose consciousness.

"I don't see any security cameras, but they must have them, right?" When she got closer to me, her jaw dropped. "Oh my God. Tory, are you okay?"

I took a few deep breaths and exhaled slowly. "I'll be fine."

"Are you sure? Because your face matches the color of your dress right now."

My exhaled breath ended with a spurt of laughter. "Um, thanks? Just felt woozy for a couple of seconds. I'm okay now." I grasped her hands to steady myself and motioned with my head to a nearby light pole. "Look. That's a security camera up there. We recommended them all over when we did the renovation. I'm not going to lie, I'm so grateful to my past self right now."

"Don't the security guards monitor the live feed? They'd have noticed any criminal activity."

Criminal. I shuddered. The thought of foul play floated in my brain. Reading about or watching reports of violence in the news was one thing. To think that someone had possibly committed a violent act against someone I loved, my husband of thirty minutes, was a whole different ballgame, and it scared the daylights out of me. I trembled as I visualized someone striking Milo's phone . . . and then him.

Ashley bobbed her head of 'fro curls around in front of me. "Look, his missing car is physical proof he's gone. Tracking down a car might be easier than tracking down a person. It's bigger and harder to hide. Hopefully, if we track down his car, we'll find him. What do you think?"

"I think we should call the police and give them the car's description."

Ashley punched in a number on her phone. "I'll call Adrian's personal cell."

She left a message referencing Milo's disappearance and missing car.

"You have his number on speed dial?"

"Doesn't everyone?"

I smiled. "Still carrying a torch for him?"

She gave me a meaningful look and smiled slightly. "Maybe. Okay, let's forge ahead and see if we can track down Milo's car. We can ask the hotel about the security camera footage when we get back."

We climbed into my car. I buckled up and called Milo's cell phone, forgetting we'd found it smashed and it was in my purse. I was officially living in a *Twilight Zone* episode. I called his landline one more time with no luck. "Should I trace the route to his town house first?"

Ashley fastened her seat belt. "Since he's not answering his home phone, I'm assuming he's not there. Why don't we circle around the hotel neighborhood first as we'd planned?"

"Right." I followed the narrow drive out of the parking lot and merged onto the main ring road around the hotel. "I'm going to focus on driving safely, Ash, so you're the main lookout."

"Okay. Good plan. Last thing we need is an accident."

"You know what's funny?"

"What?"

"Before we found the phone and the rock, my worst fear was that Milo had gotten into a car accident and was lying injured in a ditch somewhere in his mangled Fiat. That, or he'd had second thoughts and had taken off with a new girlfriend. But now . . ."

Ashley patted my shoulder gently.

A tear, then two, ran down my cheek. "But now it's probably worse than either of those. I just feel awful not knowing where he is. What happened to him? Did he get kidnapped or murdered? I can't deal with not knowing."

"I'm worried too. Let's try to keep positive."

Taking Ashley's advice, I fantasized we'd see Milo rolling into the lot. He'd greet us with a merry wave, his disarming smile, and a plausible explanation for his absence. He'd express profound regret for worrying us. My relief would wipe out any anger. I prayed for his safe return, vowing to be a nicer person if we could just find him safe and sound. I'd be grateful and all would be forgiven. I just wanted things to go back to the way they were yesterday.

After forty minutes of cruising the surrounding residential and commercial neighborhoods and entering and exiting the ramps of the 101 freeway, the main artery that ran through town, connecting San Francisco to Los Angeles, there was still no sign of Milo or his car anywhere.

I let out a sigh of frustration. "How about we backtrack now. Maybe we'll notice something when we're coming from a different direction."

We were in a residential neighborhood south of the hotel that didn't get a lot of traffic, so I made a U-turn at the next intersection. As I did so, a car a couple of car lengths behind me made the same move.

"Uh-oh."

Ashley threw me an alarmed look. "What?"

"The car behind us just made a U-turn too. I think we're being followed."

CHAPTER 4

Ashley turned around. "Oh my God. Is Ernie going undercover now? He's out of control. He can't just stalk you. We're not in middle school anymore."

"Um, I'm pretty sure he can follow me because he's a cop, but I don't think it's Ernie."

She twisted around to take another look and her eyes widened. "Then who? How do you know they're following us?"

"It's the same car again."

"What do you mean 'again'?"

I alternated my gaze between the road ahead and my rearview mirror. "I've been noticing a white car following me for the last week or so. I've been so busy with work and the wedding that I'd forget about it . . . until I spotted it behind me again. I'd mentioned it to Milo. He didn't think it was a concern."

"Whoa. Hold up, girl! I don't give a fig what Milo thought, but you're telling me you've been followed for a week by the car that's following us right now and you thought nothing of it?"

"I didn't want to overreact. I didn't think I was in danger. It reminded me of Ernie following me in high school and look how that turned out. Now he's a cop. I'm not positive it's the same car, but it sure looks like it."

"That's all you've got? You never got the license plate?"

"How could I? I was driving. You try. Easier said than done."

Now that I focused on it, it was kind of scary to think someone was watching me.

Ashley twisted around in her seat to check on the car. "It's too dark to get a good look. What's the probability of another car making a U-turn right here in the middle of nowhere?"

"I don't know. Why would anyone want to follow me? What should we do?"

She reached for her phone. "Maybe we should call Adrian again."

I rolled my eyes. "We already have two calls into him that he hasn't returned. I have to tell you, so far, I'm not impressed. Maybe we should just call SSPD proper and bypass Adrian."

"Right. And risk getting someone like Ernie who's eager to jump to the it's-always-the-wife conclusion so they can easily solve the case? Adrian might not be perfect, but as long as I've known him, he's always been a decent guy who's fair and open-minded, in other words, pretty much the opposite of Ernie. And before you get all judgey, when was the last time you saw Adrian? I hadn't seen him in ages until I ran into him at a restaurant the other day. He looks even better than I remembered. He was short in high school. Now he's tall, in addition to dark and handsome." She paused briefly to giggle. "Anyway, he probably hasn't called you back because he's busy catching bad guys. You don't move through the ranks of the SSPD as quickly as he has without being a good cop."

My aching body and fuzzy mind had drained me of the energy to argue and point out that I hadn't mentioned Adrian's looks, and that since Adrian and Ernie were both sergeants, either Ernie must have been doing something right or his bad behavior had been rewarded. Whatever. Milo vanishing had begun to take its toll. "Say no more. I'm convinced." I pulled over to make the call.

Ashley screeched at me. "What the heck are you doing? Don't stop! Are you crazy?"

"Why?"

"Because he can get us."

I looked up to see the white car speeding off in the distance. "You mean the car that just took off?"

"Oh." She chuckled. "Never mind."

"So, it definitely was a guy? You got a look at him?"

"I think it was. Hard to tell because they were wearing a

hoodie."

"I'll wait until we're back at the hotel to call Adrian again. Just to make you happy."

"Thank you."

I turned onto the Promenade, the coast road that led back to the hotel and, eventually, to downtown Santa Sofia. The Hotel Santa Sofia was a five-star luxury resort destination for the rich and famous, but the city of Santa Sofia itself was somewhat more modest, having a small-town yet sophisticated charm. An artsy community located on the California coast, it was almost equidistant between Los Angeles and San Luis Obispo. Of its two main drags, the Avenue was where most of the commercial enterprises were situated. Originating in the surrounding foothills, the Avenue cut through the center of the upscale boutique-lined downtown, past the gourmet eateries and fancy galleries, and dead-ended at the beach. There, it intersected with the Promenade, the coast road where the Hotel Santa Sofia and its adjacent Beach Resort were located along the stretch that housed a few smaller boutique hotels. A bicycle lane ran parallel to the Promenade. As we barreled along, we passed cyclists and the last of the food trucks packing up for the day. Other than an outlying regional mall and a smattering of strip malls, there wasn't a lot else going on in Santa Sofia. If you were looking for excitement, you'd have better luck a short distance south in nearby Santa Barbara.

Back in the hotel parking lot, Ashley groaned as she got out of the car. I wasn't the only one mentally and physically spent after our fruitless search. We both trudged up the spiral staircase to my suite in silence with slumped shoulders.

When I opened the door, Philip was curled up in an armchair checking his phone. "Hello, my dears! Any news?"

Ashley filled him in on our maze findings.

He sprung up and gave us each a big hug. "You poor dears. I've called all the area hospitals. No reports of Milo anywhere."

A wave of emotion suddenly hit me again, and I fought back tears.

Philip guided me to a chair. "Oh my goodness, my darling. You've been on a roller coaster of emotions today. You must be exhausted. Come. Sit. Have some tea and something to eat."

A white ceramic teapot emblazoned with the hotel's iconic gold HSS and hummingbird logo, a smaller pot for water, a large creamer, and four cups were arrayed on a large tray set on a glass-topped table. On the desk, a fruit platter and a plate with cheese and crackers lay untouched. Philip had totally tidied up the suite. The last time I'd seen my wedding gown, it had been on the bed where I'd tossed it when I changed. Thankfully, Philip had garment-bagged both my wedding gown and Ashley's bridesmaid gown so I didn't have to see them. Philip followed my gaze. He gave me another bear hug.

I punched in the SSPD number on my phone. "I'm going to try Adrian one more time."

This time I reached him and put the call on speakerphone. I brought him up to speed about everything I could think of relating to Milo's disappearance. Just hearing Adrian's confident voice calmed me down.

"We'll put out a BOLO on Milo's car."

"BOLO?"

"Be on the lookout. We'll keep a lookout for anything related."

"Got it."

"I'll let you know what time tomorrow I can get over to the hotel to take a look at the maze and the parking lot. It would be preferable if you could meet me and show me exactly where you found the phone and tire tracks."

"Okay."

"If you're followed again, next time try to get the license plate number or take a photo of the car that was following you."

Ashley threw me a smug told-you-so smile and nodded knowingly.

"I'll try. It all happened so fast. It was gone before either of us had a chance to."

Ashley gave me the side-eye.

"Meanwhile, come down to the station tomorrow morning, and I'll help you file an official missing person's report. And bring Milo's phone."

Adrian advised me to keep calling around to all the hospitals in the area. "We've done everything we can at this point. Now all we need to do is just sit tight and hope Milo contacts you. And try not to worry."

"Unfortunately, I think that's impossible right now. Thanks so much."

I glanced at my phone's screen with all the messages. "Ugh! I can't deal with everyone's questions right now when I don't know the answers myself."

Philip grabbed my phone and perused the list of callers. "I'll handle the phone calls and relatives, Tory. You and Ashley focus on the search."

I hugged him. "Thanks, Philip. You're a doll." I wrapped my arm around Ashley's and pulled her toward the door. "Let's go to the security office and try to get the video surveillance tapes."

Ashley tugged at her reception dress. "I need to go back to my room to ditch this dress first. Be right back."

My eyes must have revealed my irrational panic at the thought of her leaving.

Ashley patted my hand. "Promise."

"Be careful, please."

"I will. You should change into more comfy clothes too."

"Okay. But hurry."

She nodded and gave me a wink.

I rummaged through my suitcase. No long pants, only a pair of shorts. I grabbed them and a top and headed to the bathroom. After I changed, I sipped some tea Philip had poured for me. The warm liquid was comforting and perked me up. True to her word, Ashley was back in no time, dressed in skinny jeans and a sweatshirt. She made a beeline to the desk and started to graze on cheese and fruit.

I grabbed a long cardigan and pushed my arms through the sleeves. "Okay. Ready? Let's go."

Philip touched my arm gently. "When was the last time you ate, my dear? Eat something. Please!"

I popped a couple of grapes in my mouth to appease him and gave him a quick hug before going out the door.

The Spanish-styled main building and bungalows of the Hotel Santa Sofia luxury resort were set on a sprawling twenty-five-acre site with lush gardens and lawns. In addition to its white stucco façades and red-tiled roofs, the property was peppered with colorful accent tiles, carved wood trim, wrought iron, and numerous fountains and courtyards.

Ashley and I jogged along the main walkway to the lobby that led us past one of the pools, a courtyard, and a fountain with a cupid holding a fish. The tiled lobby of the main building had a high-vaulted ceiling and was flanked on one side by a casual restaurant, El Colibri, that shared a brick patio overlooking the Pacific Ocean with Burbujitas, a cocktail lounge. The Mar Vista, an expensive seafood restaurant noted for its stellar chef and a Sunday brunch buffet to die for, was located on the other side of the lobby and featured an ocean-facing veranda that stretched across the front of the hotel.

An attractive young black woman was on duty at the front desk. She wore a dark green blazer with the iconic Hotel Santa Sofia hummingbird insignia on the pocket. She politely directed us to the hotel security headquarters, down a short hallway from the lobby.

"Security" was painted in black block letters on a frosted glass-paneled door that opened onto an outer office, where a stocky female security guard sat behind a large wooden desk. She had tight blonde braids bobby-pinned in a tidy crisscross fashion across her head. According to the tag pinned to her pocket, her name was Officer B. Brockett.

"Good evening! How can I help you?"

"Hi. My husband is missing and I was hoping we could take a look at the video from the security camera located in the parking lot on the south wing near the Secret Maze."

Ashley chimed in. "Actually, we'd love to see footage from

any and all the cameras you have."

The friendly smile disappeared from Officer Brockett's face. "Not the missing groom from the wedding?"

I mustered a weak smile. "I'm afraid so."

She shook her head and clicked her teeth. "Sorry. Yeah, I heard about that." She clicked her teeth again. "We can only release our videos if the authorities request them."

"I've already reported my husband's disappearance to the SSPD. Well, actually to my friend who's an SSPD cop. You might know him, Adrian Ramirez?"

The woman guffawed in delight. "You know A-Ram? He's an old buddy of mine from the academy."

I wondered momentarily why their career courses had diverged in different directions but told myself I could try to find out another time, in less urgent circumstances.

Officer Brockett stared into midair, clearly reveling in her memories. "Ha, ha. Yep. Good times." She turned her attention back to me and lowered her head conspiratorially and signaled us to lean in. "I'll tell you what. Rather than wait for SSPD's formal request, I'd be happy to send A-Ram the video. How's that sound?"

Her unexpectedly helpful response caught me off guard. "Oh, that would be wonderful! Thank you so much." I gushed words of gratitude a while longer, overcome with emotion. I loved this woman for being so nice. "I'm sorry. It's been a hard day."

Her eyes creased softly and her lips melted into a sympathetic smile. I felt she looked at me the way one looked at a rescue puppy—any shortcomings were overlooked because of its sad plight. "My pleasure. I'll try to get it over to A-Ram tonight. Good luck!"

I left the security office feeling more hopeful.

Ashley whispered as we walked away, "A-Ram? Puh-leese!"

"Do I detect some jealousy?"

"Who? Me? Nah. I just think it's hilarious. I haven't heard that nickname since high school."

We checked out of our rooms and wound our way to the parking lot through the Secret Maze. I swung my suitcase and garment bags into the back of my SUV and climbed into the driver's seat deep in thought. I sighed with relief as I buckled up, happy to be heading to a reunion with Iris and the comfort of home. But I was sad to leave without my new husband. I called my next-door neighbor, Katie, who was pet-sitting Iris, to let her know I'd be home soon. Ashley followed me in her black BMW as we returned to my cozy bungalow on Mariposa Drive on the outskirts of town. My home's architectural style mirrored that of the Hotel Santa Sofia's private bungalows, as did its drought-tolerant landscaping, one of the reasons I bought it four years ago. I also loved its location—only a couple of blocks from the beach.

My headlights lit the stucco and tile roof of the garage as I pulled up in my driveway. Katie must have been on the lookout from inside her bungalow. Her front door flew open as I parked and she hurried across her lawn, holding Iris. Katie handed Iris, limbs flailing, to me through my open window.

"Hi, Iris! I'm happy to see you, too, sweetie. Thanks so much for watching her. Can you say thank you to Aunt Katie for keeping such a good eye on you?"

Iris was on her haunches, trying to lick my face.

Katie giggled. "My pleasure. Any time. She's such a good girl, aren't you, Iris?"

Iris wiggled around in agreement.

Katie started to leave. "Any word on Milo?"

I frowned. "Not yet, unfortunately."

She gave me an exaggerated sad face. "Well, I hope he turns up safe soon."

"Me too. Thanks."

I slung my handbag over my shoulder, gripped Iris, and opened the car door. Ashley parked on the street and reached my car as I struggled out of my seat. She helped me unload my suitcase and two garment bags from the back of the car and carry them inside.

Iris bucked to be let down. "Wanna go outside?"

Ashley giggled, watching Iris howl approval and dance around my legs as I walked over to the back door.

"Off you go. Burn off some energy."

I'd barely cracked open the door before she'd shimmied through it like a contortionist and zoomed away.

I turned around to inspect my home, finally resting my gaze on Ashley. "I wonder if Milo left anything here to indicate that something was going on."

"Hmm. Like what?" Ashley parked her purse on the kitchen counter and hopped on a stool.

"Oh, I don't know, maybe a business card, a receipt."

I glanced around the house. All of Milo's possessions that were kept at my place, his toothbrush, some clothes, some shoes, seemed to be have been undisturbed and in the exact same spot he'd left them before the wedding.

I shook my head. "It doesn't look like he came back here. Let's go over to his place and check things out. I should check on Otis anyway."

Otis was Milo's black cat. He'd shown up one day, out of the blue, nibbling on some goldfish crackers left outside on a deck table. I'd urged Milo to name him Otis after one of my favorite childhood films. I was well aware that movie Otis was a pug, and fiancé Milo most certainly wasn't an orange tabby cat. But, come on. How often did a Milo and Otis name pairing opportunity come around?

Iris trotted back inside, panting, and made a beeline to her bowl. While she lapped water voraciously, I scooped an eighth of a cup of kibble into her other bowl. Two years prior, Iris had been a parasite-ridden rescue dog, orphaned when her owner died. She didn't bark for the first two months I had her. Today, she sported a thick, shiny coat, along with a healthy bark. After she finished off her dinner with a Greenie, I broke the news I was leaving again. Iris paced around nervously and jumped on the back of the sofa to watch me through the big front window.

As I followed Ashley out the door, I turned to Iris. "I'll be back soon."

Ashley and I drove in my Lexus a few blocks west to Milo's town house overlooking the ocean. Moonlit waves licked the shore and sea spray was diffused in the air. I used my key to open the door.

I ventured over the threshold, holding my breath, still in shock my wedding night had taken such an unexpected and surreal turn. The open floor plan provided an overall view of the whole first floor. I sighed, relieved to not find Milo's body anywhere. His computer was on the kitchen island. I opened it and typed in the password, my birthday.

After a few minutes of skimming his emails, a soft meow broke my concentration. Otis had graced us with his presence and was rubbing against my leg.

"Hi, Otis. I bet you miss your daddy, huh? Don't worry. We're working hard to find him, aren't we, Ashley?"

Ashley shrugged and played along. "Um, yeah, we are, Otis." She leaned over my shoulder. "Find anything interesting?"

"No."

Ashley snooped around. "I've only been here a couple of times before, but everything looks normal to me. It's neat and orderly. Why don't you take his computer and you can look at it later."

"Good idea. I agree. It doesn't look like he returned here, but we haven't checked upstairs yet."

I took a deep breath and tiptoed up the circular metal staircase to the upper level. A white down comforter was spread out over his king bed as I assumed he left it the previous evening before he came over to my house. A circular indentation still warm told me where Otis had been curled up prior to our arrival. Nothing was glaringly awry here.

Ashley ambled over to the bathroom and ventured in. She emerged seconds later, her arms stretched out in cop mode, a long-standing parody we performed, whether to signal safety in dark alleys or spider eradication in bathtubs, that never failed to amuse us both. "Clear."

A laugh escaped my lips. "Thanks. I needed a good laugh. That one never gets old."

We went back downstairs. I retrieved Otis's carrier from a closet and a bath towel from a cabinet. I unzipped the carrier and nonchalantly walked toward Otis with the towel. In a quick two-step maneuver, I threw the towel over the cat then bundled him into the carrier, towel and all. I zipped it up as a muffled meow bellowed from inside.

"What was that?" Ashley chuckled.

"That was the element of surprise." I picked up the carrier in one hand and the computer in the other. "Do me a favor and grab his food, please."

As we headed out the door, both of us with our hands full, I glanced on the ground. "Oh, no."

"What?"

"Milo's boutonniere."

"Yeah, what about it?"

I put down the carrier and bent down to pick up the boutonniere. "What's it doing here?"

Ashley sucked in air and her eyes widened with surprise. "He came back here?"

"Sure looks like it." I dug my phone out of my purse and added boutonniere to my list of clues. I felt less helpless having a list. It gave me the perception of control in the emotional chaos his disappearance had created.

We packed my car with Milo's computer, Otis in his carrier, a bag of kitty kibble, his litter box, and two bags of litter without uttering a word.

I closed the hatchback. "I don't know what to make of it. If he came here, that means he's okay, right?"

"Unless someone else dropped it here."

I shook my head in disbelief. "That doesn't make any sense, though."

"Make sure to mention it to Adrian tomorrow."

I locked up Milo's town house and we drove back to my house, with Otis wailing in the backseat the whole way. Just as I pulled up to drop Ashley off at her car, Adrian called on my car speakerphone.

"I wanted to let you know I got the hotel surveillance video. I see you met my old pal Barbie."

"Barbie?"

"Yeah, Barb Brockett, a.k.a. Barbie." He laughed. "Everyone at the academy had a nickname."

"Like A-Ram, huh?"

He exploded with laughter. "Man, no one's called me that in ages."

Ashley piped in. "Except Barbie."

Adrian chuckled. "Yeah. Payback for the rest of us calling her Barbie."

"Before I let you go, we were just at Milo's place picking up his cat and computer and found something odd—Milo's boutonniere."

"From the wedding?"

"Uh-huh. Do you think that means he's okay?"

"I honestly can't say at this point what its significance is. Let's just call it another piece of the puzzle. Oh, and bring the computer tomorrow too. I'll have my tech person take a look at it."

"Okay. Anyway, thanks so much, Adrian. See you in the morning."

Ashley gathered her handbag and opened the door. "That was quick. Props to Barbie for keeping her word."

"Can you come with me in the morning to file the missing person's report?"

Ashley smiled. "One of the perks of being your own boss is not having to ask permission to take time off. And tomorrow's Sunday, anyway. How about I pick you up around eight and we can go for coffee first?"

"Sounds like a plan. See you in the morning."

CHAPTER 5

The next morning Iris woke me with soft little barks. When I didn't rouse immediately, she jumped around on the bed and barked louder. Otis, who hadn't uttered a peep all night, started meowing in response to Iris's barks.

Otis and Iris had hit it off amazingly well the night before, even without Milo's usual presence to handle Otis and intervene if necessary. After initial curiosity, the animals both went their separate ways. As a precaution, I kept Otis in the bathroom overnight. Whatever the reason for the lack of drama given that Otis's person was absent, I was grateful. I attributed their harmonious reunion to them both being rescue animals. Iris had been in foster care with many other dogs and cats after being plucked from the shelter. Otis had been winging it on the mean streets of Santa Sofia. I imagined both were thankful to have happy forever homes. In return, they were both behaving themselves, being gentle and peaceful, like emotional support animals. I was sure they sensed my distress, and I was grateful for the comforting distraction they provided to keep me from totally obsessing on Milo's disappearance.

"Hold on, guys."

I found my Uggs and pulled them on, cueing Iris to progress to shrill barks and herky-jerky posturing with her butt in the air. I caught her midair as she leapt kamikaze-style off the bed. Perhaps I'd spoken too soon. I let Otis out of the bathroom. He loped out and jumped on my bed.

"Come on, Iris. Let's go outside."

Back inside, we resumed our morning routine—coffee for me and kibble for Iris and Otis at opposite ends of the kitchen.

I checked my phone. My social media posts about Milo had garnered a lot of responses. As I skimmed them, most were sympathetic and encouraging, but no leads. I scanned my text messages. By the looks of it, Philip had done a good job getting back to all my friends and family and answering their questions. All their latest messages were expressions of love and support. A rush of gratitude for Philip filled me with warmth.

I jotted off a quick text to him: *TY. Bless your heart.*

• • •

Ashley picked me up and we drove to Starbucks on the Promenade since it was on our way to the police station. The coffee shop was packed inside, but we nabbed a table outside on the patio. I pushed the faux-fur-trimmed hood of my black puffer vest off my head, settled into my metal chair, and took a sip of my nonfat latte. Ashley, looking her usual polished and understated self in a dark green sweater, matching leather jacket, jeans, and suede booties, gulped her pumpkin spice latte and smacked her lips with exaggerated relish, making me chuckle. A half hour earlier the icy morning air had been cold enough to make steam when we spoke. Now it was comfortably brisk and by noon it would be warm enough for a T-shirt and flip-flops. Temperatures would peak around two and then recede again until dawn tomorrow, when the whole process would repeat. Welcome to October in Santa Sofia.

I fumbled for the lip balm in my purse. "My lips are super chapped. I blame the Sundowners and the Santa Anas." Both the Sundowner and Santa Ana winds were associated with high temperatures and low humidity and were the bane of Southern California. The Sundowner winds occurred mainly in the Santa Barbara area, whereas the Santa Anas occurred primarily around Los Angeles but lately wreaked their havoc as far north as Santa Sofia. Both were notorious for fanning the spread of wildfires in Santa Barbara County.

Ashley reached into her large tote. "Yep. Mine too." She held up a tube. "I love this new lip balm—so good." She smeared it on her mouth and smiled.

I nodded. "Nice. Let me write down the brand name so I don't forget it." I opened the Notes app on my phone and then, bam, back to grim reality. My last entries from yesterday clobbered me hard: *Smashed phone, blood-stained rock, footprints, tire marks, boutonniere.* I started to tremble, despite the climbing temperatures.

Ashley leaned closer. "You're shivering. Do you want to go inside?"

I mustered a brave smile and sighed heavily. "I'm afraid my shivering can't be fixed that easily." I held up my phone for her to see. "When your Notes app has a list that sounds like it's from the game Clue, it's pretty sobering."

"Aw, I'm sorry you have to go through this, Tory."

"Thanks. Me too. I guess my five minutes of denial are up for the day. Onward in the quest to find Milo."

She pointed at my phone. "Don't forget to add the white car."

In an attempt to banish my fear and anxiety, I took a deep breath and tried to think of things I was grateful for. Fire season was upon us, and any morning without a hint of smoke in the air was a good morning. I was grateful the arsonists who'd been literally playing with fire in the Santa Sofia foothills had put down their matches for the moment.

Ashley reached over and patted my hand. Matte mauve polish adorned her nails. "Never hurts to take a break for a few minutes. Allows all your emotional synapses to recharge—or something like that."

"Yeah, I guess."

She played with the heat sleeve on her cup for a few seconds, moving it up and down and then aligning its fit as if organizing her thoughts. "Hey." Her eyes twinkled impishly, her long black lashes framing her light hazel eyes like the points of a star. "Would it be too stereotypical if we stopped by a donut place and picked up a dozen for Adrian and his crew?"

"I don't know. It would depend on how much they like

donuts. How about we circumvent a possible offensive gesture and bring them some donuts and muffins from here instead?"

"Sold. I love one-stop shopping. You wait here. I'll go get them."

Out of habit, I flipped through my Twitter feed. Our local news station was reporting a new fire, arson suspected. I shook my head in dismay—so much for catching a break. I clicked to my emails. Hotel Santa Sofia Properties notified me the winner for their condominium project would be announced in a few weeks. That was so long to wait. My stomach churned with nervous anticipation that turned into high anxiety as soon as I realized Milo wasn't around to share the excitement about our joint project.

Ashley returned with a couple bags of goodies. "Want yours now or later?"

"I'll wait, thanks."

"Me too. I never dunk and drive."

"Yeah, you definitely don't want to get pulled over for dunk-driving."

Ashley and I exchanged silly grins as we headed back to her car. We drove along the Promenade up to where it intersected with the Avenue. We continued east and turned right on Juniper. We drove two blocks along the tree-lined side street until we reached a quaint one-story adobe building, home of the Santa Sofia Police Department. We parked in the adjacent lot.

The female officer at the reception desk alerted Adrian we'd arrived and buzzed us into the locked area of the station. There, another officer directed us to a cubby where Adrian, in full uniform, sat at his large metal desk.

Ashley set the bags of pastries down. "We thought you might be hungry."

Adrian's face folded into a broad smile. "All for me?"

Ashley pulled a glazed donut from one of the bags. "No, they're for everyone." She took a big bite out of the donut to punctuate her statement.

Adrian's warmth waned. "Stereotype much?"

His sarcastic tone suggested we'd insulted him. Great. Now we'd offended the one guy who could help us most.

Ashley's eyes bugged out—she looked mortified and swallowed quickly. "Not just donuts. Look. We got croissants and muffins too."

I held the other bag open, tipped toward Adrian. "We wanted to give you a variety. See?"

Adrian threw back his head and laughed before he pushed back his chair and stood to greet us, his muscular six-foot-plus frame towering over us. "I'm just messing with you." He leaned in and lowered his voice. "Actually, I love donuts, especially glazed."

Ashley cast me a look of relief.

He peeked into both bags and extracted a glazed donut and napkin and set it on his desk. "They all look great. Thanks, guys. Very sweet of you to think of us."

Adrian showed his gratitude by hugging me, then Ashley. Ashley's hug lasted a little bit longer than mine. She looked over his shoulder at me, the corners of her mouth stretched into a smile as she threw me a satisfied look, her eyes sparkling with delight.

I smiled back and then turned my attention to the baked goods, debating the pros and cons of croissants and donuts, and settled on a mini raisin bran muffin.

Adrian took a bite of his donut. "Mm, so tasty." He washed it down with a swig of coffee. "Sorry. I haven't had a chance to view the surveillance footage yet. I've been swamped. Let's watch it together now."

I finished my muffin in two bites, wiped off my hands, and reached in my tote bag for Milo's phone and computer, both of which I'd placed in plastic bags. "Here's Milo's computer and his phone we found in the maze. It looks totaled to me, but I'm sure one of your tech peeps will rise to the challenge."

"Thanks, Tory. Wow. Whoever did this wasn't fooling around."

I shuddered upon hearing him confirm my own opinion.

Ashley chimed in. “I thought it was to send a message but Tory thinks it was to destroy evidence. What do you think?”

“You both might be right.” He inspected the bag. “Hmm. I don’t see the SIM card.” He looked at us. “You didn’t find a SIM card on the ground near the phone?”

I scratched my chin. “You mean the little chip with all the data?”

“Yeah. The SIM card, micro SIM card, or nano SIM card, whatever the latest iPhone model uses.”

Ashley shook her head. “Nope. I didn’t see anything else.”

I stared upward, thinking back to when we found it in the maze. “No. I don’t remember seeing anything else either. So, wait. Then his phone isn’t much of a clue without the SIM card, right?”

“Not necessarily. We might be able to get prints or DNA off of it.”

I felt like Adrian was just trying to make me feel better.

“Ready to take a look at the surveillance video?”

We gathered around his desk as he inserted the flash drive into his computer.

“Ready.” I reached for Ashley’s hand.

Ashley glanced at me and squeezed my hand. Her main attention was directed at Adrian. Her eyes creased into a softened expression like she was looking at cute baby animal photos online. I wasn’t surprised Ashley was still crushing on Adrian. They were a lot alike. Both had kind hearts and a strong sense of justice. Both were equally attractive. But their timing had always been off. There had always been college, the police academy, law school, or other relationships preventing them from getting together as adults.

As soon as Adrian clicked on the screen, Ashley’s lovey-dovey eyes were gone, replaced by her resting lawyer face—steely stare and pursed lips—a warning to not mess with her, a look she developed during her five-year stint as a Santa Barbara County public defender before she opened her own law practice.

We watched the black-and-white footage. A person in a dark

hoodie approached Milo's car. From the angle of the camera, it was impossible to tell whether it was Milo or even whether it was a male or a female, let alone see their face. I held my breath, wondering if we'd be able to get a better look to see who it was. And then the tape went blank.

Adrian tried refreshing the video. But it was soon apparent the problem wasn't the computer. Ashley and I exchanged eyebrow raises.

I squeezed her hand. "Do you think it's the same person in the car that's been following me?"

Ashley shook her head. "I don't know. But strange they were both wearing hoodies."

Adrian picked up his phone. "A lot of people wear hoodies. I wouldn't put too much importance on that. Let me get our tech person."

A few minutes later, a slim young woman dressed in civilian clothing, her black hair twisted into a neat bun, padded into his cubby. Adrian introduced her as Sarah Ng. Her gaze barely grazed mine from behind her clear-framed glasses when I shook her limp hand.

Adrian leaned over the desktop computer and restarted the video. "Here. It just stops."

Sarah took a seat in front of the computer and replayed the video again. Once it came to the blank spot, her fingertips, barely protected by nails bitten to the nub, danced over the keys. We watched silently while she attempted to play the video beyond the same spot. After a number of tries, she concluded the problem was definitely with the tape.

Adrian crossed his arms and narrowed his thick brows in my direction. "Odd that the footage we're interested in is missing." He addressed Sarah. "Is there a way to recover the deleted part?"

Sarah stood up and retrieved the flash drive. "That would depend upon what caused the tape to go blank. Let me take it back to our lab. I might be able to recover the deleted part."

"Great. How long will that take?"

"Again, it depends. It could be as short as fifteen minutes, but if—"

"Okay, fine. See what you can do. Make it top priority and keep me posted."

Sarah nodded and then padded back to her lab without another word.

Adrian turned his attention to Ashley and me. "We'll canvass the shopkeepers around downtown and the other hotels and residences in the vicinity of the Hotel Santa Sofia to see if Milo's car was picked up on any of their security cameras. Unfortunately, since we only have limited manpower, it might take a while to complete our search. But rest assured, if it's out there, we'll find it."

I worried that the missing footage might have been deleted intentionally. "Do you think this means something bad has happened to Milo?"

"Hard to tell at this point. If we can get a better look at the person in the hoodie and identify them, we'll be able to know more. If the person has a criminal record, I'd lean toward foul play. But who knows, the person in the hoodie might turn out to be Milo. Then we're talking a different scenario."

My cheeks heated up. "What do you mean by different scenario? You think Milo vanished on purpose?"

Adrian propped himself against the edge of his desk and looked me in the eye but didn't answer right away. "Look, Tory, I know you feel there's been foul play. We have our theories too. But they all have to be evidence-based. We don't have conclusive evidence at this point to indicate foul play."

"What? How can you say that? His smashed phone is total evidence of someone's violence. And don't forget the rock with the blood on it."

"What rock with blood? You never mentioned that before."

Ashley and I both dropped our jaws in unison. Oh my God, he was right. In the commotion, we'd both assumed we'd told him but we hadn't.

I slapped my forehead. "I thought we mentioned it. Sorry."

Ashley threw in her two cents. "Yeah, and the footprint by

the driver's side of his car?" She fiddled with her phone before jamming it in his face. "Look. I took photographs of the rock and the footprints." Ashley pointed at a photo. "There's the rock."

Adrian scanned the photos quickly. "This is great. Can you email them to me? He handed one of his business cards to each of us. "What did you do with the rock?"

"We left it there."

Ashley nodded. "We didn't want to contaminate a crime scene—that's why we left it there. It's off the beaten path, literally."

Adrian's eyes glinted with admiration at Ashley. "Okay, I'll go take a look at the rock myself. But I have to play by the book. Let's start with filing a missing person's report. Here's all the paperwork you need to complete."

After I filled out the forms and handed them back to Adrian, I pulled out my phone. "Here are more pics of the tire tread. Looks wider than a bike tire, though. Ashley, show him the pictures where it looks like something was dragged from the parking lot."

Adrian viewed our photographs and handed our phones back to us. "Yeah, good work, better than some of my rookies. Send me all of these, please."

"So, now does it look like a crime was committed to you?" I braced myself, knowing whatever his answer, I wouldn't like it.

Adrian's chest heaved. "Look, Tory, I'm not saying I disagree with you. But, at this point, we still can't say for sure it's foul play. My captain expects, no, take that back, he requires, the whole department to base everything on irrefutable evidence. All of this is circumstantial and might not mean what you assume it to mean. I guarantee you at least one of my colleagues will suggest Milo might have smashed his own phone and planted the rock to make it look like something happened to him. I don't believe that to be the case, but others might because, so far, we don't have anything definitive. I'll go and take a look at the rock and the area where you found the phone. Like with all missing persons cases, we must be methodical about all leads."

Ashley patted my shoulder. "We need something indisputable to indicate foul play. Like if they found his car with blood on it."

Adrian nodded at Ashley. "Ashley's right. I'll get the missing person's report into the system ASAP. Sarah will work on the surveillance footage, and let's go from there. Meanwhile, if you find anything else that suggests a crime occurred, take a picture and send it to me. I'll investigate it further in a hot second. Promise."

I sighed with satisfaction. "Okay. That's all I needed to hear. Thank you. I'll find something else. Don't worry."

"A word of warning, though. If Milo's met with foul play, the guilty party is at large. You need to be careful for your own safety. I'd rather you call me with a lead that goes nowhere than not call me and put yourself in harm's way."

I blinked as the notion of a dangerous person on the loose registered.

He turned and touched Ashley's arm. "That goes for both of you."

I thought Ashley was going to melt on the spot. I looped her arm through mine as her eyelashes fluttered back at Adrian. We waved goodbye and I yanked her toward the door.

Ashley trotted to keep up with me as I headed out of the station. "What's the plan now?"

"The plan is to do my own detective work if the police won't do it for me. If Adrian really agreed with me, why wouldn't he start an investigation right now? I'm sure he thinks I just can't admit to myself that my husband left me."

Ashley stopped abruptly and exhaled loudly in frustration. "What planet were you just on? I didn't hear him say anything that suggested that. In Adrian's defense, he's only doing his job. He said he didn't disagree with you. That's a good thing. But from the police standpoint, he needs stronger evidence."

"Thanks for the clarification." I winced at how snotty my words sounded. I squeezed her arm affectionately. "Sorry. I'm just disappointed. You're right. It could be worse. He could have just blown me off. At least he doesn't suspect me, like Ernie seems to. Thanks for coming with me."

Ashley affectionately punched my arm. "You're very welcome. I know you'd do the same for me. I'm here for you and will help in any way I can."

I locked her in a bear hug for a few seconds. "Thanks. Seeing that hooded figure on the surveillance tape gave me the creeps, but it's a good clue. If we can identify the person in the hoodie, I think we'll be able to find out what happened to Milo."

CHAPTER 6

Ashley turned on the engine and adjusted the heat. "Now what?"

"Let me guess. Put on our seat belts and turn on the radio?"

She stared at me blankly before breaking into a smile. "Cute. No, really."

"Is it too early for lunch?"

She clicked on her seat belt. "That depends. Where do you have in mind?"

I grinned, already knowing her response. "I need comfort food—with protein. Shake Shack?"

She held out her fist for a bump. "It's never too early for Shake Shack."

We zipped down the Avenue bantering about what we were going to order. We pulled into an empty parking lot, a red flag. We parked and jumped out of the car, only to find the door locked. Our groans echoed each other's disappointment.

Ashley read the restaurant's hours printed on the glass door. "They don't open for another twenty minutes."

I pouted and sighed. "I guess it *can* be too early for Shake Shack."

We decided to wait in the car and pass the time on our phones checking our email and social media accounts.

"Wow. Tons of people responded to your Instagram post about Milo."

"Yeah, I saw that. But no leads so far. At least people are sharing the post and being nice and supportive."

"Good they're spreading the word. Sooner or later something's bound to come up."

Before we knew it, the Shake Shack doors opened. By the time we picked up our order of cheeseburgers, fries, and milkshakes, the place was getting crowded. We navigated our trays to a booth and dug in. We plowed through our food in silence, relishing the fact that, for a few minutes at least, our biggest concerns were condiments, napkins, and straws.

I was bagging our trash when Adrian called. I put it on speaker.

"Can you meet me at the hotel lobby? I want to take a look at the rock and the other evidence."

"Definitely. We're at the Shake Shack on the Avenue. It'll take us about ten minutes to get there."

"Cool. I'm rolling from the station now. See you soon."

It actually took us more like fifteen minutes since we got held up at a train crossing two blocks away from the Promenade. We waited five solid minutes for the cargo cars to rumble by. Once the crossing barrier lifted, it was clear sailing to the hotel. We entered the same remote lot where the hooded figure appeared on the surveillance footage. Today the lot was nearly full, making it seem less isolated and sinister.

I pointed to a car pulling out. "They must be having some function here today."

Ashley parked in its place, one of the last remaining spots. "Good thing we came here yesterday and took pics before all the clues were driven over."

I led the way through the Secret Maze, the fastest and most direct route, but only if you knew its twists and turns. Most people followed the pathway around its perimeter. We trotted down the long outdoor corridor and arrived at the lobby just as Adrian walked in from the front of the hotel.

"Sorry—"

"We know. The train. Us too."

Ashley tugged a stray wisp of hair off her face and smiled in a slightly simpering and uncharacteristic fashion. "Better safe than sorry, that's what I always say."

I gave her the side-eye. I'd never once heard her utter that phrase in the umpteen years I'd known her, and it made no sense in this context. I cut her some slack since many of us spewed nonsense when we flirted. I subtly cocked my head at her and raised my brows as if to say, "This is your best game?"

She furrowed her brows momentarily and jerked her head toward me in a silent message, "Stop it! I'm rusty and trying my best."

Seemingly unaware of our secret sign language, Adrian followed us back to where we'd found the rock in the Secret Maze. It was still there. Right where we last saw it. Adrian took some photographs of it and then retrieved a few tongue depressors, a pack of plastic bags, and latex gloves from his backpack. He snapped the gloves before pulling them on. He poked at the rock with a tongue depressor and flipped it over. A larger stain was on the underside of the rock. But that wasn't all. Underneath the rock was a SIM card. A nervous rush went through my body, knowing it could possibly answer what happened to Milo.

Adrian poked at the SIM card. It was cracked and almost broken in half. He let out an expletive as he pulled a plastic bag from the pack and carefully deposited the SIM card in it. "We'll let Sarah take a look at it to see if she can get something off of this, but I doubt it."

Ashley patted my hand.

Adrian poked around in the gravel near the rock with two tongue depressors.

I couldn't stand the suspense. "Does it look like blood to you?"

Adrian carefully bagged the rock. Then he scooped some gravel up, using the tongue depressors, and put it into another bag and placed both bags into his backpack, along with the SIM card. When he raised his head to look at me, I didn't like what I saw. His expression had changed. His face was somber. His mouth was set in a grim line, and his eyes hardened into a determined stare. The atmosphere in the maze had flipped from morbid curiosity to serious business in a split second. "Yup. The lab will analyze it and tell us for sure."

Ashley squeezed my arm, and I mouthed a swear word to her in response.

"You said you talked to one of the groundskeepers about hearing an argument? Did you catch his name?"

"Yeah. Only his first name—Octavio."

Adrian zipped his backpack. "Let's see if we can find Octavio." He turned to me. "Why don't you lead the way since this is your stomping ground."

We silently tromped through the hedges of the maze to the Hidden Garden exit. As luck would have it, Octavio was planting some azaleas.

Adrian flashed his badge. "I understand you heard an argument in the maze yesterday?"

Octavio stood straight, knocking dirt off his gloves. "Yes, sir."

"Could you hear what they were fighting about?"

"No, sir."

"Did you hear or see anything else out of the ordinary?"

"No, sir. Like I told these ladies yesterday, only the loud voices arguing. Oh, and the rustling in the bushes before that. I guess that was one of the guys or both of them running through the maze before they met."

"What's the watering schedule here at the hotel?"

The tension that had gripped Octavio's face eased as the topic turned to more familiar ground. I groaned at my pun silently. I swore I'd probably have a pun on my tombstone, something like "I told you I was dead tired," or some such nonsense.

Octavio adjusted his wide-brimmed straw hat. "The grounds are controlled by several control centers and each center has five or six zones. Like the Hidden Garden here—it has five zones."

Adrian nodded. "What about the hedges in the maze?"

"Oh, those have a drip system. No sprinklers."

"Do you know the drip schedule? Or is it continuous?"

Octavio's facial muscles tightened into defensive mode. "We keep to the city's drought schedule. We only water on the drought schedule days, Sunday, Tuesday, and Thursday."

Because of our drought conditions in California, the city imposed rules for when and how everyone could water so as to optimize water conservation. As a landscape architect, it was part of my professional responsibility to keep up to date on all the latest regulation iterations.

"And you also adhere to no watering between daytime hours of nine to five, right?" I nodded to him encouragingly.

"Yes, ma'am. Always." He offered a tepid smile.

We waited for Octavio to continue, but he seemed done.

Adrian handed Octavio his card. "Please give me a call if you remember anything else. Appreciate your help."

As we walked away, I turned to Adrian. "Octavio looked terrified when the watering schedule was questioned. Like he thought he was going to get in trouble for breaking the watering rules."

Adrian bobbed his head. "Yeah, I noticed that too."

"You know what's weird, though? Yesterday was Saturday and, theoretically, a non-automatic watering day, yet the maze was super saturated when Ashley and I found the phone. Also, we were there around three thirty but drought rules mandate manual hosing be limited to the hours between four in the afternoon and ten thirty in the morning."

Ashley shouldered herself between us. "Yeah, Tory's right. It was so squishy we had to walk on our tippy toes to keep our heels from constantly sinking."

Feeling validated, I threw her a quick smile. "Which leaves us with a couple of explanations for why the maze was so wet."

Adrian twisted toward me. "The drip system could have a leak. Although it wasn't muddy today, so that would rule out that explanation."

"Good point." Ashley touched his arm lightly.

His eyes twinkled at Ashley. "Or someone could have hosed it down for some reason."

The phrase "for some reason" hung over us like a dark cloud. He didn't have to elaborate. What with the bloodied rock and what I suspected was blood in the gravel sample he'd collected, we all knew "for some reason" was to wash away blood.

"Look, I'm not going to lie, Tory. It's not looking good. But that being said, this evidence is still open to interpretation."

"Meaning?"

"Meaning, even if we think the evidence suggests Milo might have been attacked and abducted, I know some of my more skeptical colleagues will theorize Milo smashed his own phone because he's staging it to look like a kidnapping, especially since he disappeared moments after you were legally married. We always look at motive early on, and your family's business is a symbol of wealth in Santa Sofia. In other words, kidnappers look for victims whose families have the means to pay a ransom. And you said you only knew Milo for a short time before he proposed, correct?"

I nodded as my face warmed.

"They'll look at your brief relationship as an opportunistic move on his part to create a strong bond quickly so you would want to pay a ransom to get him back. Again, let me be clear. I don't believe that. I just know my fellow officers and want to give you a heads-up. They might say the same thing about all of this alleged evidence—the SIM card and rock—that it's been planted to make it look like Milo is the victim. But let's find out if it's blood first and if any data can be retrieved from the SIM card. We'll worry about theories later."

I flinched like I did when the ophthalmologist puffed air at my eyes. I was shaken, reeling in both body and spirit. I appreciated Adrian's honesty and guessed their cynicism served them well as cops. I almost wished he was right, because then, at least, Milo would be alive, albeit despicably so. But my heavy heart and pounding headache told me otherwise. I believed Milo had been killed. I just knew it.

The buzz of Adrian's phone broke my thoughts. He wasn't on the call for more than a minute. "That was Sarah. She's managed to retrieve the deleted portion of the surveillance video. Meet me back at the station?"

Adrian headed back in the direction of the lobby. Ashley and

I meandered back through the maze to the parking lot. Patrolling the lot was the hotel security guard, B. Brockett, a.k.a. Barbie. She greeted us with a hearty hello.

"Thank you so much again for sending the footage over to SSPD so quickly. Adrian was here with us just a minute ago. The tape had a blank part but his tech person has retrieved it and we're going back to watch it at the station right now."

"Yeah, I know. Luckily, our CCTV video is automatically saved on a hard drive. Sarah took a look at our hard drive and found the missing footage. Apparently, it was a computer glitch or software issue, who knows. Glad I could be of help."

Had we been in a western movie, I pictured her tipping her cowboy hat.

Ashley and I waved goodbye to Brockett, jumped in the car, and hightailed it back to the police station.

Once again, we gathered around Adrian's computer. Adrian started the video. The hooded figure opened the car trunk and then went out of view. The hooded figure came back with a huge wheelbarrow filled with plants. Adrian paused the tape on the hooded figure. The longer I studied the hooded figure, the more I was convinced it couldn't be Milo. The person looked bulkier than Milo. But I still couldn't be sure. At least it wasn't Milo in the wheelbarrow.

Ashley hit my arm. "That's what the tracks we saw were—from a wheelbarrow, not a bike."

I nodded. "I should have thought of that."

"I know. Me too."

The video continued. After all the plants were unloaded from the wheelbarrow to the car trunk, the hooded figure bent over and reached into the wheelbarrow. It looked like a jumbo-sized black trash bag. The figure struggled to load it into the trunk. It was long and looked heavy. It looked like a body.

CHAPTER 7

Adrian clicked off the video and faced us. We all were speechless for a few seconds. Ashley threw her arm around my shoulders and pulled me close, her squeeze giving me strength as I willed myself to stay conscious, despite the clamminess that had descended upon me. I took a few deep breaths to ward off my lightheadedness, each successive breath bringing me more back to life, like the re-inflation of a deflated balloon.

Ashley's voice was tremulous. "Was that what I think it was in that trash bag?"

Though I'd regained my composure, my voice sounded thin. "It was a body in the bag, wasn't it?"

Adrian chewed the inside of his cheek. "Based on the way the trash bag was handled, it seemed heavy and jointed. Yes, it looked like there was a body in it to me. Looks like someone hid a body in the bag, put it in the wheelbarrow, and then covered the bag with plants. Do you recognize the person in the video? Could it possibly be Milo?"

"I don't think so." My voice quivered. "The person in the video looks taller and huskier than Milo. But you know what's weird? The hooded person was lucky the car's backseat had been folded down or there wouldn't have been a trunk to put plants and a body in."

Adrian perked up. "Milo's car normally didn't have a trunk?"

"No, it did. He kept the backseats folded down most of the time. So, no real point. It just strikes me as weird. Sorry."

Adrian paused. "Don't be sorry. That was a good observation. You're starting to think like a detective—question everything and think outside the box. For instance, that bag could have also just been a big bag of soil or fertilizer."

I turned to Adrian. "Don't get me wrong—as much as I'd love it to be a bag of soil or fertilizer—in all my years in the landscape business, I've never seen bags of soil and fertilizer that big unless they were customized for a large job."

He patted me on the shoulder. "Okay. I'm going to have our dispatcher update the report right now to reflect suspected foul play. Be right back."

Ashley and I exchanged mournful looks.

"I can't believe that might be Milo's body." I sank into a chair, my shoulders heaving as I gasped for air in between sobs.

Ashley rubbed my back. "Try to calm down, Tory. You're hyperventilating. Take a few deep breaths."

I inhaled deeply and, after a few minutes, I felt better.

Adrian came back to his cubby and gave me the thumbs-up sign. "We're all set—just updated the missing person's report."

He turned the video back on. "Let's see what else we've got on here."

The monochrome footage continued. The hooded figure got in the driver's side of the car and then drove out of the parking lot. Adrian fast-forwarded for another minute and found nothing more of significance.

He clicked it off and turned to me. "Okay, we really need to look at all the footage from the other hotel cameras now. Maybe we can see which direction the car went after this. I'll let you know if we find anything."

Adrian patted the side of Ashley's shoulder, and he and Ashley locked gazes for a second.

Ashley and I left the police station, walking arm in arm to the parking lot.

I waited on the passenger side of her car. "I saw that."

Ashley beeped open the doors. "What?"

"That look. Your chemistry with Adrian—it was like an electric current emanating from both of your eyes."

Ashley laughed, bubbling over with giddiness. "You saw that? I felt like I was beamed up to another level. I think I like him."

"I think it's mutual."

Ashley squealed in response.

While Ashley drove me home, I checked my Instagram post. The only new comments were those sending well wishes and prayers. Nothing new related to Milo's disappearance.

Ashley tossed concerned glances my way as she drove. "I've got a great idea. I'll interview you on my podcast."

"What podcast?"

"The one I'm going to start. I was thinking of calling it *Where's Milo?* You know, like *Where's Waldo?* It could help spread the word."

I guffawed. "I'll do anything that'll help. But who's going to listen?"

Ashley patted my hand. "Oh, child. I didn't double major in marketing and communication for nothing. Trust your friend."

"Okay. Knock yourself out."

"Thanks. Meanwhile, keep checking your social media posts to see if anyone has seen him or knows anything. In this day and age, I'm convinced you can run but you can't hide—for very long, at least. Also, try reaching out to the local paper. Do you know anyone who works there?"

"I don't know anyone personally at the *Santa Sofia Sentinel,* but Benning Brothers advertises there. I'll ask Uncle Bob and Aunt Veronica who our contact is."

"That's the spirit. Also, have you heard of Disappeared.com? Try contacting them to see if they'll put out a *Where's Milo?* post too."

"Don't tell me you're trying to brand the investigation now."

"You want to find him, right?"

"I do. What's next? T-shirts?"

"Hmm. Not a bad idea. Let's hope we'll find him before that. If not, that can be part of Plan B."

"We could post signs around the hotel and the surrounding neighborhood and in the neighborhood around his town house too."

"All phenomenal ideas, Tory. We could mention the podcasts in the signs. Way to cross-reference. Go, you."

• • •

Two weeks passed without any significant news on Milo. I'd gotten into the habit of reading online articles about other missing persons each night for tips to make sure we were doing everything we could to find Milo. It only depressed me more. Many cases took months or longer to solve, some never were.

I received a call from Adrian. "We've looked at footage from several home and business surveillance cameras, but so far Milo's car hasn't been captured on any.

Both he and his car had vanished into thin air.

"I know you're frustrated, but I assure you our investigators are doing all they can."

I didn't doubt that. My doubt lay in their limited experience and skill in investigating anything more than a missing dog. Most of those cases usually had happy endings, thanks more to technology and microchips than to the detective skills of our local police force. I was crossing my fingers that the one exception might be Adrian. His updates demonstrated a bulldog-like tenacity, a trait I hoped that, combined with his ambition, would lead to solving the mystery behind Milo's disappearance.

"Make sure you let me know if you remember anything else out of the ordinary, even if it seems unrelated or insignificant. Some of our most challenging cases have been cracked from a simple clue. Don't worry. We'll get to the bottom of this."

I scoured my brain to remember any crime story I'd ever read about in the *Santa Sofia Sentinel* that could be described as "challenging." I decided I'd give Adrian's detective skills the benefit of the doubt. No use second-guessing him at this point. Better to keep my own antennae up and hope I noticed something the police could follow up on.

I'd emailed my aunt Veronica, our former finance VP who'd

also overseen marketing and advertising, about her contacts at the *Santa Sofia Sentinel.* I was browsing through our latest Benning Brothers Nursery ads she'd placed in the *Sentinel.* The page was filled with pictures of seasonal plantings, summer stuff on clearance, wheelbarrows, and hoses. That triggered my thoughts about the wheelbarrow treads from the parking lot. I drove down to our nursery to check out our wheelbarrows. The tread patterns varied, but all of them were more or less around the same width. I decided to go down to the hotel and take a look at their wheelbarrows, which were stored in a large shed at the rear of the property.

Before I started my car, I texted Ashley to let her know where I'd be. Heeding Adrian's warning, I'd gotten into the habit of letting her know where I was going anytime I explored a lead. I drove to the hotel and parked in a remote lot that backed onto the railroad tracks. Since it was dinnertime, the groundskeepers had already left for the day. As I headed to the shed, I reflected on the last several days. It was hard to believe that this time two weeks ago Ashley and I were tiptoeing through the maze hoping to find Milo. So much had happened in a short period of time. His smashed phone and the rock had shaken me up, but the video showing what was almost certainly a body in a bag had dashed any hopes I'd ever had we'd find Milo alive.

The narrow, hedge-bordered walkway leading to the shed was deserted. I shuddered as I experienced the same feeling of isolation as I did when I was in the Secret Maze. For peace of mind, since it was getting dark, I decided I'd follow the less secluded driveway back to my car after I looked inside. I padded up to the structure that looked like a small barn. Huge double doors made up one whole wall, permitting one end of the shed to be opened up for easy access to all the equipment. The dirt driveway to the shed was only sparsely covered with gravel, making it possible to pick out different types of tracks in the dirt. The big double doors had a padlock, so I went around to the side where there was a door. That was locked too. I peered through an adjacent window and gasped. There were eight wheelbarrows lined up as neat as a fleet of cop cars. But it wasn't the wheelbarrows that stopped my heart. It was what was parked next to them—Milo's car.

CHAPTER 8

> **Instagram Post** @ToryBenning: UPDATE: Monday, October 16. Milo Spinelli's red Fiat was found last night in a Hotel Santa Sofia gardening shed. In addition, hotel parking lot CCTV footage has revealed suspicious activity suggesting foul play. Milo's phone and a possible bloodstained weapon were found in the Hotel Santa Sofia's Secret Maze shortly after he disappeared two weeks ago. Today the SSPD has officially declared Milo's disappearance a suspected homicide investigation. If you have seen Milo or have any information about his disappearance, please contact the SSPD or their anonymous tip hotline. I'm asking for your help to spread the word and hopefully someone will have seen something that might help the police investigation. Thank you for all of your love and support. Love, Tory.

I studied my phone screen and tweaked my copy, proofed my edits, and scanned the whole entry one more time. With my lips pursed in resignation, I breathed in deeply and posted it, leaving out a lot of the gory details that had recently come to light. In a span of two weeks, I'd cycled briefly through each of Kübler-Ross's five stages of grief: denial, anger, bargaining, depression, and acceptance.

Initially, I'd denied Milo's disappearance, hoping it had been a huge misunderstanding. I'd bargained that all would be forgiven if he returned. I'd been depressed about the loss of the love of my life and best friend. Last night, I was forced to accept that someone had probably killed Milo when Adrian informed me the Secret Maze gravel samples had revealed blood in the mix. As I'd feared, it turned out the boggy state of the maze path Ashley and I had tiptoed through sixteen days earlier had resulted from someone hosing down the area to wash away blood. SSPD's forensic team, and by team I meant two officers, collected more samples that indicated someone had lost a significant amount of blood in the maze. An analysis had found the blood to be a match to a sample of Milo's DNA obtained from his hairbrush. Adrian's theory was Milo knew his killer and had agreed to meet that person in the maze, they argued, and the killer flew into a rage, smashed the phone, and struck Milo. Adrian didn't think it was random, a small consolation to those of us wondering whether a homicidal maniac was on the loose. Instead, we wondered what on earth could have been the motive to spur such violence.

Adrian's explanation of what he thought happened thereafter was equally puzzling. The killer, a.k.a. the hooded figure, had wheelbarrowed the body to Milo's car. The killer then had driven Milo's car somewhere to dump the body. Then the killer hid the car and, presumably, the wheelbarrow, in the gardening shed sometime during the next two weeks. The blood found in the Fiat's trunk was also expected to match Milo's DNA, but analyses were not yet completed. All the wheelbarrows were being checked for evidence.

A number of questions remained in my mind. Even though the groundskeepers used the shed for storage, they rarely frequented it since another shed was for everyday use. If any of the groundskeepers had found Milo's car, for some reason, no one had reported it. I wondered why.

I doubted the police statement claiming they'd checked the shed before and Milo's car hadn't been there earlier. I thought they were just covering their behinds because they failed to conduct a thorough search of the hotel grounds. Adrian had told me it had been Ernie who'd sworn he'd checked the shed himself and saw nothing but wheelbarrows. My hunch was that Ernie had been too busy trying to make the existing evidence fit his theory that I was the culprit to conduct a thorough investigation of the grounds. When I told Adrian I believed Milo's car had been there all along, he didn't disagree, but he cautioned me to be wary of Ernie, because when Adrian questioned the thoroughness of Ernie's search, Ernie had countered by questioning my alibi, confirming my hunch. Ernie had even wondered aloud whether Ashley and Philip were "in on it" with me, the old "best defense is a good offense" strategy. Adrian assured me that he'd try to keep Ernie at bay. But now I was convinced if I wanted the mystery of Milo's disappearance solved, it was up to me to solve it, and fast, before Ernie sucked me into his own agenda and charged me with murder.

I'd regressed back to the angry stage of grief. And by angry, I meant fighting, bull-by-the-horns angry. I owed it to Milo to get to the bottom of his murder and bring his killer to justice, however long it took. And by the looks of things, it was going to take a while. Our hope of a clue from his SIM card was dashed when Sarah informed us it was mangled beyond repair. SSPD was in the process of obtaining phone logs from Milo's phone carrier. Adrian telling me to be patient did nothing to slow the burning rage that fueled my quest for justice, not to mention my burning curiosity about the series of events that might have led to such a horrific outcome.

...

As days passed following Milo's disappearance, my focus, out of necessity, had turned back to work. I had a business to run and bills to pay. Uncle Bob had agreed to come back from his recent retirement to assume his former role again as chief financial officer and help me run Benning Brothers. I was taking over my father's creative management role and needed someone I could trust to help with the financial aspects of running the business.

One morning as I sat at my desk mainlining coffee to keep myself awake while I waded through an unusually long

Request for Proposal (RFP) document, Uncle Bob sauntered into my office. He'd given up watching his waistline years ago and wore both suspenders and a belt to work every day to hold up his pants. Aside from his major fashion faux pas, Uncle Bob was savvier than he let on to be, mostly by design. I think he enjoyed portraying himself as unsophisticated because people perceived him as less of a threat that way, a strategy that gave him the upper hand in his dealings with employees and business associates alike.

He snapped his suspenders in greeting. "Benning Brothers has been approached by Chandler International. They want to acquire us."

Chandler International, an American multinational architecture and engineering company, had been Milo's employer at the time of his disappearance. They had many different divisions, including design, consulting, construction, and management services to a wide range of clients and were noted for gobbling up stellar architectural and landscape design firms for their global network. Benning Brothers fit their acquisitions profile.

Chandler's MO was to retain the prestigious reputation of an acquisition by keeping their top architects and landscape architects. But the downside was, more often than not, Chandler ended up letting go the rest of the acquired company's full-time employees, or sometimes firing them then hiring them back at lower pay with fewer or no benefits.

I set down my coffee mug. "You told them no, right?"

Uncle Bob plopped down in a leather side chair. "They've given us a month's notice to consider our options. They didn't have to give us a heads-up at all."

"They're probably feeling guilty because one of their rising-star employees left me in the lurch. And by left me in the lurch, I mean disappeared off the planet."

"Don't forget Milo had friends there, Tory. They're feeling his loss too."

"Can you please not talk about Milo like he's dead."

"Sorry, kiddo. I thought you'd come to grips with the realization he's probably been murdered. You posted on social media to that effect, didn't you?" With that he had a coughing fit for a few seconds.

What had I done? Was I trying to give the poor man a heart attack? He was just stating a fact. It didn't mean I had to spit back a sharp retort like a snapping turtle. "Sorry for being snappy, Uncle Bob. It's just that the word 'loss' hit me the wrong way. We didn't lose Milo—someone took him from us. Don't know why that distinction matters so much to me right now, but it does. Sometimes I feel like I'm barely hanging on."

He'd stopped hacking and wiped his mouth with a cloth handkerchief he'd plucked from his pants pocket. "Sorry, pumpkin, didn't mean to upset you."

My heart filled with love for my uncle. He hadn't called me pumpkin in years.

He stuffed his handkerchief back in his pocket. "Just to be perfectly clear, the SSPD have called it a *suspected* homicide investigation. No one knows for sure."

It was that very uncertainty that drove me crazy. At times, I didn't know what to think or what my true thoughts were. The constant turmoil had me swinging between extremes. One minute I found myself doubting whether I'd ever really known Milo, and the next minute I was positive I had known him better than anyone I'd ever known. If I trusted what my heart and gut told me to be true, that I had indeed known Milo, then I had to face that Milo might have been murdered, as the mounting evidence suggested. But with him still missing and without a body to prove it, I felt if we kept one iota of hope he was alive, the police would have a greater sense of urgency to keep looking for him.

Uncle Bob reached for my hand and patted it. "You've been doing so well running the company, I sometimes forget how much you've been through lately." He gave my hand another pat and his voice cracked. "I'm very proud of you, and I know your father would be too."

"Thanks, Uncle Bob. And I don't even want to consider an acquisition unless Chandler promises to keep everybody on."

"My sentiments exactly. I already ran that by them. They said no dice. But the fact they're giving us a month to mull it over wasn't something they needed to do. They did imply even if we reject their offer, they're still planning to open a landscape architecture division here in Santa Sofia. Hopefully we can work out a compromise where everyone wins."

"Like what?"

Uncle Bob gave me a sly wink. "That's the part I'm still working on."

• • •

A few days later, I was at my office computer drawing an irrigation plan in AutoCAD, a computer-aided design and drafting software app, for a new client when Uncle Bob tapped on my door.

"Got a minute?"

My gaze didn't leave the computer. "Of course. Let me just do one more thing on this." When I looked up, my heart stopped. All the color had drained from Uncle Bob's normally ruddy face.

"What's wrong? Are you okay?"

He shook his head. "I have an awful feeling that somehow Benning Brothers is inexplicably on the verge of bankruptcy."

I spun my chair around to face him. "What? How can that be?"

"I don't know. When I retired six months ago, we were in tiptop shape. Somehow, our funds have been drained. I'm going to go back and recheck the books from the time when I left and start carefully reexamining our expenses and revenue since then. But my quick take, looks like someone has been embezzling."

I leaned back hard in my chair. "Embezzling? Who?"

We never had gotten around to replacing Uncle Bob when he'd retired. We were going to start interviewing potential replacements after the wedding. In the meantime, my father had been handling the financial management.

"Do me a favor, Tory, and go through your dad's records to see if you see anything that looks odd or out of the ordinary."

Realizing my mouth was agape, not my best look, I clenched it shut. "Okay. I'll get right on it. But I'm warning you, Uncle Bob. I might have to start locking my door if all you do is bring me bad news."

He winked again. "Welcome to running a business. There are always ups and downs. Hang in there, Tory. I'll know more after I go over everything more carefully. Hopefully I'll find some glaring error and we can set things right."

After my dad died, I hadn't moved into his corner office right away, partly out of respect and partly due to my chaotic schedule leading up to the wedding. When I finally did, I left his office pretty much undisturbed, again, partly as a sign of respect and love, and partly because I didn't really have time to go through all his papers with my wedding day rapidly approaching. Since the roller-coaster ride of getting married and Milo's disappearance had my stress level off the charts, I still hadn't gotten around to clearing out my father's personal files.

I scooted my chair back a bit and started to go through my father's papers in his desk file drawers. About ten minutes into going through his files, I found a green folder of receipts for the premiums he'd been paying for a two-million-dollar insurance policy. He'd paid through to the end of the year. In another green file I found the policy documents stating I was the primary beneficiary. My dad had never mentioned the policy to me. It felt like a gift he'd sent from heaven—the answer to Benning Brothers' financial fix. I could invest the money from the insurance policy back into the company. I stood up, ready to go tell Uncle Bob about our unexpected windfall, when my phone rang. It was the insurance company. I sat back down and clicked on the speakerphone while I resumed flipping through files at my father's desk.

The woman on the line identified herself as Janet. "We're

calling about an insurance policy your father had taken out on himself."

"Funny you should call. I was just going through his files and discovered the paperwork on it. I had no idea he had it."

"We wanted to let you know we're investigating the circumstances of your father's death. You'll be getting a written notice in the mail shortly."

"All right. What does that mean exactly?"

"It's pretty routine for accidental deaths, especially in cases when the deceased has only had the policy for a short period of time, like in your father's case. We investigate policies that are less than three years old more closely.

"Our investigation will focus on whether any negligence occurred on the part of the owner of the pier. We'll examine whether or not they maintained the upkeep of the pier to keep it safe. Things like the condition of the guardrail and the wooden planks. Also, we'll determine whether there've been any similar claims. If we think there is evidence they failed to maintain the pier properly, we would go after the pier's insurance company to make the payout we owe to you. It's called subrogation."

"Okay. How long will that take?"

"It varies. The pier's insurance company has also opened an investigation of its own regarding his death—"

"Because they don't want to be held liable and pay, yes, I understand that."

"They will probably try to make the case it wasn't accidental, especially because your father only took it out six months ago. If they can show other possibilities, they can argue more strongly they're not liable to any degree."

"Like what other possibilities could there be?"

"They'll probably look into factors that might suggest a possible suicide. Like your father's health status, his mental state, his finances, things like that. I'm assuming you know of no health or financial problems he had, correct?"

As soon as she said "financial problems," I froze in my seat. My heart pounded hard against my chest. I shut my eyes for a moment and inhaled slowly to calm myself down.

I exhaled and deflected Janet's inquiry with my own question. "Why are they questioning it was an accident?"

Why wouldn't they? I'd questioned it being an accident since it happened, as had Ashley. But still I'd balked when I found out the medical examiner would perform an autopsy on my father. It wasn't until Ashley informed me autopsies were required in all accidental death cases in Santa Barbara County that I became more amenable to the idea. The results were due any day now. But that was before I'd known the company was in financial trouble. Could my father have been so upset he just gave up? That response was the last one I would ever have imagined from my father. He'd always been an active problem solver. He'd have gone into overdrive had he found out someone had been embezzling. His way would have been to confront whomever he suspected, go to the authorities, and work out a plea bargain that included a plan for restitution.

"Insurance companies conduct investigations all the time. That's what we do. It's how we fulfill our due diligence."

I sighed. "Okay."

"We'll also need access to Benning Brothers' books. You'll be contacted by one of our investigators in the next week or so to set up an appointment. In any event, whatever the outcome, the payout, if any, won't be paid out until our investigation is completed. It's possible it might be delayed several months."

"Several months?" My heart sank. The anticipated windfall wouldn't happen soon enough to save the company.

Janet ended our conversation by reminding me to be on the lookout for their investigator's phone call or email. As soon as we hung up, I went to Uncle Bob's office to brief him.

He gulped before speaking. "We need to find out who was embezzling. You need to keep looking through his files to see if there are any clues to what happened."

"You don't think my dad would have killed himself over it, do you?"

"Not for one moment. Your dad would have contacted

whomever he suspected and made it a teaching moment. Depending upon who it was, he might try to bypass going to the authorities and handle it himself, so as not to give the offender more trouble."

"Yeah. That's exactly what I thought immediately."

Time stood still as my mind raced through the events of the last few weeks as if they were animated pages in a cartoon flipbook. First, my father's death, then Milo's disappearance, then Milo's firm trying to acquire Benning Brothers, then our financial trouble due to embezzling, and now my father's suspected suicide. It was bad enough that my father was dead. I couldn't imagine him ever even contemplating suicide or mismanaging company funds. I was convinced neither could be true but was at a loss how to convince everyone else. For the time being, at least.

CHAPTER 9

To keep Benning Brothers afloat, I responded to as many landscape architecture RFPs and Requests for Quotation (RFQ) as possible. I guess you could say I was too busy minding my p's and q's to worry about the helplessness I felt in every area of my life. Coupled with managing all our existing projects, I didn't have a whole lot of time left over to wallow. Throwing myself into my job worked at keeping me sane for the moment. The suspicions swirling around my father's untimely death and Milo's disappearance were soul-sucking—that they occurred within two weeks of each other was a one-two punch that had left me down for the count. I struggled to regain my emotional equilibrium. I didn't know who to believe, or who to trust.

Therapy twice a week helped. My therapist's main message was that tough times never lasted, tough people did. Ashley was the best, as usual, putting up with all my endless conversations when I rehashed everything over and over again. I didn't know what I would have done without her support.

I was wrapping up for the night at the office and making a to-do list for the next day when Ashley called.

I hit Accept. "Speak of the devil!"

"What? Who's talking about me?"

I laughed. "No one. But I was thinking about you and all you've done for me lately. I'm so grateful to have you as a friend, Ash. I don't thank you often enough, so . . . thank you!"

"Aw, you're so sweet. I know you'd do the same for me. I was calling to see if you wanted to grab a bite tonight? A new kebab place opened at Olive Branch Mall."

"I was planning to work out."

"Of course you were. When you're not working, you're working out. Ironic much? Like you need to lose any more weight. I can't see you anymore when you turn sideways. You need a good square meal."

"I eat."

"Girl, you're going to disappear, too, if you keep it up."

I could almost feel her cringe over the phone.

"I'm so sorry, Tory. I wasn't thinking."

"Don't worry about it."

She cleared her throat. "Have you heard from Adrian lately?"

"No new leads as far as I know. They're still analyzing evidence and waiting on phone and credit card records. Everything takes so long."

"Apparently. I thought if you had any news you could fill me in over dinner."

"No news. Sorry. But I'd think you'd hear it yourself from Adrian, no?"

"Um, no. We've both been busy with work. You know how that goes. No white car sightings either, I hope?"

I hesitated. "Not really."

"What the heck does that mean? Someone is still following you? Did you tell Adrian?"

"Every now and then I think I spot a white car behind me. Then it's gone and I don't know whether it was ever really there or not."

"Great. Please, Tory, tell Adrian so he's aware."

"Okay. I will." To be honest, I doubted my own sanity sometimes. Was I being overly paranoid when I thought I was being followed? Or too cavalier when I dismissed it? We were working on moderating my mood swings in therapy.

Ashley quickly regrouped. "Okay. I get the message. You'd rather spend your time with that new boyfriend of yours instead of me. What's his name again? Oh that's right. Gym."

I groaned.

"Too soon?"

"No. I'm fine."

I worked out each night at the local fitness club because it was the only activity guaranteed to make me feel better on every level. For at least an hour every day, after turning my iPod volume high and hopping on the treadmill, I could zone out and be carefree and forget about my problems. Cardio was my therapy.

While time had eased the initial shock of Milo's disappearance and probable death, even though I'd stopped the bleeding, my wounds were still fresh and my emotions raw. I wasn't going to lie, in my weaker moments, or when the charge ran out on my iPod, ugly doubt seeped into my thoughts. *Did Milo only marry me for some nefarious scheme to, at some later date, come back and take my money? Why did I agree to marry someone after only knowing him for such a short time? Was Milo really a victim of foul play or did he stage the whole thing, like* Gone Girl, *only in reverse, Gone Guy?* But then a good night's sleep restored me and I got a grip and came to my senses. In my heart of hearts, I knew our love had been real. And I knew in my gut he was really gone forever, as in dead. But on one level, I'd wished we'd found his body so I would know for sure. Overwhelming guilt filled my being every time that thought popped into my head.

Ashley let out a loud breath. "You don't sound fine. You need to get out once in a while. I'm starting to get hearing issues from spending so much time on the phone with you. Next thing we know you'll have thirty cats. I know working out is therapeutic —you have to take care of number one first and foremost. But you have to take care of business too."

"Uh-huh." I knew where she was going with this. Taking care of business was Ashley's code for filing for divorce. Every conversation I'd had with Ashley sooner or later ended with her urging me to file.

She sighed. "Without a body, we can't know for sure what happened. No one knows whether he's pushing up daisies or coming back or what happened to him. Maybe he had a girlfriend on the side. We don't know whether that person in the surveillance video was male or female. You see where I'm going with this?"

"I see where you're going. If you're trying to make me feel better, this is not helping. This makes it seem like he's still alive. And he's not . . ."

"Sorry, Tory. As your lawyer *and* friend, I'm just trying to protect you and your assets. Ninety-nine percent, he met with foul play. But in the one percent chance he didn't meet with foul play, you want to protect your assets and limit your liability. Have you given any more thought to filing?"

Up until now, I'd dragged my feet and refused to file for an annulment or divorce until I knew what had happened to Milo. Plus, given the state of Benning Brothers' current finances, whose money woes I hadn't even shared with Ashley, out of respect for Uncle Bob, if we didn't figure out a way to avoid bankruptcy, there might not be any family fortune left to worry about protecting.

Ashley responded to my lack of response with a frustrated sigh. "Okay, I don't know how to tell you this gently, Tory, so I'll just say it. Milo once hit on me, but I shut him down. It wasn't a big deal. But still. I don't think you knew him long enough to really know him that well."

"Again, if this is supposed to make me feel better, it's not." I didn't know whether or not to believe her. Ashley wasn't a liar, but she was a lawyer. She'd always been notorious for her love of debate, never passing up an opportunity to negotiate and persuade everything and everybody. Sometimes, when she got carried away, she even exaggerated to make her point. I'd never pegged Milo as a cheater, but given all the unpleasant surprises I'd experienced lately, I wasn't as confident in my own judgment as I used to be.

"I'm just sayin'."

"Okay, you win. You've worn me down. I'll file for legal separation. Baby steps. I know it's for my own good."

"Thank you! I'll get the paperwork to you first thing in the morning. Two pages, fill in the blanks, and boom, you're protected."

"I know you're right. I need to move on. Happy now?"

"Not quite. If you really want to move on, you've got to put yourself out there. Come with me Friday night to the Halloween Firefighters Fundraiser at the Hotel Santa Sofia. My plus-one flaked on me."

"Adrian flaked?"

"Yep. He claims he regards it as a work function so he can't go with a date. I think he's playing hard to get. But I'll show him."

"Aren't you overreacting a tad? Adrian has never been a game player. If he said it's because of work, it is. Don't take it personally. I think he really likes you."

"Whatever. I don't need any more flaky guys. I want to get someone who cares about the world and thinks about other people, not just their own pitiful, narcissistic self. What I need is one of those fine firefighters."

"You realize that description matches Adrian too, don't you?"

"Whatever."

I chuckled. "And you do know it's not a singles mixer, right?"

"Whatever."

I hadn't been back to the Hotel Santa Sofia since I found Milo's car in the gardening shed. The thought of returning filled me with dread. But I was already feeling guilty for not planning to attend my own company's fundraiser for an extremely worthy cause, our local firefighters' emergency fund that benefited fire victims. In the recent Olive Branch Fire, firefighters had risked their lives knocking on doors warning residents to evacuate when the wind had changed abruptly. Several homes in the hills were lost that night and the fire had burned down to the parking lot of the Olive Branch Mall. A smaller fire had even threatened the grounds of the Hotel Santa Sofia. The Santa Sofia Fire Department had prevented bigger disasters in both cases, but that wasn't much consolation to the victims who lost their homes, especially when it was revealed both fires were the work of a yet-to-be-apprehended arsonist.

In addition to Benning Brothers donating trees to reforest the burn sites, we cosponsored the fundraiser with the Hotel Santa Sofia. Our participation was not only charitable, it was good PR, a commodity we desperately needed right now, given all the takeover rumors that had somehow been leaked in landscape architecture circles, according to Uncle Bob. I also feared my absence might suggest I was out of commission due to Milo's disappearance, a perception our company couldn't afford. I felt obligated to show everyone I was able to conduct business. We still hadn't heard about our entry for the Hotel Santa Sofia's new condominium project up the coast. The winning bid would be announced soon, according to the latest email from Hotel Santa Sofia Properties. Showing up to schmooze could only help our chance of getting the job.

Agreeing to fill Ashley's need for a buddy to pal around with while she flirted with all the hunky firefighters in attendance was the least I could do to repay her for all the kindness she'd extended to me. I felt I owed her a favor since she'd listened to all my problems nonstop during the past few weeks. I needed to pull on my big girl panties and face the world again. I didn't have to stay long. I planned on making an appearance and leaving early.

• • •

When Friday evening rolled around, I was at my computer, focused on selecting a planting palette for a downtown plaza and putting the finishing touches on my AutoCAD drawing, applying hatching, a shading technique drawn with close parallel lines, to the flower beds. I'd lost all track of time. When I glanced at my phone and saw it was already seven, the time the event started, I packed up and locked up my office. Our offices were located in a one-story, designated-historical adobe building on Manzanita Street. I waved to our nursery manager, Jed Barnes, who was locking up the gates of our nursery and garden shop across the street, as I hurried to the parking lot in back of our building. Benning Brothers was at the opposite end of town from the Hotel Santa Sofia. At this hour, I figured there'd be light traffic and the trip would only take about ten minutes.

I jumped in my car and zipped down the Avenue, making good time until I approached the railroad tracks that cut through the center of town. The crossing lights flashed red, the bells dinged, and the barrier arms lowered. I was stuck. A freight train lumbered by, boxcars extending forever. I texted Ashley to let her know I was held up.

A few moments later she responded, *I just got here. Hurry up.*

At the hotel, I splurged on valet parking since the self-park lots would be full. The shortest route to the Hidden Garden fundraiser would be through the Secret Maze. I hesitated, paralyzed with fear as a host of horrible images rose in my consciousness—the smashed phone, the bloodstained rock, and the mud. My therapist had told me that my old associations needed to be replaced by new ones. I imagined myself a Mylar balloon floating through the maze, impervious to anything bringing me down, my buoyancy rising above dark memories. I took a deep breath and plunged into the Secret Maze, repeating my therapist's words, "The best way out is through."

Again, the mud and gravel path played havoc with my heels. *Stay in the moment. Be mindful of now.* As I wound my way around the twists and turns, raised male and female voices echoed from somewhere else within the maze's lofty, dense hedges. I paused, turning in the direction of the voices, straining to hear what they were saying, but their words sounded muffled. I turned quickly to resume my trek and my foot slipped out of my right shoe. I wiggled my foot back into its three-inch-heeled shoe. Despite the darkness, I didn't need a floodlight to immediately recognize I had a problem. I'd broken my heel. It'd snapped off like the bottom of an asparagus stalk. A few choice swear words escaped before I decided to keep my shoes on anyway and tough it out till I caught up with Ashley.

The party noises grew louder as I hobbled toward the exit like a peg-legged pirate. At last I exited the maze and entered the

Hidden Garden.

Making it through the maze with my only casualty being a broken heel filled me with pride. The journey had been short, measured by physical steps, but long in emotional gains. I felt like I could stand taller now having faced my fears. As I hung out at the entrance to the Hidden Garden and scanned the festivities, a man's deep voice from the maze behind me suddenly got louder.

I spun around to see a man with his head down and a phone to his ear rushing straight for me. Surrounded by thick hedges on both sides, I had nowhere to go but back. I stepped back and shouted a heads-up, "Hey!"

He whipped his head up but not soon enough to avoid crashing into me, each of us grabbing each other's arms to prevent a head-on collision. When our eyes met, for a moment my heart fluttered. *He's gorgeous!* He apologized brusquely and continued on his way, his mind clearly on his phone conversation more than his physical surroundings. Given his muscular build and rugged good looks, I assumed he must be one of the firefighters being honored. No wonder they fought fires. They were pretty hot themselves. Ashley would be thrilled if there were more firefighters like him in attendance. I wondered if it had been his voice I'd heard in the maze earlier.

I looked around and summoned my extravert self to help out her introvert sister to mingle as I took in the scene in front of me. The Hidden Garden was packed with noisy revelers mingling beneath strings of jack-o'-lantern lights and fake cobwebs suspended from tree branches, festive decorations for the Halloween season upon us.

Of course, Ashley was nowhere to be found. Probably checking out all the hot firefighters before launching her speed-dating version of working the crowd. I spied some familiar faces. Hard not to anytime you attended an event in Santa Sofia. Adrian was engaged in an animated conversation across the lawn with a couple of fellow cops and gave me a wave when he caught my eye. My maternal aunt, Marian Wall, the

Santa Sofia head librarian and town gossip, was holding court with a few of her friends, among them Uncle Bob and my aunt Veronica. Her back was turned to me, but I'd recognize her silver bun anywhere. Judging by everyone's smiles, Jed Barnes, our longtime nursery manager, appeared to be entertaining a small circle of fellow employees, among them our secretary, Raquel Okada, and receptionist, Claudette Dunbar. Philip, his hair loose and unbound from his workaday man-bun, who chatted to some people I didn't recognize, raised his arms in delight when our gazes met and he immediately headed toward me.

"So nice to see you, my darling. How are you?" He surveyed my hair with a disapproving eye. "You should have called me. I'd have done your hair."

I'd swept my locks up into a messy updo because I was overdue for a shampoo. The gym played havoc with my beauty regimen. "I know. I would have, but I've been so busy at work."

He bubbled with conspiratorial delight as he leaned in and whispered in my ear, "OMG have you ever seen so many hot men?" Out of habit, Philip arranged a few stray strands of my hair. "Come join me for a drink and then you can tell me all about what's going on with your shoe."

"I need to sign in first. I'm supposed to meet Ashley here. Have you seen her?"

"I haven't, but if I find her, I'll tell her you're here. Come and find me when you're done registering."

We parted and the handsome stranger had disappeared into the crowd. I walked in the direction of the registration table to check in. The Halloween theme was in full force. The perimeter of the Hidden Garden was dotted with booths that housed a variety of psychic services offered by different types of fortune-tellers, from mediums to palm readers to astrologists. While I waited to check in, attendees who were eager to have their futures predicted lined up outside the booths.

Ashley emerged from one of the palm reading booths. She dazzled in an off-the-shoulder black dress and strappy heels. As soon as she spotted me, she rushed over. As she approached, her hoop earrings swung gently, peeking through her mass of perfectly coiffed crimped curls.

I hugged her. "You look gorgeous!"

"Thanks. I know, right? Gotta step up my game if I want to snag one of these fine firefighters. You look gorgeous too."

I was wearing the same black top and pants I'd worn all day at work. But she was kind to say so. I dangled my broken-heeled shoe in front of her.

"What the heck happened? Those are the ones from Nordstrom, right?"

"Yep."

"Hope you're gonna give them a one-star review. Now we know why they were on sale."

"I blame the maze. Again. It's a long story."

"Give me that. I'll fix it. Wait here."

"Where would I go with only one shoe?"

Ashley laughed and gave me a fist bump. "I'll be as quick as I can."

In less than five minutes, Ashley returned with my shoe. Duct tape encased the heel shaft and the back of my shoe. It looked like a middle school avant-garde art project.

"Wow! Thanks, Ash. Where did you get the tape?"

Ashley grinned from ear to ear. "I asked the cutest firefighter here. It was a perfect icebreaker. 'Excuse me, kind sir. I don't suppose you could help a damsel in distress?'" She chortled.

"Please tell me you didn't actually say that?"

"Of course not, silly. But that was the gist. And it worked! See?" She pushed the shoe into my hands.

I tried moving the taped heel. It didn't budge. I had to admit it looked like a good fix. "I didn't know they taught shoe repair as part of EMT training. Thanks again."

"It's not Cinderella's glass slipper, but at least you can walk now."

Her glass slipper reference stirred a sad, fleeting memory of my wedding. I slipped on my shoe and immediately brightened. "Wow. I'm impressed. Good as new! Now, if only all my other problems could be solved so easily."

"Can you believe all the gorgeous guys here? I feel like a kid in a candy store, only I'm thirty-two and it's eye candy." She squealed softly. "Don't look now, cute guy at two o'clock."

I looked in the direction of two o'clock. A small group of firefighters stood in a circle talking. "Which one? They all look cute to me."

She did a little dance in place by stomping her feet a few times. "I know! I'm talking about the black guy. He's the one who fixed your shoe."

"I hope you thanked him for me. Props for the creative icebreaker, by the way."

Ashley nodded. "His name is Tate and he was so-o-o nice, too."

"What happened to Adrian? I thought you two were really hitting it off."

"We were, but I think he only wants to be friends."

That certainly wasn't the vibe I picked up when I saw them together, but I had too much on my plate at the moment to play cupid too. "He seems into you to me. Time will tell. Where are you going now? They have a hypnotist. You always said you wanted to try one."

She scanned the garden. I assumed she was following my recommendation and was searching for the hypnotist's booth. She turned and gave me a quick hug and whispered in my ear, "I'll be in whatever line has the cutest guys, and by cutest guys, I mean Tate."

Soon after, I was all set, equipped with my name tag. I sipped a glass of white wine I'd swiped from a passing server's tray as Ashley and I exchanged texts. She told me she was at the fortune-teller's booth, which didn't really narrow it down much. I wandered around for a few minutes before finding Esmeralda the Fortune-teller. As an added bonus, her booth didn't have a line, but I soon realized why. Stuck to the front of the booth was a little note written on a yellow Post-it that read "Back in five." Puzzled, I was about to pull out my phone again to text

Ashley when, with a sweep of the curtain, the booth was open for business. A woman I assumed to be Esmeralda appeared in the doorway. Her slight frame was draped in a long, ornately embroidered vest over a white blouse and long black skirt. A heavy black veil covered her face.

She coughed a few times then cleared her throat. Her husky voice sounded like she was a smoker. "Hello, my dear. Please come in and have a seat."

Even though I normally didn't believe in such nonsense, I had to admit I was intrigued with the prospect of hearing my fortune predicted. A small brocade-covered table and two wooden chairs had been squeezed into the cramped space. I set my phone and my wine down and faced Esmeralda across the table.

She grasped my hands. "What's your first name, dear?"

"Tory. Actually, that's my nickname. My given name is Victoria."

She winked at me. "Date of birth?"

"July fourth, nineteen eighty-four."

She stared at me for a few seconds and gently squeezed my hands. She slowly lowered her eyes, her lids fluttering like Iris's when she dreamed. "You are an extraverted introvert. You like spending time by yourself because it brings you peace, the same reason you love nature. You're independent, but sometimes you can be headstrong to a fault. On the other hand, your kindness and intelligence attract others to you, and you connect with a few like-minded close friends. You help others by teaching them to help themselves. You will make a good mother someday. Your high intelligence is manifest in your insatiable curiosity and problem-solving skills. You like to solve puzzles, both jigsaw and those in real life. However, be warned! Curiosity killed the cat. Don't let your impatience in finding solutions make you throw caution to the wind. Your worst fear is not being in control of a situation."

My mouth slacked in awe. "Wow." She had described my personality to a T. Even the part about teaching others to help themselves, a trait I picked up from my father. There was something about Esmeralda that made me trust her. Her spirit came across as authentic, rather than playacting. I felt like I knew her.

Next, Esmeralda turned my right hand upward and studied my palm. With her index finger, she traced the lines in my palm and examined them as if they were roads on a map leading to my future. Her eyelids fluttered shut for a few seconds before she spoke. "You have recently lost a loved one."

A chill went up my spine and I sighed mournfully. "My father —"

Esmeralda put her finger to her lips and hissed at me. "Shh! His death was not what it appeared to be."

I froze in fright. Did she mean my father had committed suicide? There was no way I'd ever believe that. I was ready to get up and leave.

She closed her eyes. "Another loved one also left you. This one you had a romantic relationship with. A boyfriend?" She shook her head. "No, a husband. I see a good aura around him. I have a message from your husband."

I nearly fell off my chair. "From Milo?"

Esmeralda's veil prevented me from seeing her expression, but her heavy nod spoke volumes of sadness that chilled me to the bone. "He loves you and he's sorry. He was only trying to help. He never meant to leave you."

At that moment, my worst fears about Milo's fate, that I'd tried to repress, surfaced from the back of my brain. Compliments of a rent-a-psychic, no less. The one percent of hope I'd held out that he was still alive was dashed. It was bad enough when the police reached their conclusion based on circumstantial evidence. But to have a totally different source confirm the same conclusion was like having a different brand of pregnancy kit duplicate the first test result. My palm was still in Esmeralda's grip, now a whole lot sweatier, but her hold kept me anchored to the moment. I reached for my wine with my other hand, taking a few swigs while she continued.

"Both of your lost loved ones are now your guardian angels. They're looking out for you. They're reaching out to show you signs. The answer to your husband's disappearance lies in the Secret Maze."

Just then a crack of light pierced the darkened booth as someone parted the curtains that hung at the entrance. Someone peeked in at us. I kept my eyes on Esmeralda, practically entranced from what she had just said. She looked over my shoulder and shook her head sharply. At the same time, my phone pinged. It was a text from Ashley. These interruptions broke Esmeralda's spell. She took both my hands in hers and patted them before standing up. I gathered up my purse, phone, and glass and thanked her.

"Think about what I've told you. Here's my card. You can call me with ten questions you want answered related to what I've said."

Before I could articulate any follow-up questions, she'd ushered me out of the booth and disappeared behind the curtains, shutting them tight.

At once I texted Ashley back. We met near the beverage table. I was typically a light drinker, but I needed more wine.

"She said what now?" It was noisy and Ashley's attention was elsewhere, distracted by the attractive scenery. "That you're nosy and bossy?" She chuckled.

I pushed my shoulder sideways into hers. "No. She called it independent, curious, and intelligent, thank you very much, and that Milo is going to send me a sign to explain his disappearance, and that the answer lies in the Secret Maze."

"Hmm. Weird that she got so much stuff right, though."

"Yeah, I know she's basically a psychic for hire, but she blew me away with her accuracy."

Ashley did a double take. "Wait, you're not going to tell me that the queen of logic, Ms. Victoria Benning, really buys any of this crap, are you?"

I remained silent.

"I can't believe you! She probably read about Milo's

disappearance in the *Santa Sofia Sentinel* and saw your photograph, like everyone else. You've got to admit, his disappearance has made you somewhat of a minor celebrity. You're the biggest thing that's happened in Santa Sofia since they found that naked dude stuck in a chimney last Christmas."

"Umm, thanks? Could you just humor me for a minute, please? It makes me hopeful that I still have a connection with my dad and Milo, even if it's in another realm. I felt like Esmeralda knew what she was talking about. Come with me. I want to ask her what she meant when she said the answer was lying in the Secret Maze. You always ask such good lawyer questions."

"Okay. But let's make it quick. I have firefighters to meet and places to go."

I rolled my eyes as she shot me an impish smile. The dinner hour was upon us and the crowd had reached capacity. We wiggled through the throng, but when we finally reached Esmeralda's booth, it was empty. Esmeralda was gone.

The voice over the loudspeaker announced that dinner would start in ten minutes.

I pleaded with Ashley. "Can we at least check out the Secret Maze to see if we can figure out what Esmeralda meant? Maybe it'll inspire us to see it from a different perspective, to think outside the box. Now we're looking for some kind of message."

"We've gone through that maze more times than is healthy. I think it gave me maze-brain last time. I couldn't think straight. I'll give you five minutes. Then I need to scope out the dining room. I want to make sure I'm sitting at a good table. And by good, I mean one populated with cute guys." She flashed me a toothy grin.

Once in the Secret Maze, I led the way. After we'd turned a few corners, Ashley checked the time on her phone. "Welp. Nothing new to see here."

We arrived at a small clearing, near where I'd overheard a man and a woman arguing earlier. Stumped, I didn't know what Esmeralda wanted me to look for. Ashley glanced at the time again.

"I know you think I'm stupid thinking we'll find a message from Milo."

"Not at all. I'm a skeptic and a big believer in logic, but I also know I don't know everything."

"Well, I know one thing—you didn't like him. You told me he was a player and that he'd hit on you. So, you probably think I'm better off without him anyway, right?"

"Yes and no. Yes, you'd be better off without him, obviously, if he were up to no good. But I never said I believed he was. So, technically, I might have stretched the truth when I said Milo hit on me. I'll admit that was a fib, but I did it for your own good. I acted like that because I wanted to protect your sorry butt just in case we had all been wrong about Milo. You weren't in the frame of mind to listen to reason. So, I appealed to your emotions. If I told you how great he was and what a perfect match you two were, you would have never agreed to the precaution of legally separating. Sorry. I'm goal-oriented, what can I say."

The wine and this rare self-revelation from Ashley made me grateful for our friendship more than ever.

"Aw, that's so sweet." She wasn't the only one feeling the effects of alcohol.

We hugged it out and resumed our search for another ten minutes but came up empty.

I sighed. "Okay, I give up. That's enough excitement for me for one night. I'm going to head out to the gym." I gave Ashley a hug. "Don't break too many hearts."

Ashley went back to the party, and I continued along the dark maze on my way to my car. Around the next bend, I tripped over something. I flashed my phone light downward and flinched. Esmeralda's body was sprawled across the path in front of me, slumped on her side. Her veil was rolled back and rested on the top of her head like a padded headband. A knife stuck out of her chest.

CHAPTER 10

The bloodstain was huge and her blouse was saturated. Esmeralda tried to speak but only a gurgle came out. *Oh no!*

Adrenaline pumped through me big-time. My voice and lungs combined to emit a thunderous out-of-body roar that threatened to awaken the dead in the nearby cemetery.

"Help! Somebody! Call nine-one-one! He-lp!"

I turned my phone light to illuminate Esmeralda's face, spotlighting the fear in her shocked eyes. She blinked and I flinched, jarring a vague recollection, again, that I had known her in a previous life. I immediately redirected the beam to the ground, noticing a footprint in the dirt as I did so, causing me to flinch once again. I was no expert, but it sure looked exactly like the footprint left near Milo's car. I shuddered with dread. I clicked the camera on my phone and took a couple of shots before turning my attention back to Esmeralda. She seemed to acknowledge my presence with an ever-so-slight movement of her head.

I leaned in closer and whispered, "Oh my God, Esmeralda, who did this to you?"

A raspy, guttural utterance that was indecipherable escaped from her barely parted lips.

With the only light coming from my phone, I panned my surroundings, squinting at the hedges in the semidarkness and listening to a rustling in the hedge. My whole body trembled and the possibility that the killer was still lurking in the bushes did nothing to quell my tremors. The rapidly growing crimson stain on Esmeralda's white blouse discouraged me from moving her for fear I might make matters worse. The unnerving sight of the knife sticking out of Esmeralda's chest didn't help either. My only consolation, the killer was no longer armed. Hopefully.

My shrieks had effectively raised the alarm. The maze buzzed with activity and voices were approaching. Help was on the way. I tried to comfort her by gently stroking her face. Her eyes focused beyond me in an earnest stare. I nervously turned around to see if someone was behind me. No one was there. Her lips barely moved as she tried to speak. But the effort was too much for her. Her chest heaved, once, twice, three times, as if she were expelling her own soul. Her last breath escaped as a loud rattle, signaling the end. She went still. The realization she was gone hadn't yet sunken in as the crunch of gravel made me aware of the group of people now gathering around me in the tight space.

Ashley broke through the crowd, aghast at the sight of Esmeralda's body. "Are you all right? Is that Esmeralda? Oh my God, she's not . . . ?"

My eyes brimmed with tears as I nodded. "I think she is."

Ashley wrapped her arms around me in a comforting hug. The handsome stranger I'd encountered near the maze earlier was right on her heels. He steered both of us over to a clearing to make room for the line of firefighters trotting behind him. I then realized how lucky we were to have Santa Sofia's entire emergency response team in attendance at the special event. Some were off duty and in business casual attire for the event, but others were on duty and dressed accordingly, their flashlights shining on the scene.

Adrian pulled up the rear. He bent his head to consult with the firefighters attending to Esmeralda for a moment before he started to bark orders at two of his fellow police officers to cordon off the area and not let anyone in or out of the Hidden Garden and Secret Maze.

He came over to me, resting a hand on my shoulder. "I take it you were the one who found her?"

I nodded.

"Epic scream, by the way."

"Um, thanks?" I'd been called many things before but epic screamer was a first.

A long whistle escaped Adrian's puckered lips. "Another murder?"

I dipped my head in assent.

"And in the maze again?"

A multitude of emotions festered inside me—fear, sadness, shock, and anger. I didn't know how much longer I could keep it all together. Finally, words erupted from me as hot and intense as lava flowing from a volcano. "Why does everyone I encounter keep dying?" I was beginning to feel more like the Grim Reaper than a landscape architect.

He jerked backward. "You knew her?"

"She just read my fortune about ten minutes ago."

"No way." He shook his head and his shock registered for a second longer before he returned to his professional demeanor. "So, tell me what happened. Take it from the top."

Ashley had been stewing silently next to me, listening to my interchange with Adrian. She pushed her face in front of Adrian's. "Tory screamed bloody murder because that's what she saw. She's probably in shock. Poor thing attracts trouble like a magnet."

"Um, hello. I'm right here, in case you forgot. I can hear what you're saying." I might have been a bit in shock, but these two and their wisecracks told me I wasn't the only one acting strangely.

Ashley's eyes kind of crossed as if she'd just heard what she said about me. "God, sorry, Tory. I didn't mean that." She whispered to Adrian, "But it's kind of true."

Adrian flashed his palm in a stop gesture. "Take it easy, Ash. I wasn't judging her. I'm trying to get the facts straight."

Ashley swayed. "It's just that I've never seen an actual murder victim close up like this before." Her voice was shaky and she started to stagger to maintain her balance.

Adrian blinked with concern, and he put his arm around her waist to prop her up. "You need to sit and take some deep breaths."

She dropped to the ground and followed his instructions. After a few minutes of Lamaze-worthy deep breathing, she seemed back to normal.

Satisfied Ashley was okay, Adrian faced me. "What were you doing in the maze?"

"I was taking a shortcut to get my car at the valet parking near the lobby."

"Kind of early to leave, before dinner, wasn't it? Were you alone?"

I paused.

Ashley perked up and got to her feet, chiming in before I could respond. "She was with me first. But then I needed to get back to the event. The dinner service was starting."

"So you were in the maze earlier? Before using it as a shortcut. Why?"

I got his subtext—why would I ever want to use the maze again after what had happened to Milo here. "Because I had my fortune told by Esmeralda earlier this evening and she told me I could find a clue about Milo's disappearance here."

Adrian raised his eyebrows and stared at me quizzically. "All right. What did she tell you exactly?"

"That the answer to Milo's disappearance lies in the Secret Maze."

Ashley's eyes widened. "Oh my God. Did she predict her own death? Because technically, she's lying in the Secret Maze."

I turned to Ashley. "You think Esmeralda is the answer to Milo's disappearance? How does that even make sense?" My thoughts were in turmoil. "I honestly think if that was the case, she would have avoided the maze, don't you?"

Adrian shifted his weight. "Did she know Milo?"

Before I could answer, Ashley responded. "Anyone who reads the *Sentinel* knows about Milo. I'm sure that's where these so-called fortune-tellers get their info for these charitable event readings. There are always well-known philanthropists and society types at these events. All she had to do was read up on the latest scandal or self-promotion."

"I believe I can shed some light on this." The stranger I'd almost forgotten about handed Adrian his business card. "Jake Logan. I'm a private investigator."

"Please. By all means, enlighten me." Adrian could barely hide his contempt.

"I don't know for certain whether Mr. Spinelli and Madame Esmeralda actually knew each other. But I'm certain Madame Esmeralda knew Ms. Benning."

Heat flashed to my face. "What are you talking about? I never even knew Esmeralda existed before tonight. And how do you know my name?" I threw him a withering glance, wondering whether he was one of those guys with good looks but an ugly personality, and hoped he wasn't going to ruin my impression of him by continuing to mansplain to me about what individuals I did or didn't know.

Jake opened his mouth to speak, but I cut him off before he could.

I took a deep breath. "Okay, to be honest, she did look familiar. But I swear, tonight was the first time I ever laid eyes on her."

Jake turned to me. "Actually, that's not true. Her real name is Josephine Benning. And I believe she's your aunt."

CHAPTER 11

"That can't be. My aunt Jo is dead."

"Well, you might have been led to believe that by your family, but, up until now, she's been very much alive."

Ashley and I stared at each other in open-mouthed surprise and locked arms to bolster each other up, like dancers in a chorus line.

Adrian instructed all of us in the maze to regroup at a table in the Hidden Garden. When we did, the entire Santa Sofia police department appeared to be out in force, methodically taking names and contact information from all the people milling around who'd been in attendance, before letting them leave the premises. Since the attendees hadn't yet been served their dinner and some were forced to remain until given permission to leave by the SSPD, the hotel catering manager had very quickly improvised and instructed the kitchen to box up the dinners so anyone who was hungry could eat now or take the meal home with them. Even in stressful circumstances, the hotel staff upheld their stellar reputation for attention to detail, endearing them to me even more. As a testament to my own state of mind, I didn't even worry about grabbing my own meal . . . too much.

Adrian had asked for friends of Esmeralda, as well as anyone who had interacted with her or observed her at the event, to remain. That statement dismissed the majority of the crowd, many of whom filed by a long buffet table to grab a boxed dinner on their way out. My late mother's younger sister, Aunt Marian, or Marian the librarian as we affectionately referred to her, raised her hand to say she'd known Esmeralda since her homeless days when Esmeralda used to camp out in the library. Paloma, a palm reader, and a medium named Blanche stepped forward and identified themselves as her friends. To my surprise, so did Philip. He identified himself as her hairdresser and said Esmeralda was a longtime client.

I mouthed "What!" to him. He smiled back with an inscrutable Cheshire cat grin as one of the officers directed him to a table where they were taking statements. Some of the guests who'd known or seen Esmeralda were told they'd be dismissed after their particulars were taken. Others, like us, stayed for questioning. I pulled up a chair next to Adrian. Ashley sat on my other side. Uncle Bob, Aunt Veronica, Aunt Marian, and the private investigator, Jake Logan, joined our table, as did Paloma, the palm reader. Hovering behind us, a handful of Benning Brothers employees hung around chatting. That left about twenty people, half of whom were police personnel, still lingering in the Hidden Garden.

In the commotion of finding out Esmeralda was actually my long-lost Aunt Jo, I'd failed to consider the impact of her death on my uncle Bob. Whereas I'd barely known her, she and Uncle Bob were siblings and had spent their whole childhood together. Even in the dimmed light of the Hidden Garden, I could see all the color had drained from my uncle's face. He was visibly shaken to learn of his sister's death.

His wife, Aunt Veronica, wasn't doing well either. Fighting back tears, she gripped my uncle's arm. "I need to be the one to break the news to Sam."

Adrian scrutinized her and she met his gaze.

"I need to talk to my son before he hears about it from someone else or sees it on the news."

I wondered why it mattered how Sam found out about the death of Aunt Jo. Sam was sixteen. Surely, like me, he must have only known she existed through the stories shared by Uncle Bob and my father. Aunt Veronica's hysterics attracted the attention of the small group of Benning Brothers employees and Ernie, who'd been questioning them. Ernie met my gaze with a "wazup" chin jut and pointed at me and then his pad to indicate he wanted to question me next. Jed Barnes, our nursery manager, turned and approached our table. He looked at Uncle Bob first and then Adrian.

"I can drive Veronica back to your house if you like, no problem."

Aunt Veronica stood up. "That would be great, if it's okay with the officer."

Jed rested his hand on the back of my chair, and I sniffed subtly to make sure he wasn't reeking of alcohol before I let him drive my aunt anywhere.

Adrian studied my aunt and uncle and Jed for a moment. "Okay. Only on the condition both of you set up an interview time with one of the officers before you take off. We have more than enough to do tonight. And make sure you leave your contact information with us too."

Jed bowed his head in agreement. "Will do, sir."

Uncle Bob stood up and grasped Jed's hand before patting him on the back.

Aunt Veronica smiled with relief. "Thank you so much. I really appreciate it. I'll be sure to leave all my information with your colleague." She squeezed my shoulder before she and Jed were shepherded to another table by a uniformed officer.

Adrian wasted no time getting back to his questioning while multitasker Ernie lurked in the background. "Okay, Bob. How about you tell us about your sister. When was the last time you saw her?"

"I saw her tonight, but I didn't realize it was Jo. She was wearing that heavy veil. I just saw this veiled woman in costume known as Madame Esmeralda wandering around the party like the other entertainers we hired. But prior to tonight, I've only kept in touch with Jo a couple of times a year through email. I haven't seen her in person in many years."

"Did you speak with her tonight?"

"No. I had no reason to speak to a fortune-teller. I was busy making the rounds thanking all the donors for their contributions. Of course, had I known it was Jo, I'd have been civil. But she made no attempt to speak to me either."

Adrian jotted something down. "Okay. Can you tell me why you weren't in touch more often? Did you not get along?"

"It's a long story. She's been estranged from our family a long time."

"Can you tell me how that came about?'

I couldn't stay silent any longer. "Why did you tell me Aunt Jo was dead? I thought she died in a car accident when she was a teenager."

Uncle Bob winced like he'd just realized he'd swallowed a bad oyster. "We told you she was dead to protect you. My father, your grandfather, Robert Benning, disowned Jo when she was seventeen."

"He disowned his own daughter? Why? I wish I would've known she was alive. I would've at least liked to have met her."

After an awkward pause, he gave me a mournful stare. "You have met her, a number of times, when you were a little girl. Don't you remember?"

I fell back into my chair. "No. When? Where?"

"At your house. Your father told me she used to bring you a huge lollipop every time she visited."

Ah. "That was Aunt Jo? Yeah. Now I remember . . . I loved those big lollipops." Nothing like a food association to jog my memory! My thoughts spiraled back to when I was about four. I recalled a friend of my parents who visited us every now and again. "She always brought me a giant sucker with a candy stripe swirl."

Uncle Bob smiled at the recollection. "Your father told me you were always so sticky after she visited."

Ashley guffawed, and I gave her the side-eye.

I looked back at Uncle Bob. "So why did she get disowned? She must have done something awfully bad."

"She made a series of bad choices, despite warnings from our parents. She was too pretty for her own good. All the boys liked her. That gave her a cocky confidence. That was the problem. She got too big for her britches and scorned our parents' advice. Jo liked the attention and fell in love with a biker gang guy several years older than her. He was divorced and had a little boy from a previous marriage. She wanted to drop out of high school and marry the guy. Our parents told her she was way too young to be married, let alone be a stepmother. They wanted her to finish high school and graduate from college first."

"She was still in high school?"

"Yup. Our parents had her best interests at heart. But Jo was having none of it. She was always headstrong and had a false sense of impunity because men worshipped her. Dad threatened to disown her, cut her out of the family business, if she went against his wishes. Her response? She eloped with the guy."

"Wow. So what happened to her after she got married?"

"They moved out of state, somewhere in the southwest, Texas or New Mexico, I believe, and we lost touch for a while."

"For how long?"

"For a couple of years, maybe three. Her marriage didn't last long. No surprise there."

"She got divorced?"

"Yup. And moved back to Santa Sofia and stayed with our brother George for a while."

I jerked forward in my seat, spluttering. "Wait! You have another brother? Uncle Bob! How is it I've never heard of him?"

I couldn't get over that my staid uncle Bob and my dear father had kept all of these family secrets from me. My life had been a charade. I felt like I was dreaming or on an episode of *The Bold and the Beautiful.*

Totally flabbergasted, words sprayed from me. "How many more secret siblings do you have? Please don't tell me you're from a family of ten and I've only known two of you. Or that I'm a twin."

Ashley put her hand on my shoulder to calm me down.

I patted her hand and rolled my eyes. *Can you believe this?*

Uncle Bob cleared his throat. "No more, just the two siblings. And no, you're not a twin . . . that I know of." He chuckled.

Not the time to fuel my already shaken feelings about my identity, Uncle Bob.

He wiped the smile off his face and assumed a more serious expression. "Unfortunately, George was a real bad influence. He has been in and out of jail since high school. George and Jo were the babies of the family. Your father and I, as you know, were close in age. I'm sixty-five, your father was two years younger than me. It was just the two of us until George was born eight years after me, and then Jo five years later. When your dad and I were kids, your grandfather had just started Benning Family Landscape Design and Nursery, as it was known then. The business was still becoming established while your father and I were teenagers. By the time Jo and George reached adolescence, the company was doing very well. So, you can say Jo and George were born with silver spoons in their mouths. They grew up knowing they were rich kids. Your dad and I often wondered if that was why he and I ended up with a good work ethic and the other two didn't. Wealth is a double-edged sword, especially when you haven't personally done anything to earn it. It certainly seemed to contribute to George and Jo's lack of motivation to make anything of themselves—though you've always been ambitious."

I dipped my head, grateful for not being lumped together with spoiled brats.

Ashley nudged me with her shoulder. "Don't forget competitive."

Uncle Bob winked at Ashley and me. "Anyway, Jo started running around again with some bad seeds she knew from high school. Druggies. She drank too much and did too many drugs."

"How did she support herself?"

"Right before your grandfather died, he changed the company name from Benning Family to Benning Brothers, essentially transforming it into a new company, because he didn't want Jo or George trying to come back after he died to claim a share of it. After your grandfather died and it became crystal clear he'd cut Jo out of the will, she finally realized she had to depend on her own devices. Jo worked in bars mainly. Cocktail waitress. She always wanted to party because she got so much attention. After several years, she took up with a no-good layabout and got pregnant, and he left her right before she had the baby."

"Wow. How old was she then?"

"Her mid-thirties. We foolishly hoped that having a kid would motivate her to be more responsible. That she'd change her ways. But no. It went from bad to worse. She got postpartum depression and started drinking big-time. Her alcohol abuse got the best of her. She started to have blackouts. Thankfully, a neighbor called Social Services and they contacted us and clued us in. A social worker told us they were making plans to remove her baby."

"Oh my goodness. What happened?"

"The baby was adopted. Jo went to rehab."

"So, all her visits with the lollipops stopped way before that?"

"Yes. Your father thought it best to sever her in-person visits. He was worried about you being kidnapped more than anything else. She had so many drug-dealer and druggie friends. We've all heard stories where desperate drug addicts turn to crime to support their habit. Jo was a kindhearted person but not very discriminating when it came to whom she hung out with. It wasn't Jo we were worried about so much as her circle of friends. You never know what a desperate person might do to get drugs. Especially if a friend's young niece comes from a wealthy family."

I got it. I didn't have children, but I did have loved ones, although their numbers were, sadly, dwindling of late. The current love of my life was Iris, my dear Pomeranian, and I feared I was developing an unhealthy attachment to her since she was such a little buttercup. Especially since my father and Milo were no longer around. I had to rein in my constant impulse to protect her and shield her from danger. Lately, mail carriers, delivery persons, and passersby who'd stopped to admire her had all come under my intense scrutiny, all potential dog-napping suspects in my eyes. I was hoping it was only a passing stage in my grief journey since I hadn't been quite so paranoid prior to all my loss. But as it stood, for now I definitely fell into the helicopter pet parent category.

I shook my head to stop my wandering thoughts and refocused.

Adrian addressed Uncle Bob, while continuing to take copious notes. "How long had Jo been reading palms and telling fortunes as Esmeralda?"

"I can help with that." Paloma, the palm reader, fiddled with her cuff of bangle bracelets as everyone's gazes turned to her.

All the other people at our table had been silently listening up until this time, equally engrossed in the story of our family history.

Paloma clinked her bangles. "Jo and I became friends when I moved into her apartment building about ten years ago. We both moved in the same month and started to meet at the pool a couple of times a week. I was building a special event clientele and business was booming. All the fundraisers wanted me, as did weddings, birthday parties, and company functions. I had more business than I could handle alone, so I suggested she help out. She devoured the books I gave her to read up on the paranormal and supernatural arts and, like me, what started out as hocus-pocus turned into something deeper, where we helped people feel hopeful about their futures. Plus, we were both entertainers at heart and liked the exotic costumes."

Paloma paused to adjust the shawl she'd wrapped tightly around her. "People are surprised I'm able to make a living off of palm reading. But the high-roller vacationers who visit Santa Sofia are big tippers. Plus, a good portion of my income is from my online astrology business, and Jo helped with that too. She made enough to sock away some cash to buy her kid gifts."

"She had contact with her kid?" Adrian perked up like Iris spotting a squirrel.

"He actually contacted her about a year ago." Paloma lowered her voice. "I'm not sure whether or not his adoptive parents knew he had found her and established a relationship with her."

Uncle Bob moved restlessly in his chair. "I can tell you with certainty they did not."

Adrian shot his eyes at Uncle Bob. "How can you be so sure?"

"Because I'm his adoptive father. Our son, Sam, is Jo's biological child."

CHAPTER 12

I pushed back my chair and shot up like a rocket. "What! Sam is Jo's son? Why didn't you tell me?" It was now official. I *was* living in a daytime TV soap opera.

Uncle Bob let out a whistle. "I don't know. The longer we waited, the harder it got because then it seemed like an intentional deception. We didn't plan for it to work out that way. It just happened. And then I didn't want to rock the boat."

"Did my dad know?"

Uncle Bob nodded.

"Oh my goodness! What else haven't you told me?"

"That's it. No more surprises."

"Good. Because I don't think I can handle any more." I settled back in my chair.

Adrian put his hands on the table and directed his gaze at Uncle Bob. "So, you're telling me nobody knew Esmeralda was your sister Jo."

"That's right, none of us did. Sam knew he was adopted. We had told him my sister Jo was his birth mother. He knew she was alive. I thought that we'd all left it at that. I had no idea the two were in contact. I had no idea Jo was Esmeralda. I'm assuming Sam didn't either."

Adrian continued, "Then why did your wife insist on breaking the news to your son herself? If your wife and Sam didn't know Esmeralda was his mother, Jo, why would your wife think Esmeralda's death would upset Sam so much?"

"I didn't say Sam didn't know Esmeralda. I'm guessing she was one of the fortune-tellers he'd been working for part-time. He got a part-time job with a moving company. I'm assuming he met her through his job, moving their equipment, their booths, and other props for their various engagements. He'd worked for a theater company, moving their sets and equipment, too. He got odd jobs posted on his high school job board. He was always working part-time at random jobs. He moved furniture, washed windows, even worked for our nursery division putting up residential holiday lights. He's a great kid, very ambitious."

Adrian could barely hide the doubt in his voice. "So, you think your wife knew Esmeralda might be one of those he moved stuff for and he'd be upset to hear the news from anyone other than your wife?"

Uncle Bob paused to ponder Adrian's words. "Yes, I'm assuming that's what she thought."

"How often did he work at his moving job?"

"I don't know exactly. Maybe a couple of times a month or so."

"And when did he start the job?"

Uncle Bob tilted his head back "I'd say about four months ago."

"So, after moving equipment for Esmeralda and her fellow fortune-tellers only a few times, they formed a strong bond?"

Uncle Bob literally had to wipe the sweat off his brow with his sleeve. "I guess. Maybe my wife knows more about their relationship. I'm just trying to piece it together myself right now."

I consciously worked to not let my jaw slacken as I watched my friend Adrian in tough-cop mode pummel my Uncle Bob on inconsistencies. And doing a darn good job. Why was my Uncle Bob lying? What was he still hiding?

Adrian was relentless. "But you don't think he knew Esmeralda was his mother?"

Uncle Bob gazed back at Adrian in a daze. "I . . . I don't know. Even I didn't know Jo was Esmeralda. He knew his biological mother was Jo. He didn't know that Jo was Esmeralda, is my understanding."

"And your wife never mentioned to you that Sam knew

Esmeralda was Jo and, in fact, his mother?"

"Yes, er, no, um, I can't remember for sure."

Adrian dug in his heels. "Bob, let's cut the BS, okay. I think you knew Esmeralda was in fact Jo. I think your wife knew. I think your son knew she was his biological mother. Am I correct?"

"Do I need a lawyer?"

"I don't know. You tell me."

"I haven't done anything wrong."

"No one said you did. I just expect total honesty. This is a murder investigation. Let me be the one to decide what's relevant, okay?"

Uncle Bob nodded.

I extracted my phone from my purse. "Speaking of relevant, Adrian. Look at these photos I took of a footprint." I handed him my phone. "I took them when I found Esmeralda. I wanted to make sure I took a photo of them before they got trampled."

Adrian studied the photos and then looked at his watch. "Okay, everyone. These officers will finish up collecting your information and will contact you in the morning. Please be available tomorrow for further questioning. Thank you for your cooperation."

I looked up beyond our table, and Philip caught my eye. He blew me a kiss and gave me the "call me" gesture before he scurried away.

My aunt Marian slid over a couple of seats. "Let's have lunch soon, Tory dear. It's been too long." She kissed my cheek.

I patted her hand. "I'd like that. I'll call you soon." I stood up ready to go and winked at my uncle Bob across the table.

Uncle Bob gave me a weak smile and looked lost for a moment before Aunt Marian rounded the table, linked arms with him, and ushered him away.

Adrian stood up too. "Tory, can you stick around for a few minutes. I'd like Ashley and . . ." Adrian dug a business card from his pocket and squinted at it. "Er . . . Mr. Logan to hang around too."

An officer came up behind Adrian. "Sir, a moment please."

"Excuse me. I'll be right with you guys." He walked to a corner with the officer, where another cop joined them.

Ashley smiled at Jake. "So, you're a private investigator?"

Jake's gaze studied her. "That's right. And you are?"

"I'm sorry." She stuck out her hand. "Ashley Payne. Lawyer. Used to work in the Santa Barbara County Public Defenders division. I know a couple of PIs from there. What types of cases do you work on?"

He never got a chance to respond because Adrian returned to the table. "Okay, let's go back to where you found Esmeralda in the maze and take a look at those footprints. When I got to the scene, it was only you three and the firefighters. So how did you two end up being the first two at the scene after Tory?"

Ashley and Jake took turns filling Adrian in on their activities and whereabouts up until they found me in the maze with the body. Jake told him he was near the entrance of the maze and had heard my screams for help.

Adrian turned to me. "How many tickets were sold to the fundraiser? And I'll need a list of donors who attended tonight."

"I don't know how many offhand. Our bookkeeper would know and have a list."

"Who's that?"

I paused. "Aunt Veronica is temporarily handling our bookkeeping duties. She and Uncle Bob had both retired last year, but after my father died, they both came back to help during the transition." I didn't think it was critical to announce to the world that she came back to help figure out who was embezzling from Benning Brothers. We had enough stuff going on to fuel the soap opera for the moment.

"Okay. Could you do me a favor and find out for me? Just in case she's not feeling up to an interview tonight. I'd like to get on it and follow up."

"Of course. I'll get on it first thing in the morning."

"Good."

The four of us, Ashley, Adrian, Jake, and myself, walked back to the maze. Adrian lifted the yellow tape at the entrance and we entered. The body had just been removed and two forensic personnel were packing up. After they left and it was only the four of us, I looked around to make sure no one else was within earshot.

I dug out my camera. "Adrian, I want to show you something interesting. Here are the photos of the footprints I took tonight."

"Uh-huh." He nodded. "Yeah, thanks. You already showed me."

"And here are photos of the footprints I showed you after Milo disappeared. I took one set in the maze and another set from the parking lot next to Milo's car."

Adrian studied them. "Yeah. I remember. These are great. You're the best kind of witness—one who pays attention to details. Do me a favor and email both sets of pics to me. I can have our tech people blow them up to see if they're the same. I don't know whether our forensic folks have such good photos."

I stood up straighter, flattered by his compliment. "Okay, great. I'll email them tonight."

He patted my shoulder. "Good job. Hang in there, girl."

"I'm trying."

Ashley chimed in, her eyes drilling in on Adrian. "Tory's trying, all right, trying my patience. I had to guilt her to even attend tonight when my plus-one bailed on me."

Adrian threw up his hands. "I told you I had to work. Doesn't it look like I'm working?"

I glared at Ashley. "Hey. It hasn't even been a month since Milo disappeared, Ashley. Forgive me if I'm not applying to go on *The Bachelor* just yet. Cut me some slack."

In response, Ashley pursed her lips and sniffed, barely veiling her mild contempt for Adrian and me at the moment.

Jake had been intensely following our conversation. "Sorry to snoop, but it is my profession." He laughed lightly and his cheeks dimpled as he did.

He's adorable, I thought.

Adrian regarded Jake. "What is it?"

Jake turned to me. "I take it you're referring to Milo Spinelli, the guy who disappeared on his wedding day. I've read about the case. Puzzling."

Ashley crossed her arms. "He was her husband."

Jake raised his eyebrows. "Yes, I figured that out earlier when you were talking about what Esmeralda said about him. You're the Tory mentioned in the posters. You still haven't heard from him, I take it? You think he's met with foul play?"

Adrian answered, "Several factors indicate that's the case. We've found evidence that's suspicious. We continue to search for him . . . or a body."

I gazed at Jake intensely. "There were footprints. And a creepy person in a hoodie caught on surveillance footage."

Jake said, "Really? So the footprints weren't Milo's? You think they belonged to the person in the hoodie?"

"Exactly." I was impressed how quickly Jake connected the dots. But then he was a PI. If Benning Brothers hadn't been in dire financial straits, I'd think about hiring him to help find Milo.

We exited the Secret Maze and gathered together in the Hidden Garden and said good night. Adrian escorted Ashley to her car in the parking lot. Jake had also valet parked, and we walked together along the regular walkway, bypassing the yellow-taped maze.

While Jake spoke to one of the valets, I found myself staring with appreciation at his effortlessly trendy look, well put together without trying too hard, his neatly tousled hair and the five-o'clock shadow enhancing his square jaw. He turned and caught me staring at him. I waved my ticket randomly, pretending to flag down a valet.

Jake strolled back to me and leaned over my shoulder to whisper in my ear, "You just need to show your parking ticket at the kiosk. It's valet parking, not a New York taxi stand."

When I turned to face him with my skin burning, his eyes twinkled impishly.

I tittered like a teenager. "Ya, I know. I was just trying to pay."

"Right. You need to do that at the kiosk. But it's okay. I took care of it and paid for both of us. If you give me your ticket, they can call up your car."

"Oh, I can't let you do that."

He took the ticket from my hand and gave it to the valet while I foraged in my purse for my wallet like a blind squirrel searching for a buried nut. Finally I pulled out a twenty-dollar bill.

When he returned, I tried to shove the money into his hand. "Please. I insist."

He dodged my attempt to hand him the money by lifting his arms in the air as I lunged forward. Revved up by the dual needs to end my embarrassment and to pay my own way, I tucked the bill into one of his front pants pockets.

He laughed. "Now I know how the guys from Chippendale's must feel."

My face burned like it was on fire. Mortified, I couldn't think of a quick comeback. "Oh, by the way, I've been meaning to ask you, how did you know Esmeralda was my aunt Jo?"

The valet pulled up in Jake's white Tesla and parked it first in line. Then another valet drove up in my black Lexus. Jake ran to his car and jumped in. He rolled down the passenger's side window and signaled me to approach. "Catch up with you soon." He reached over and pressed the twenty-dollar bill into my hand. Before I realized what he'd done, the valet urged me to step back on the curb to make room for a big white Land Rover. Behind it, a silver Infinity and a black Mercedes followed in quick succession. While I was complying with the valet's command, Jake had driven off and then turned back around onto the ring road that circled the hotel. Odd. I wondered if he had forgotten something or was staying at the hotel. But then why get his car?

I drove home feeling alternately puzzled and sad, as I'd been feeling the last few weeks. But tonight, despite my aunt's murder, inexplicably I also felt a slight hope for the future for the first time since Milo had disappeared.

Iris greeted me in her typical overly exuberant fashion. When I opened the back door, she flung herself outside to take care of her business and, just as quickly, trotted back inside. I grabbed her fuzzy little body and plopped into my desk chair. Otis jumped on my desk, coiled up, and purred like an idling car.

Iris cast Otis a smug look, conveying she'd bested him in premium seating for the night and curled into a contented ball on my lap, like a little bunny, as I sent the two sets of footprint photos to Adrian. I also sent them to my own email and opened them on my computer to compare them. I was convinced they were from the same boot. I leaned back in the chair, pleased with my good eye for detective work.

Then a realization hit me. Esmeralda was murdered. Milo had probably been murdered too. A chill went up my spine and radiated throughout me. Grabbing Iris in one hand, I got up and bundled a cashmere wrap around me. But even with the wrap and Iris on my lap, I couldn't get warm. I turned up the heat a few degrees and hugged Iris tighter as I sat staring at the footprints. Thinking about the hooded figure. Remembering Esmeralda's warm grasp of my hands. Wishing I could unsee the knife sticking out of her chest. No wonder I couldn't warm up. No matter how tightly I held Iris, pulled the cashmere wrap around me, and turned up the heat, the chill wasn't going away until the mystery of their deaths was solved.

CHAPTER 13

I awoke to a ping from my phone. Iris was snuggled up into a little fluff ball between the pillows next to me. Without getting out of bed, I stretched from head to toe, arms over my head and toes pointed. Iris didn't budge. I felt rested. The last thing I remembered was my head hitting the pillow like a felled tree.

Iris sprang into action as soon as I swung my legs out of bed. She had two settings: hyperactive and comatose. Hyperactive mode in full throttle, she pranced around on my California king bed for several seconds, soon thereafter adding intermittent soft barks. No smell of coffee brewing. Darn. I'd forgotten to turn on the coffee machine last night.

I checked my phone—eight thirty. Ashley had sent me a text: *Want to meet up for coffee?*

Perfect timing. I smiled and texted back I'd meet her in twenty minutes. And then I remembered. Yesterday. Esmeralda. The knife. The footprint. All the unsettling images came crashing back into my consciousness. I also remembered Adrian's request to get the fundraiser donor list. I sent a quick text to Aunt Veronica asking her to send it to him directly. My aunt was good at her job and liked to help people, and I was hoping being of assistance to Adrian would make her feel better than she'd felt last night. As for my own current fragile state, coffee with Ashley was definitely the Rx I needed. Thank God it was the weekend.

I caught Iris in midair as she leapt off the bed and set her down on the hardwood floor, where she increased her game to full-on nonstop yapping, like a track on repeat. I quickly changed into gray sweatpants and a sweatshirt and jammed my feet into an old pair of chestnut-colored Uggs. I shuffled through the hallway to the living room, stepping over Otis, lying right in my way, as Iris dashed ahead, beating me to the door. Once outside, I forced myself to trot around the perimeter of my small backyard a few times to get my blood circulating while Iris darted around, looking for squirrels.

After about ten minutes, we headed back inside. I filled matching red polka-dot dishes with Iris's and Otis's respective premium kibble before I went back to the bathroom to brush my hair and teeth. By the time I'd returned to the kitchen, they'd eaten all their food, the cue for Iris to dance around me on her hind legs like a circus animal until I gave her a Greenie. She snatched it from my hand as if it were a relay race baton and scampered away, determined to leave everyone behind her. Otis padded out of the room after her in hot pursuit. I followed them into my office, where Iris was lying on her sheepskin bed gnawing on the Greenie propped between her paws, gloating, while Otis watched in envy. I made a mental note to order Otis some feline Greenies, but in the meantime, I found his catnip toy in his bed and threw it to him. He immediately started to play with it by wrapping his paws around it and kicking himself in the chin. After Iris finished, I dried off her chest fur with a paper towel and put on her leopard-print harness. I threw on a light quilted jacket, grabbed my purse in one hand and Iris's leash in the other, and locked up before jogging the two blocks to the local Starbucks with Iris at my side.

Ashley was already sitting outside. "I just got here and haven't ordered yet. I wanted to snag the last empty table."

"Good thinking. What do you want? I'll go order if you stay out here with Iris."

"Hello, Princess Iris. How are you today?" Ashley bent down and scooped her up.

Iris commenced to slather Ashley's face with kisses.

"I need to find me a man with Iris's personality. She's always happy and loving, worships me, and does everything I say. I'd like a nonfat latte, please . . . and I wouldn't mind splitting a goody—your choice."

"You got it." Chuckling, I headed into the shop.

A couple of patrons ahead of me were finishing up their transactions, giving me time to peruse the pastry case replete with massive muffins, cinnamon buns, and croissants. I ordered and paid for two nonfat lattes and one huge pumpkin bran muffin—seasonal, yet healthy-ish.

The barista put the muffin on a plate on the counter.

"Thanks so much. I'll be right back for the lattes." I grabbed some napkins and a knife and trotted back to the table. Ashley put Iris on the ground, cut the muffin in half, and divided the napkins. I skipped back to the counter and the lattes were ready. I grabbed one in each hand and whipped around—and slammed right into Jake Logan.

"Oh, I'm so sorry." Fortunately, the lids had been secured properly, otherwise he wouldn't be flashing that dazzling smile nor flexing those adorable dimples.

"No problem. But I've got to say, we have to stop meeting like this."

What? Oh, the collision by the Secret Maze exit. For a moment I was jarred back to my first date with Milo when he'd said those exact same words after I'd tripped and fell into his arms like I had at the site visit. I smiled apologetically. "Sorry. I always get in trouble when my eyes and feet aren't pointed in the same direction." I tittered like a teenager. Again. *But those blue eyes and dark lashes.* I was melting like the butter on my bran muffin, while at the same time feeling guilty I might be attracted to Jake. *Slow your roll, girl.*

He laughed softly. "At least the collisions are getting gentler."

"Yeah, that's true." More tittering from me, and then an awkward silence followed. That was all I got. That I enunciated an articulate sentence in light of such male pulchritude was huge for me. I was a big believer in quitting while I was ahead.

But, of course, I was also a big believer in inclusivity, which apparently overrode everything. "Um . . . feel free to, er . . . do you want to join us outside? I'm here with my friend, Ashley, from last night. We're sitting outside." Since my hands were full, I jerked my head in the direction of the patio. "She snagged the last table outside. It's crowded today."

He somehow gleaned the meaning from my stuttering redundancies and graciously accepted my invitation. "Thanks. Sounds good. I'll be there in a sec after I order."

I hightailed it to the table. OMG he's polite and kind too.

Ashley had already taken a small bite of muffin from her half. "That PI is here. Jake, from last night."

"I know. I asked him to join us. Hope that's okay with you?"

She swallowed hard and nearly choked on her muffin. "You did? That's my girl! Good for you. He seems nice."

I handed her one of the lattes. "He does seem nice."

Jake came to our table a few minutes later, borrowing a free chair from an adjacent table. Iris danced around his feet and licked his hand when he petted her. While she was a very affectionate dog in general, she didn't always warm to males. She'd adored Milo and Jake seemed to pass the Iris litmus test as well.

"How are you both doing today? That was quite an eventful evening last night, to say the least."

"Hanging in there." Ashley looked him up and down. Her eyes sparkled with approval. "Would you like some of this muffin? It's huge—plenty to go around."

I broke off a small piece of muffin. "I sent the footprint photos to Adrian but haven't heard back from him yet."

"I'm sorry about your husband's disappearance. I've actually been following it in the local paper. Missing person cases always attract my attention since they make up close to half of the cases I work on."

"Really?" I popped the muffin piece into my mouth.

"Has there been any activity on his credit cards?" Jake asked before taking a sip of his coffee.

I sighed hard. "None that I've found online. The police have submitted warrants for his phone and credit card records. We're still waiting for the companies to comply with their requests.

Apparently, unless there's proof of a life-threatening situation, it can take a month or longer to obtain them. I'm positive something bad has happened to him. I can feel it. If he wanted to leave me, he would have told it to me straight. That's what I loved about him. He was honest. Kind. In fact, I worry it was those qualities that somehow got him in trouble. He was almost altruistic to a fault."

"Huh. That seems to be the consensus from everything I've read and heard about him. Sadly, not knowing more, I would tend to agree with you. His profile certainly doesn't fit that of someone who drops out of sight of their own volition, usually to dodge responsibilities or other nefarious reasons. Sorry. But it seems you've reached the same conclusion."

I hung my head. Tears welled up. I took a deep breath. "I can see why you're a detective. You're good at reading people. What brings you to Santa Sofia? I'm assuming you're not from here. I saw you turn around and drive back to the hotel after you drove away last night."

"You're quite the detective yourself. You're right. I'm up from Santa Barbara. Working on the bread and butter of our business, insurance investigations."

I almost blurted out what a coincidence because our insurer was going to conduct an investigation for my father's insurance policy but caught myself, too embarrassed to discuss the embezzlement and insinuation of suicide. Besides, I was cognizant of Uncle Bob's sensitivity and desire for privacy. Maybe once we figured out what happened, I could pick Jake's brain. For now, I wanted to keep it general.

Ashley set down her cup. "Oh? What type of insurance investigations?"

"All types—life, property. Any claim that's five figures and over gets investigated before the insurance pays up. It's pretty run-of-the-mill these days."

Ashley listened intently. "So, how does that work exactly? The insurance company hires you for specific cases? Are you on a retainer?"

"We're on retainer for a few smaller companies. For the larger insurers, once they've worked with us and like us, they zap us their cases almost automatically. We're fortunate we've had a high success rate, which, in turn, keeps us busy."

I nodded. "Same with my family's landscape architecture business. Once we've been hired by a big corporation like Hotel Santa Sofia Properties, our foot is in the door. If they're pleased with our design and construction work, it's almost a guarantee for future work." At least I was hoping that would be the case for their condominium project.

Ashley rested her chin in her hand, engrossed in our conversation. "Always better to have too much work to keep you busy than too little. It's hard building a clientele. My law practice is at the stage where it's either feast or famine."

Jake tipped his cup for the last of his coffee and rose up. "Well, very nice talking to you guys. He handed us each a business card. "In case you ever need a PI."

Ashley whipped out her card and handed it to Jake. I followed suit.

He patted Iris. "See you around."

Ashley and I watched in silence from the patio as Jake walked halfway down the block and jumped into his Tesla, as if we were ogling a model strutting down a runway.

Ashley took this in and turned to me. "Umhm. Mighty fine dude, that one. He must be doing well if he drives a Tesla."

I couldn't get over this good-looking guy was also green —driving a sexy electric car, showing he cared about the environment. He was so much like Milo—I was a sucker for eco-friendly men.

I picked up my phone. "I should call Aunt Veronica. I texted her earlier about the donor list and she never responded, which is unlike her. I've been thinking about how upset she was last night."

She answered after a few rings.

"Hi, Aunt Veronica. How are you doing? How's Sam?"

"Tory, how sweet of you! I was just about to text you to

let you know I sent the donor list. Sam is very sad. He'd just connected with Jo in the past several months and was working on building a relationship with her. So, this has been quite a blow."

She and Sam knew. If Aunt Veronica had been aware that Jo was Esmeralda, it was a good bet that Uncle Bob had known too. Why had he lied about it?

"I'd say. Especially losing her in such a violent manner. I could take Sam out to lunch. Do you think he'd be up for that? Having lost both my parents, I can really relate. Losing someone you love is never easy."

"Thanks, Tory. I'll ask him. My guess is he'd like that. He and Bob had planned on lunch today, but that police officer from last night called, the one I sent the donor list to—"

"You mean Adrian?"

"Yes, Adrian. He called Bob and wanted him to come down to the station right away to sign a formal statement."

I flinched in surprise. "He did?" I flashed an anxious look at Ashley and took a deep breath. "Okay. Let me know when a good time would be for me to pick Sam up for lunch. I'm pretty flexible."

As soon as I hung up, Ashley asked, "What's wrong?"

"Adrian called my uncle and asked him to come to the station for a formal statement."

Ashley whistled. "That's not good. Didn't he sign one last night? If he did, that probably means they have more questions to ask him. I'm not surprised, though. Your uncle is a lousy liar."

"You noticed? Horrible liar. But the real question is why did he lie to Adrian last night about not knowing Jo was Esmeralda? Aunt Veronica acted like it was common knowledge. How weird is that?"

"Pretty weird. I wonder why he lied? What's he got to hide?"

I was about to posit some reasons when my phone rang. I checked the screen. "It's Adrian. Can't wait to hear what he thinks about the matching footprints."

Ashley hunched her shoulders in anticipation.

"Hi, Adrian!"

"Hi, Tory. I'd like to know when you can come down to the station."

"Come down to the station?" I repeated for Ashley's benefit.

She grasped my arm.

"Yes. We have some additional questions for you to include in your formal statement that you need to sign."

My stomach flipped. "Um, okay. I can drop by right now."

"Great. See you soon."

"He wants me to come down to the station now too. He said he has some additional questions for me. He said I have to sign a formal statement."

Ashley winced. "Honey, that's never good. I'm coming with you. I'd say it sounds like, at the very least, you're what the cops call a person of interest. Translated, that's cop talk for being one degree away from being a suspect."

CHAPTER 14

We arrived at the police station just as Uncle Bob was leaving in his silver Prius. I went up to his car window. "Hi, everything okay?"

His face had better color than the night before, but the bags under his eyes told me he probably hadn't gotten a good night's sleep. "Depends on how you'd define okay, I guess. Adrian, or rather his colleague, Sergeant Gomez, seems gung ho on wrapping up Jo's murder today. He's more interested in pinning it on me, it seems, than protecting our community and finding the real culprit."

"You mean Ernie? Or Ern the Worm Gomez, as some kids used to call him. Join the crowd. He's trying to pin Milo's murder on me. Mainly because I pointed out to Adrian I suspected Ernie failed to properly search the Hotel Santa Sofia grounds for Milo's car. Ernie has always tried to wiggle out of everything he does wrong by blaming someone else, anyone else, as long as it isn't him, since I've known him. I wouldn't worry too much. We all know he's a jerk. Plus, he's competed with Adrian on everything since high school. I think he just became a cop because Adrian became one."

Uncle Bob shook his head woefully. "Great."

I patted his shoulder through the window. "Don't worry. Adrian mentioned in passing that Ernie is notorious for arresting first and questioning later, so be happy he's asking you questions and not arresting you."

Uncle Bob's mouth curled into a sneer. "For now. He's hell-bent on making an arrest soon. I can tell you that."

Ashley chimed in. "Really, don't worry about it. Adrian called

Tory in to answer more questions too. It's routine."

"Thanks. Hope you're right."

We waved and as Uncle Bob pulled away, Ernie followed him in an unmarked white car. Ashley and I exchanged uneasy frowns and turned to mount the steps of the station.

Ashley grabbed my arm and spoke under her breath. "You two are definitely suspects, mark my words."

"Then why on earth did you lie to my uncle?"

"He looked sad. I wanted to cheer him up."

"By lying to him?"

"Whatever works."

"Apparently."

Adrian was sitting at his desk. He pointed to the two chairs across from him. "Have a seat."

Ashley started right in. "My client, Victoria Benning, answered many questions last night. Why do you want to ask her additional questions today?"

I turned abruptly to look at Ashley. What had gotten into her?

"You can knock it off, Miss Payne, is it? I'll be asking the questions."

My head snapped back to look at Adrian. Adrian and Ashley stared at each other for a few seconds. Adrian's eyes twinkled. Ashley's did too. Then Ashley's dimples puckered and the corner of Adrian's mouth tugged upward. Now I got it. They were flirting with each other—law and order style.

"I hate to break this up, whatever this is." I paused to gesture with circular hand movements. "But what additional questions do you need to ask me?"

Back to business, Adrian scanned the file folders spread over his desk and slid one out that had been buried beneath the others. He gathered up the rest of the files, shuffled them into a stack, and then slammed them into alignment with a sharp crack on his desk like a blackjack dealer squaring a card deck. He opened the selected file. "I want you to clarify your relationship with your aunt Jo, also known as Esmeralda. You had no idea when she told your fortune that she was, in fact, your aunt?"

"None. She seemed vaguely familiar, for some reason. But honestly, with that thick veil, I could barely see her face, other than that she seemed attractive compared to my stereotype of a fortune-teller, which was more grotesque and sinister." A flashback from my youth popped up, of a pretty lady presenting me with a massive lollipop that had immediately won me over. "I don't know, maybe if she hadn't had a veil, I might have recognized her. But remember, I thought my aunt Jo was dead, so that wasn't even a logical possibility in my mind."

He nodded as he wrote in my file. "Did Milo ever mention going to a fortune-teller?"

"No. Neither of us believed in that sort of thing. Only as a lark."

"Did you tell him about your aunt Jo?"

I thought back on our first weeks together. We both made a lot of self-disclosure. "Yes, I did. We exchanged family history stuff. I told him she died in a car accident, as I'd believed."

Adrian wrote some more.

Ashley sat up straighter. "Why are you asking about Milo?"

I wiggled to the edge of my chair. "It's the boot print, isn't it? I knew it!"

Adrian nodded. "Calm down. Yes. I had Sarah, our techie, blow up the photos you emailed me of the prints near where Milo's car was parked and the ones near Esmeralda in the maze. She compared the prints and concluded they are, in fact, from the exact same boot."

Ashley's eyes grew huge. "Wow!"

I sucked in air. "I knew it. They looked identical to me, but to have an expert verify it, just wow. So that means whoever killed Esmeralda was involved in Milo's disappearance . . . so that means . . ."

It was hard for me to admit the possibility that Milo was dead, but nothing indicated he was still alive. I gulped hard. "Does this mean the same person most likely killed them both?"

Ashley gave me a big hug.

Adrian looked up. "Yup. I'm afraid that's the conclusion I've come to. A double homicide by the same perp. But the problem is the footprint is from a brand that's pretty common, Wallington Boot Company."

Ashley leaned an elbow on Adrian's desk. "But that doesn't preclude a definite match, does it?"

"We sell them at the nursery. We don't keep a lot in stock because they're sold online too. But they're popular work boots for gardeners and contractors. And hipsters. Can you tell from the print what the size of the boot was?"

Ashley spoke before Adrian had a chance to answer. "Great. That really narrows it down. In other words, a lot of freakin' legwork to find the owner. Ha! Did you hear that clever pun, legwork, boot . . . don't I get any love?"

Adrian laughed. "A pun, yes. I don't know about clever."

"Okay, you two." I gestured to my eyes. "Eye. On. Ball."

Adrian sat up straighter. "Unfortunately, we can only estimate a size range. Trouble is the range includes common sizes for both men and women. The only exclusions are the smallest and largest sizes. So, not much help there."

I felt defeated. Ashley slumped back in her chair.

Adrian continued, "It's true that they're standard-issue work boots owned by every construction worker and hipster in town. And, for that reason, when Ernie catches up on the case, the amount of work involved in tracking down the owner of the boot will discourage that line of theorizing for him. He'll probably claim the boot was destroyed by now anyway, making our theory even more tenuous. So, he'll take the easy way out and focus on your statements, which I guarantee he'll claim incriminate both you and your uncle. I know how the guy thinks."

The news wasn't getting any better. Ashley and I looked at each other. I saw my distress reflected in her eyes.

Adrian added a few more notes to my file. "But while they're not as rare and distinctive as the Italian-made Bruno Magli shoes in the O. J. Simpson case, I do think I have an ace up my sleeve.

Luckily for us, the boot print we have shows a nick in the tread that makes it unique when compared to other similar boot prints. So, if we find the boot with the nick that matches the print, we find our killer."

I clapped softly and fist-bumped Ashley. "That's great! FYI, Adrian, next time can you please lead with the good news?"

Adrian directed his gaze at me. "Okay. I'm going to switch gears for a moment. Benning Brothers had a big role in the fundraiser, correct? Did anyone you know mention they knew Esmeralda? Did anyone recommend her for your event?"

My heart stopped for a moment as I recalled a situation about six months ago that, up until now, I'd totally forgotten about. When the fundraiser was in the preliminary planning stages, when the planning committee was brainstorming ideas for the theme, someone suggested Esmeralda by name. My face had a rush of warmth as I reeled from the storm of thoughts in my head. "Yes. My father suggested Esmeralda."

Ashley eyes widened. "He did? Why didn't you mention that before?"

"Because I'd totally forgotten about it. Once he died, I stepped back from the planning committee. All the groundwork had been laid, anyway. It was a matter of tracking all the vendors' progress to make sure everything was on time and executed as promised. I passed those duties on to Aunt Veronica."

"I wonder if your dad knew Jo was Esmeralda." Ashley scratched her chin.

I was wondering the same thing.

Adrian was taking copious notes, like a student learning what would be on the next test. He finally looked up. "My guess, both your dad and your uncle knew Jo was Esmeralda and were on somewhat okay terms with her."

Looked like my uncle's bad job of lying hadn't fooled Adrian for a minute.

I avoided Adrian's gaze. "Maybe you're right." Covering for my uncle was pointless. Pinocchio was a better liar. "But I'm sure they had their reasons for keeping it on the down-low." They must have. All my life my father and uncle had been my ideal image of upright citizens. I couldn't imagine I'd read them wrong.

Adrian straightened the files again. "Whatever. You need to hammer home to Bob that honesty is the best policy. You should clue him in that lying to a police office is an offense, punishable by jail time. I told him I'd give him twenty-four hours to reconsider his statement and be more straightforward before he signed it because he just fed me the same lies he told me last night, which help no one except the actual perpetrator. I was hoping you could talk some sense into him, Tory, between now and when he comes back in tomorrow to sign his statement. Make him understand his lies not only incriminate him but you."

That got my attention and I shot Adrian a glance. "Me? How?"

"Because it makes it seem like he's trying to distance not only himself but his whole family as possible suspects. But it has the opposite effect. If one family member lies, it immediately draws our suspicions to the whole family. It makes us wonder what he's trying to cover up or, more to the point, *who* is he trying to protect? So far, you're the last person who saw your aunt alive."

I gulped. "But what about the person who peeked in? I think she met with them after I left."

"Do you have anyone else who can verify that? Because, so far, we have no witnesses to corroborate your story."

"No."

Adrian leaned in as if Ashley and I were his co-conspirators. "And by 'we,' I mean Ernie. He wants that promotion to lieutenant as much as I do. And he'll do anything it takes to get it. Even if it means making an arrest that isn't justified. He's capable of making an arrest, any arrest, just to show progress on the case. I'm trying to run interference between you and your uncle and Ernie, but sooner or later he will want to talk to both of you directly. It would help if your uncle came clean and told the truth. Because we don't want him contradicting anything you say."

"What do you mean by that exactly?"

"The last person to have seen Esmeralda alive would be at the top of our suspect list. And that person seems to be you."

"I have no motive to kill Esmeralda. In fact, in the short time I spent with her, I liked her. She was pretty accurate about reading me and she did give me a clue."

Ashley rolled her eyes. "Clue? You mean telling you the answer to Milo's disappearance was in the Secret Maze? Hmph."

"Apart from no motive, I bet I wasn't the last person to see her alive either. Surely someone must have seen her go into the maze, and maybe even saw someone follow her there."

"And in terms of Milo . . ."

"What? You have news?"

"Not exactly. But typically, the spouse is the prime suspect. I know you supposedly have an alibi, you were with the photographer right after the ceremony and then with Ashley and Philip right before the reception. But did anyone see you between the time you left the photographer and the time you joined Ashley and Philip?"

I threw my hands up to cover my mouth. "You have got to be kidding!"

Adrian shook his head and stared me down.

I blinked in disbelief. "I don't recall seeing anyone. It took me all of a minute to walk from the garden photo shoot back to my room. I wouldn't have had enough time to use the restroom, let alone meet Milo, smash his phone, change into sweats, get a wheelbarrow, and dump a body in his car. Hopefully Simon, the photographer, has time stamps on the photos. Philip and Ashley ordered room-service champagne. I'm sure they can pinpoint the timing of my arrival more accurately by looking at my room charge transactions. Surely we can pinpoint a timeline using those things to corroborate my movements and show my whereabouts can be almost continually verified by others and prove there was no way I could've murdered Milo. "

Adrian riveted his gaze on me. Then a smile crept onto his lips. "Good answer."

I blew out a breath. "Phew! Adrian, you don't seriously think I could have been involved in Milo's disappearance, do you? That I killed him? Are you insane?"

"Not me, Tory. Ernie. I wouldn't put anything past him. He'll ask about a prenuptial agreement."

"Good try. We didn't have one."

"That could work against you in terms of motive. Maybe one of you became enraged because the other one did or didn't want one. Guarantee Ernie is capable of coming up with a compelling theory either way. He'll also ask if Milo had a will. Do you know if he did?"

"He already asked me about that, but Ashley told me not to answer. But, for your information, we both drew up new wills and were each other's beneficiary."

Adrian responded with a grim smirk and shook his head. "Doesn't help your case much that Milo's beachfront town house alone is worth a couple of mil."

Ashley pulled me back down by my jacket as I started to stand. "Calm down, Rambo. Adrian is only playing the devil's advocate. Giving you a heads-up. He's on your side."

"Ashley's right. I'm not saying it will happen, but all Ernie will need is another piece of evidence or two, like the will, and the whole case can go south for you. Granted, we haven't completed our interviews with everyone that was there last night. But so far, nada. You're it. I know you, Tory, and your family. You're good people. But I can't help you if anyone is hiding anything. I need you all to be totally honest for me to do my job and put the right suspect behind bars."

Ashley shook his hand, and their clasp lingered as she spoke. "Thanks, Adrian. I know Tory will urge Bob to cooperate."

Adrian couldn't tear his gaze away from Ashley. "Good. If we keep an open line of communication and work together, we'll get to the bottom of this."

As we walked out of the office and cleared the lobby, I

couldn't resist teasing Ashley. "For goodness sake, get a room. Told you. So much for just being buddies."

Still starry-eyed, Ashley smiled. "Was it that obvious?"

"Um, yeah. I think you two would be a good pair. You both have a lot of similarities. You both have a strong sense of justice."

"Plus, he's hot. That never hurts." Ashley swooned and then redirected her attention back to lawyering. "Okay. You need to go talk to your uncle and find out why he's lying. He's hiding something."

"On it. I need to talk to Aunt Veronica and Sam too."

My phone pinged with a voice mail message. I winced and held the phone away from my ear as I listened to Ernie bark out an order. *"This is Sergeant Gomez. I need to ask you some questions. Call me back ASAP."*

I cast a nervous glance at Ashley. "And I have to move fast."

CHAPTER 15

The next day I drove over to Uncle Bob's and Aunt Veronica's house. They had lived in the same sprawling hacienda-styled home with a horse corral in the back since I was a little girl. I drove south along the Promenade, turning before I hit the Avenue, and continued for about a mile inland to Ryder Ranch, a gated old-money enclave with a strict set of homeowner association building and landscape guidelines created to preserve its natural beauty and rural setting.

I breezed along the empty road until I came to the hitching post gate that marked their turnout and meandered along their winding driveway bordered by low shrubs. Their two-acre property featured succulents and other drought-resistant plants that aptly reflected Benning Brothers' environmental sensibility and drought-tolerant landscaping practices.

Aunt Veronica opened the Dutch door as I raised my fist to knock. "Tory! You're early. I thought your lunch with Sam wasn't 'til noon. He's over at our neighbors' feeding their horses. Come on in."

"I purposely came early because I wanted to talk to Uncle Bob beforehand. Is he around?"

She pushed back a highlighted strand of her chin-length bob and straightened out the beige Williams Sonoma apron she wore over a long-sleeved T-shirt and jeans. "You just missed him. He went to the store. He'll be back soon. Can I get you some coffee?"

Perfect timing. Now I could quiz my aunt on what I believed to be untrue statements made by Uncle Bob. "That would be great. Thanks."

I followed her into their large kitchen. She poured some

coffee into two Franciscan Strawberry Fair cups, a cozy vintage pattern I'd come to associate with the hominess I'd always found at my aunt and uncle's place.

"How's Sam doing today?"

She reached over and patted my hand with her French-manicured hand adorned with a simple gold wedding band. "Thanks for asking. He seems to be okay. But you know teenagers, especially boys. Still waters run deep. But I consider it a good sign he's channeling whatever he might be feeling into productive activity. He was up early to go to work at the nursery this morning and, like I said, now he's feeding our neighbors' horses."

Knowing my uncle was due back, I delved right in. "How's Uncle Bob? How'd his interview go at the police station?"

For a moment, she looked lost in thought as she pushed another loose strand of hair behind her ear. "He was annoyed because he said they asked him the same questions they asked him the night before."

"They called me in too. Adrian implied that Uncle Bob might be lying because he's hiding something or protecting someone. Do you think he is?"

She furrowed her brow, adjusted her round tortoiseshell glasses, and appeared baffled as she shook her head. "Gosh. I really don't know, Tory. Did Adrian mention what he thought he was lying about?"

"He didn't tell me. But I was there when he asked Uncle Bob questions the night of the murder after you left. Uncle Bob seemed very uncomfortable talking about Jo, especially about whether or not you and Sam knew she was Esmeralda. He implied that even though Sam worked for Esmeralda, he didn't know Esmeralda was actually Jo, his birth mother."

Aunt Veronica's eyebrows shot up in surprise. "That's ridiculous. Of course we knew. Sam is the one who found out about her by searching online on an ancestry site, I believe. Then he told us."

She pushed back in her chair, shaking her head. "We had told

Sam he was adopted years earlier and that Bob's sister was his biological mother. Your dad and Bob thought writing Jo out of our lives was the best route. Hence, they concocted the story she died in a car accident. But I couldn't sit back without telling Sam his birth mother was still alive. Of course, at that point no one knew where Jo was living. We certainly had no idea she'd moved back to Santa Sofia. It was Sam who figured that out and tracked her down. As soon as we found out, we had her over for dinner one night. We were all very civil to one another because we were united in putting Sam first. I didn't know how Sam or Jo would react, but they liked each other right from the get-go. Took it slowly. Sam working for her was a good way for them to hang out without any pressure."

"When did all this happen? And why on earth would Uncle Bob lie? Or feel what appears to be a need to protect you and Sam? Why would the police care?"

She took a long sip of coffee. "The dinner was about six months ago." She tilted her head back slightly, staring past me out the window. "Privacy, maybe? I can't think of any other reason."

A car door slammed. Uncle Bob entered, carrying a grocery bag, his thin gray comb-over doing a poor job of hiding his glistening pate. "Hi, Tory. You're here early, aren't you?"

"Yeah. Actually, I wanted to talk to you before lunch. I know Ernie gave you a hard time. How'd your interview with Adrian go?"

When I looked at his feet, my heart stopped for a second. He was wearing Wallington work boots, like those of the prints found in the parking lot and the maze. I did my best to maintain a poker face.

He peered through his wire-rim glasses, following my gaze, and the smile left his face, replaced by the eye shifting he displayed during questioning the night of the murder. "Okay, I guess."

"Uncle Bob, I'm going to cut to the chase. Adrian knows you're not being straightforward with him. He asked me to find out why. Because if you don't come clean and you continue to not tell the truth to the police, it's bad for all of us, particularly me."

He set the bag down on the counter. "He said that?"

I nodded.

"Well, tell him that's my story and I'm sticking to it. I don't need any young upstarts messing in my personal business. And that's that."

"Bob, don't be rude! What are you hiding? Now you have me concerned. This isn't like you. Do you understand what Victoria just told you? Not telling the truth to the police gets them very suspicious. It makes it seem like you're hiding something criminal . . . you aren't, are you?"

His face reddened as he became agitated. "Of course not. Trust me. I know what I'm doing. The truth, in this instance, will appear more damning to the police than my evasiveness."

Exasperated, Aunt Veronica sighed loudly. "You're impossible sometimes!" She threw up her hands and marched out of the room.

Uncle Bob gave me a weak smile and grabbed a bunch of carrots from the grocery bag. "Come on. Let's take a walk."

I'd always loved their spread-—the horses, the expansive property. To me, it represented the Old West part of Santa Sofia. We strolled over to their stable and dusty paddock. Uncle Bob handed me some carrots. I took them and then purposely dropped one, hoping to get a better look at his boot soles as I bent down to pick it up. But since the telltale nick of the killer's boots was on the bottom, looking at the mud-caked edges didn't help much. Star, a sorrel with a white blaze, and Luna, a smoky black roan with two white socks on her rear legs, galloped to the fence. Watching them enjoy their treat made it feel like old times, a feeling I wished I could freeze and preserve forever.

"So, tell me. What's going on? Why are you acting so weird about Jo?"

"It's nothing, Tory. I forgot Sam knew Jo was his birth mother. Simple as that."

"You forgot? That's a pretty important fact to forget, don't you think?"

"Look, Tory. Don't make this into a drama like everything else. Just let it go for once. Okay?"

Burn. "Ouch." Like my father, Uncle Bob had a tendency to lash out when cornered. "Now I know for sure you're hiding something. I could understand more if it only affected you, but you might take me down by lying. But that's okay. I know you'll come to visit me in jail unless, of course, I get the death penalty. But, God forbid you involve yourself in my drama. Thanks for your help. Not!"

I spun around to leave but my uncle tapped my shoulder with a carrot. "Luna and Star want another carrot."

I grabbed the carrot and fed it to Star, while he fed Luna. My face was prickling with heat, but watching Star chomp the carrot while taking care to avoid my fingers cooled me off. I patted both horses and strolled back to the house with Uncle Bob in silence.

The quietude was broken by the sound of leaves crackling behind us. When I turned around, Sam was approaching on his bike. He was dressed in jeans and a T-shirt and, like his father, Wallington work boots. I was momentarily taken aback and tried to conceal my reaction to his footwear with a hearty "Hello."

"Hi, Tory. I hope you haven't been waiting too long. I was feeding—"

"Your neighbors' horses. Yeah, I heard. No problem. I got here early. Just catching up with your folks."

"Let me change into some decent clothes. Back in five."

Bob mumbled something about needing to talk to Aunt Veronica, ending any opportunity to inspect the soles of his boots. I waited for Sam in my car. I turned on the engine and listened to the news. The lead story was Jo's death. I reflected on the revelation that both Benning males owned Wallington work boots like the ones that left footprints. The ones assumed to be those of the killer. Would the killer be so brazen to continue wearing the same boots out in public? Perhaps a reverse psychological strategy, to make it seem they weren't the killer because the killer would have ditched the boots?

The other news on the radio was a wildfire update. The latest wildfire was only five percent contained and arson was suspected. Strong winds were predicted for the next twenty-four hours, with warmer temperatures.

The passenger door opened and Sam climbed in. His sandy-colored hair was slicked into spikes and he smelled like soap. He had changed into a fresh T-shirt and a darker pair of jeans. He still wore the Wallington work boots. Was it a sign of innocence or was it well played? And how could I sneak a peek at his soles to see if they had the incriminating nick? His parents stood in their doorway, waving us off.

I rolled down my window. "Uncle Bob, please think about what I said and talk to me before you sign your statement. Okay?"

Uncle Bob shrugged.

Aunt Veronica elbowed him. "Don't worry, dear. I'll make sure he calls you."

"Thanks, Aunt Veronica! Bye!"

After a ten-minute drive, we pulled up to Cheeseburger Boutique. The restaurant had recently opened in a standalone building in the Olive Branch Mall. Located in the foothills of Santa Sofia, the mall had splendid mountain and ocean views. One of the reasons I'd chosen Cheeseburger Boutique was that lately I'd been craving comfort food. Who could blame me, given everything I'd been going through? Despite increasing my intake of burgers, pizza, and desserts, I'd been losing weight, a not unwelcome consequence I attributed to the stress I'd been experiencing since the deaths of my family members, coupled with my newfound, stress-relieving gym addiction.

Another reason I'd chosen Cheeseburger Boutique was we'd done the landscape design for their outdoor seating area, and I'd wanted to see how the landscape had developed. That was one of the things I loved most about landscape architecture. Unlike buildings, plants thrived and became more attractive over time. Plus, I'd always tried to patronize our clients' businesses. But the most important reason I'd chosen Cheeseburger Boutique was because of Sam. I figured the best way to get to a teenager's secrets was to ply him with burgers and fries.

The furnishings were hipster chic—lots of wood surfaces and natural materials. I had specified both the exterior and interior plantings. I pointed out to Sam one of the live-plant wall hangings that had turned out better than I'd expected. I made a mental note to mention how happy I was with the installation to our nursery people.

I ordered a single cheeseburger with all the fixings and a vanilla milkshake. Sam opted for a double cheeseburger, fries, and a chocolate shake. There were plenty of empty tables, so we hung around the counter waiting for our order until it was ready.

"How's work at the nursery? Are they keeping you busy?"

Sam's eyes widened for a second then returned to normal. "It's okay."

"What do they have you doing?"

"I'm basically helping Jed move stock, keeping up the nursery inventory, unloading truckloads of soil and fertilizer, stuff like that."

"Cool. Do you like that?"

"It's okay."

He was a strong strapping young man who was perfect for such a job. But Sam had always been more than simply brawn. He did well academically, a regular on the Dean's List. "How's school?"

He blushed. "Did my mom snitch about my grades?"

My emotions took a dive, as if his statement opened up the floor of a guillotine. But I tried hard to keep my facial expression unperturbed. "Um, no. What about your grades? I take it not good?"

"Not lately. I can't get over my counselor sending my mom a notice because my grades dropped a little." He swore under his breath.

Again, I was taken aback since, in my mind, my cousin was still a little freckle-faced boy who didn't even know swear words existed. "I'm sure that was done because your counselor cares and knows you're capable of better. Why have your grades gotten worse? You must be upset about your birth mother's murder. But that just happened a couple of days ago. Something else troubling you?"

He avoided eye contact and started to fidget. We'd always had a good relationship with open communication, and I could tell by his pursed lips he was ready to clam up.

"I don't mean to pry. Just know I'm always here if you want to talk. I know it's hard with your parents, even though they're well-intentioned. Sometimes they can come off as being super judgmental."

He nodded. "It's just with school, sports, and then working for the nursery and everyone else, I'm sometimes too tired to stay on top of my homework."

"Maybe consider cutting back on jobs. Do you need to work so much?"

"I feel like everyone depends on me. Not Esmeralda now, obviously." His voice caught when he uttered her name. "But Jed, Paloma, Blanche. I hate to let them down."

"That's a lot of pressure. I'm sure you help all of them a lot, but I think they'd survive if you cut back your hours. Also, it's all physical work. Lugging and lifting. You must be exhausted every day."

He nodded. "I am. I can barely keep my eyes open some nights."

His words percolated in my mind for a minute. "Hey! I have an idea. I'll be finding out soon whether Benning Brothers wins the bid for the Hotel Santa Sofia condo project. If we luck out, I'll need a temporary part-time project assistant with technical skills. You've always been so good with computers. Maybe substituting one desk job for a couple of manual labor jobs for a while will let you conserve your energy better for studying. And you can also do your homework here in the office in between assignments. Hopefully that will help you bring your GPA up again. Would you be interested?"

"Seriously? I'd love that." His animated response said it all.

"Great! We should hear any day now. If we get the bid, the job is yours."

"Cool. Thanks, Tory."

Our burgers were ready. We grabbed a table on the patio by another living wall hanging that looked spectacular and were silent for a couple of minutes, save for our raving about how good the food was. A thriving landscape, a cheeseburger and shake, and a happier cousin. My day was made. It was great to see him act carefree again, and I hoped I'd be able to hire him so his parents and I could keep a closer eye on him while he was grieving the loss of his mother.

We got back in the car. I smelled smoke in the air I hadn't smelled earlier. I pulled out of the shopping center lot and stopped at a four-way intersection. "I sure hope they can contain the fire before the wind picks up again. Smells like it's getting close to civilization."

Sam sighed. "Hopefully they will. I didn't know it was going to get windy."

"Yep. Heard it on the radio while I was waiting for you earlier."

We continued down the highway that led us out of the foothills and back to town. I glanced in my rearview mirror and let out a sigh of annoyance. There was a white car three cars behind me that had been with me since we left the shopping mall. This was getting old. I decided to not get upset until I got closer to town, where there would be more street choices to go in different directions. The road we were on was the main highway between the mall and downtown Santa Sofia. I was so intent on the white car, wondering if it was even the same one I'd thought had followed me before, that I flinched when I saw, too late, a white pickup truck loom ominously close in my driver's side mirror. The next second the pickup truck pulled even closer and then purposely sideswiped us. Luckily, I had seen it in the nick of time and was able to steer off the road onto the gravel shoulder to dodge the full impact. I then swung back to the highway in time to avoid the steep cliff beyond.

"Whoa! What the . . ." Again, Sam swore under his breath. But this time I couldn't blame him. We could have been killed.

At the next turnout, I pulled over to get my wits about me. My hands trembled on the steering wheel. "Wow. That was intense. That truck sideswiped us on purpose. I saw it approach us in my mirror."

Sam looked at me. "Whoa, that was some serious road rage."

"Road rage? For what? Driving in the slow lane?"

"I don't know." He twisted around in his seat. "Someone's parking behind us."

A white car pulled up in back of us and I locked the doors. "Great. Now what?" I tried not to let my burgeoning hysteria show in front of Sam as my imagination galloped away, thinking the sideswiping truck and the white car were in cahoots to make me stop and pull over. I was still shaken from our near miss but grateful for my apparent race-car-driver quick reflexes and pretty darn proud of my Wonder Woman ability to dodge danger.

I watched in the rearview mirror as the driver's door opened. Jake Logan stepped out and trotted over to my window. "Are you guys okay? I saw your near miss."

I let out a deep breath of relief and turned to Sam. "It's okay. I know him. He's a PI."

Sam and I both got out of the car.

"Wow, I've never been so happy to see a familiar face. Jake, this is my cousin, Sam. We were just run off the road. Luckily my hands are always at ten and two on the steering wheel and I managed to keep control of my car and strong-arm us back onto the pavement to keep us from pitching off the cliff."

"Yeah, I saw the pickup swerve into you, but that's all I saw. You think someone ran you off the road on purpose? Did you see who it was?"

"Yes. I'm positive it wasn't an accident. And no, it happened so fast I was too busy steering the car to get a look at the driver."

Sam peered over the cliff. "Yep. Definitely road rage. We were lucky. We could have been splattered all over the ravine."

I bit my tongue over Sam's graphic image and rolled my eyes apologetically to Jake. I was so relieved that it was Jake that it wasn't until later I reflected on the coincidence of Jake being right there after we were run off the road. Jake insisted on following us back to Sam's house to make sure we got there without further incident. Then he did the same while I drove myself home, not leaving until I was safely inside.

A half hour later, I decided to take Iris for a walk along the beach. We both had nervous energy that needed to be burned off. I threw on a quilted puffer vest and buckled Iris into her leopard harness. We trotted the couple blocks to the beach in unison, both of us taking in the brisk sea breeze. The wind was already picking up, boding ill for the firefighters. On the walk, I had a lot to think about. What was Uncle Bob hiding? What got Sam upset enough to affect his grades? Why did a road rage incident happen randomly? Why was Jake Logan everywhere I went?

As the wind kicked up, I told Iris it was time to head home. We forged the two blocks back from the beach, bucking the invigorating blast of air that blew my hair straight back away from my face and gave Iris the look of a troll doll. I'd left my car in the driveway but, after seeing twigs and branches being blown down on the walk home, I decided to move it into the garage for the night. As I approached, I noticed a note on my windshield tucked under my wiper blade. A shiver went down my back as I read its menacing, all-caps warning: MIND YOUR OWN BUSINESS OR NEXT TIME YOU WON'T BE SO LUCKY!

CHAPTER 16

A clanking noise from the kitchen jarred me awake. My body flinched.

My mind geared into overdrive as I remembered the threatening note on my windshield, the road rage, Ernie Gomez, and the feeling someone was out to get me. Trembling, I drew the gray polka-dot duvet up closer, suddenly chilly and vulnerable.

Iris's foxlike head popped up from the mound of pillows like a vigilant soldier's from a bunker. Another bang of metal and Iris was having none of it. In a second, she cracked the air with one shrill bark followed by nonstop yapping. Before I had a chance to catch her, she'd made one of her kamikaze leaps off the bed and shot out of the room in a flash of cream sable fur. I threw off the covers and jogged after her, or tried to. The best I could muster was a wobbly stagger, making me feel like a bobble-head toy. It didn't help that Otis chose to lope in front of me, freezing to a standstill every few steps.

As I hobbled down the hallway in unsteady strides, I heard a soft thud and Ashley shout, "Oh, fudge!" After I'd found the note on my windshield, I'd phoned Ashley and Adrian and sent them both a photo of the note. Ashley insisted on coming over to spend the night. Adrian thought that was a great idea and made us promise to lock up well and call him at any hour if we felt unsafe.

When I walked into the kitchen, Ashley was picking up a heap of Cheerios from the floor and dumping them into the trash bin. Two frying pans were on the floor as well.

"Good morning?" I couldn't help but chuckle at her

predicament.

"Not so far, apparently." She stood and stepped back to survey the remaining mess, hands on her hips. "I'm sorry. My plan was to make you breakfast."

Iris was having a field day with the Cheerios. She snorted like a little pig as she lunged at them furiously, in a race to chug them down faster than Ashley could clean them up.

"Iris, no!" I bent down to scoop up handfuls of cereal while Iris gobbled at a more frenetic pace.

Ashley observed Iris, laughing. "I like the way she obeys you."

"She's been trained by food rewards. Obviously not the best system when food is what you don't want her to touch."

"I can relate. The struggle is real."

"Stop or you'll explode!" I made a grab for Iris, but she sashayed away, gorging herself on cereal as she did. I succeeded on my third attempt and swept her up into my arms as she still snapped at the Cheerios stuck on her fur.

Ashley guffawed. "Iris, you like it when Auntie Ashley comes for a sleepover, don't you?"

"Yep. Fun times. You clearly have made her day."

Ashley winked. "Hmm. Maybe I should try the same tactic with men. Just throw food at them."

I laughed while I poured myself some coffee. "Worth a try. It might work. Is it okay if I take a rain check on breakfast? If we're lucky enough to get the Hotel Santa Sofia bid, I'll be slammed with work for a while. So I want to catch up on all my other stuff, just in case." And by other stuff I meant looking through my father's files for evidence of any financial improprieties.

Ashley looked at her watch. "Yeah. I should actually get going too. But let's go out for breakfast soon."

"Definitely. It's a date."

I walked around my backyard with Iris. Usually I let her out to run around and do her business on her own or, when I'd had the time, I'd take a few laps around the yard to add steps on my Fitbit watch. But in light of the menacing note, we stayed outside only as long as necessary. I couldn't bear the thought of anyone hurting my little nugget.

I quickly showered and pulled on a camel sweater dress and chestnut suede boots. When I arrived at my office in the main building, the nursery parking lot across the street was full, despite it only being seven thirty. Most nursery employees arrived at the crack of dawn. My idea of early coincided with their breakfast break, marked by the arrival of Cynthia's food truck, a Santa Sofia fixture for as long as I could remember. Cynthia did a thriving business at our nursery since her tasty fare was a favorite of our employees and all the itinerant workers who congregated outside our gates looking for landscape jobs. Many of the workers lined up at the truck wore Wallington work boots. Jed and Matt Ortega, Jed's second in command, stood near the truck chowing down their breakfast. My gaze panned to their feet—both of them wore Wallingtons too. Well, crap. What I'd hoped would be a slam-dunk clue to ID the killer had totally missed the mark. It seemed everyone and their brother owned a pair of Wallingtons. Unless I figured out a way to discreetly examine all their soles, I was back to square one.

I sipped coffee at my desk and resumed digging through my dad's files. Tucked into a folder marked "Loans" was a spreadsheet of various small loans made to employees over the last couple of years. Most were small loans to nursery workers, gardeners, and clerical staff. Matt Ortega had been loaned fifteen hundred dollars early last year and repaid it six months later. As I scanned the spreadsheet, one name leapt out from the page, Veronica Benning. She and Uncle Bob each had become wealthy from Benning Brothers' success and both had drawn good salaries as Chief Financial Officer and Vice President. Why on earth had she needed to borrow two thousand dollars several months ago? I ran my finger along the row. She'd paid it back a couple of weeks later. Well, that was strange. But at least my father had it marked as paid in full. So, no harm no foul. I wondered whether Uncle Bob knew she'd borrowed the money. And if he did, I wondered whether Aunt Veronica knew he knew.

In about an hour, I'd gone through all the files in my dad's desk, happy I'd be able to report to Uncle Bob that nothing seemed out of line since no loan was over five thousand dollars and all had been repaid. None would have anything to do with embezzling, I presumed.

I took a break to check my emails. One was from the Hotel Santa Sofia Corporation with the subject line "Hotel Santa Sofia Condominium Landscape Design Competition: Announcement of Winning Bid." My heart palpitated with excitement and I took a deep breath. As soon as I glanced at the first word in the message, "Congratulations," I let out a whoop. I opened the email and danced in my seat as I read further, "Your bid has been selected as the winning proposal for the Hotel Santa Sofia Condominium project in North Santa Sofia, California."

I ran to Uncle Bob's office. "We got the condo job!"

He jumped out of his seat. "That's fantastic! Congratulations, Tory!"

"Thanks!"

We high-fived each other.

He gave me a big hug. "Your dad would be so proud of you!"

"I only wish he and Milo were both here to join in the celebration."

Uncle Bob paused. "I have a feeling they're both smiling down at us right now."

I nodded rapidly, struggling not to cry and feeling all the emotions. Joy for the accomplishment and income. Sorrow that my dad and Milo weren't here to share in the jubilation.

Uncle Bob gave me a pat on the back. "Good job, kiddo!"

"Thanks again for always being there for me through thick and thin."

"My pleasure. Like I said, your dad would be proud."

Nothing like good news benefiting our company to minimize our differences. Uncle Bob acted as if I'd never gotten annoyed with him about his statement to Adrian, and so did I. I floated back to my office on cloud nine, reveling in the exhilaration of winning such a competitive and large bid. Back at my desk, the enormity of the upcoming job started to sink in. I now had tons of work to do and was ready to dig in. Reaching for my phone in my purse, I came across the note left on my windshield. My neck and shoulder muscles knotted up. When I spoke to Adrian last night, he'd asked me to drop the note off at the station at my earliest convenience. I figured I'd do it on my way home later today.

Sam would be in class. I called and left him a message, "We got the Hotel Santa Sofia condo job, which means I need an assistant. Hope you're still interested. Call me!"

Ashley had texted me. *Something came up. Can't make lunch. Sorry. What did Adrian say when you dropped off note?*

I texted her back, *Haven't seen him yet.*

Ashley responded after a few minutes. *Wait a minute. You know legit PI. Call Jake and see what he thinks. Can't hurt. Plus, he's hot.* She ended her text with a winking emoji.

I dug around in my purse and found Jake Logan's card. Normally, I might hesitate. Was I being too obvious and forward? *Because those blue eyes!* But this wasn't personal. This was business. And, after all, he'd been a witness to yesterday's road rage incident. That cinched it. I was in a kickass mood anyway and was impatient to check "threatening note" off of my to-do list. Besides, I kept running into him everywhere I went. I still wasn't sure whether those meetings had been coincidences or intentional. He just might welcome a call from me.

He picked up on the second ring. "Hey. What's up?" Playfulness emanated from his warm drawl.

"I'm afraid this is a business call. I wanted to get your professional opinion about something that happened last night. When I came back from walking my dog, I found a note on my car's windshield telling me to back off. Is it common for people to leave menacing notes? Have you seen that a lot?"

His voice lost its warmth and his words became clipped. "Common? Not really. I've seen it a few times."

"I've never received a menacing note before. But since it appeared on the same day someone tried to run me off the road, it definitely got my attention."

"Yeah. Doesn't sound like a coincidence."

"Right? I'm positive they're related. I called Adrian and he thinks so too."

"What did the note say exactly?"

"I'll read it to you. 'Mind your own business or next time you won't be so lucky.' It's all in caps."

"That's definitely a threat. And, in my opinion, I'd say it's definitely referring to the earlier incident. I wouldn't take it lightly."

"Don't worry, I'm not."

He chuckled. It was a warm, hearty chuckle. Dare I say a sexy chuckle? Was there such a thing? If there was, he nailed it.

"I'd like to see the note. Are you free for lunch?"

I mumbled a "Yes," suddenly nervous about getting through a lunch with those darn blue eyes of his.

I texted Ashley that Jake and I'd agreed to meet at Sadie's Seafood Restaurant at noon. A few minutes later, she responded with a thumbs-up emoticon and a heart.

• • •

Sadie's lobster rolls were absolutely to die for. I fantasized about the butter-drenched lobster chunks cradled in the crust-trimmed bun as I sailed down the Avenue toward the ocean. Soon I was cruising along the Promenade, taking in the expansive view of the encroaching high tide, with frolicking whitecaps frosting the surface of the sparkling indigo sea. I turned onto the pier, bumping along, the weathered wooden planks clicking and clacking loudly under me, and pulled into the wharf parking lot, a wide area at the base of the pier spanning both the beach and ocean. I continued on foot along the pier as it extended over the water, invigorated by the brisk breeze tousling my hair yet warmed by the sunrays peeking through dollops of puffy clouds that dotted the baby blue sky. October in Santa Sofia was a grab bag of weather extremes.

One day I wore shorts and flip-flops. The next day I wore Uggs and cashmere. Today's dense morning fog had dissipated into low clouds currently in the process of burning off, keeping temperatures cool and creating the semblance of an East Coast autumn. When I reached the restaurant, Jake was at an outside table soaking up the fall sunshine in a gray shawl-collared cardigan over a white shirt and jeans, wearing shades, basically looking like he'd stepped out of a Ralph Lauren ad.

Focus. This lunch might be more challenging than I'd originally thought.

The waiter took our drink orders and returned quickly with two sturdy white mugs filled with steaming coffee. He placed them on the table and then waited for us to order.

Jake studied the menu. "Everything looks great."

"It is. Well, everything I've tried. Which is pretty much the hot lobster roll. It's so good I can never order anything else."

Jake chuckled heartily, apparently charmed by my wit.

That chuckle!

"Okay, I'll make it easy. Two lobster rolls, please."

The waiter expressed a strong approval of our choices and nodded approvingly when we both opted for the coleslaw side.

"Now that all the important decisions have been made, did you bring the note?"

I reached into my purse and laid it on the table.

Jake studied it. "This was pinned under your wiper?"

"Uh-huh."

He took out his phone and clicked a couple of shots. Just then it occurred to me I could have simply taken photographs of the note and sent them to him too. A few seconds later, I realized he could have requested I do the same. Was it really necessary to view the note in person? Or was it me Jake wanted to see in person? My face heated at the thought and I turned away from Jake, pretending to intently observe a group of noisy seagulls at the table behind me.

When I turned back to face Jake, he'd taken off his sunglasses and his eyes were twinkling with amusement. "I didn't know you were such a wildlife aficionado."

Oh, man. Why did he have to take off his sunglasses? His incredible blue eyes were so distracting. I stuttered a response. "Um, yes, er, no, well, seagulls, they can get aggressive."

"Thanks for the warning. You have a protective streak. Good to know."

Heat rose up to my face again. "So, what do you think about the note? Should I take it seriously?"

"In my professional experience, nine times out of ten, threatening notes are just that, an empty threat. But . . ."

I gulped as he hesitated, blurting out my worst fear. "One time out of ten they follow through?"

"Yep. The good thing about this note, if you can call anything about it good, is that it isn't specific. It doesn't say, for example, next time they're going to kill you. It's just a general threat."

"If that's the good part, I'm almost afraid to ask what the bad part is."

"The bad part is the timing. You got this right after someone actually ran you off the road. That's assuming you didn't go on social media and describe your near miss in detail immediately afterward?"

I shook my head. "I didn't mention it to anyone between the time it happened and when I got the note. Only Sam, Ashley, and the police knew about me being run off the road, besides you and me. I'll ask Ashley and Sam if they mentioned it to anyone else. You didn't tell anyone, right?"

"Correct. So, if we assume the person who wrote the note was the same person who ran you off the road, we know we're dealing with an individual who doesn't make idle threats and has already resorted to violence."

I shuddered at the thought. "In other words, I should mind my own business, as the note cautioned." I gestured with air quotes. "The scary thing is I pretty much was minding my own business before I was run off the road."

"Here's the thing. We really don't know what 'mind your own business' refers to. Does it refer to Benning Brothers' business?

Is Benning Brothers involved in any disputes with former employees? With competitors?"

I scrunched up my face. "We just got awarded a big job. The other two companies on the short list are our competitors, but neither of the teams is local. One firm is based in Santa Barbara and the other in LA. And while jobs are scarce, I can't imagine anyone I know from those firms acting in a threatening manner."

"But sometimes something can trigger a seemingly normal person to become deranged."

"Yeah, I guess so." I poured milk into my coffee as I reflected on my elation at hearing we won and imagined my disappointment had we lost. We'd have to scramble for several smaller jobs to stay afloat. If a firm was already in the red, losing out on a big bid could be catastrophic.

Jake took his turn with the milk. "I know so. I've seen it many times. Everyone has a breaking point."

"All I'd done that day was go to the police station as requested, visit my aunt and uncle, and take my cousin to lunch. I asked each of them questions, but how is any of that not my business? They're my family. It's not like I was interviewing Jo's friends or anything like that."

The warmth left Jake's eyes and he leaned in. "You're not thinking of doing anything like that now, of course, are you? Because you value your life, right?"

"Well, I need to find out who killed my husband and aunt before the SSPD decides to pin it on the low-hanging fruit—yours truly."

He stirred his coffee. "My understanding is you're on good terms with the police, especially the guy from the other night, Adrian, the one you just referred to." He pulled a business card out of his wallet. "I have his card—Sergeant Adrian Ramirez."

"Yeah, I am with Adrian. But one of the other cops, Ernesto Gomez, not so much. He'd do anything to make himself look good at the expense of harming others in the process. I'm not going to stand back and let Ernie get promoted to lieutenant by arresting the wrong person—me. I didn't kill my husband, and I didn't kill my aunt Jo or Esmeralda or whatever name she called herself, even if I was the last one to see her, which I'm sure I wasn't. And I'm certainly not going to let my uncle get arrested because he's being evasive, for whatever reason. I know he wouldn't hurt a fly, let alone his own sister."

"Tory, let Adrian find the killer. He strikes me as a good guy."

My phone rang and Sam's name appeared on the screen. "Let me get this. It's my cousin."

"I got your message about getting the condo job. Awesome. Congratulations."

"Thanks. So, is that a yes on my assistant job? Flexible hours."

"Definitely. And thank you. I really appreciate it."

"Great. Can you come into the office this afternoon to fill out some paperwork?"

"Yes. What time? I get out of school at two today and I can come by right after that."

"Sounds good. Oh, Sam, while I'm thinking of it, did you mention to anyone about us being run off the road yesterday?"

"I told my parents."

"Okay. Anyone else?"

He hesitated. "No. Why?"

"Someone left a note on my car yesterday warning me to mind my own business. It seemed to refer to us being run off the road, so I was wondering if you'd mentioned it to anyone. I'm trying to figure out whether it's a real threat or a prank."

He gulped loudly and his voice cracked. "Did the note say anything else?"

"That next time I won't be as lucky."

"Whoa! That's cold."

"That's putting it mildly. Anyway, let's keep it on the down low, please, and let the police deal with it."

"You told the cops?"

"Yeah. And the private investigator you met yesterday, Jake Logan." I smiled at Jake. "Anyway, see you at the office later."

When I looked up, Jake's stare unnerved me. "Sorry. I wanted to tie that down. That was about the big job I mentioned earlier —we won the bid for the Hotel Santa Sofia condo project."

"Congratulations. If I'd known, I'd have ordered champagne."

"I'll have to take a rain check on that. Champagne would make me conk out."

"We'll have to schedule an evening celebration then. How's Friday evening for you?"

Heat whooshed up to my face as I went through the motions of checking my blank calendar. I didn't think Gym would mind. "It's a date. I mean an appointment scheduled on that date." *Great. Way to be awkward.*

His stare made my heart flutter. "Great, how does seven sound?"

"Sounds perfect."

He put it on his calendar in his phone as our food arrived.

As usual, the lobster rolls didn't disappoint.

"This is incredible." Jake held the delicacy like a harmonica.

"Told you." I patted my mouth with my napkin.

Jake blotted the butter dripping on his hands with his napkin. "I don't think I've ever tasted better coleslaw."

His phone buzzed. When he checked its screen, he frowned.

"Everything okay?"

"Duty calls." He took out two twenties. "Sorry. I have to take off."

"Let's split it." I handed him back one of the twenties.

"If you insist. He stuffed the bill into his pocket, stood up, and laid his hand on my shoulder. "See you Friday night."

...

Two hours later, I was back at my desk. Ernie had left another message in a gruff voice. *"This is Sergeant Gomez again. I still need to talk to you. Call me."* Why so formal with the "Sergeant Gomez," I wondered. I supposed intimidation was a tactic he'd found useful to get people to comply with his requests. Well, it wasn't working with this girl, at least the compliance part, but the intimidation was definitely taking its toll as I fidgeted with files on my desk and had a sudden craving for chocolate. I needed to put Ernie off until I had some concrete evidence to eliminate myself as a suspect. If I got railroaded into an arrest, then I wouldn't be able to search for the real killer. I needed a plan. I pulled out a pad and pencil and made a list of people I needed to talk to, starting with my own family. Something was up with Uncle Bob and Aunt Veronica. I wondered what they weren't telling me.

A tap on my office doorjamb interrupted my thoughts. Sam stood in the doorway. "I'm here to fill out my paperwork."

"Great. Let me get you the forms." I went to the cabinet where we kept tax forms and handed them to him.

In the hallway outside my office, Jed Barnes, our nursery boss, paced.

"I'll be right back, Sam." I got up and pulled the door of my office shut to let Sam work undisturbed.

I motioned Jed to an office across the hall and closed the door. "Hi. Can I help you with something?"

He lowered his head, avoiding eye contact. "I'm sorry to tell you but some of my workers are upset about you hiring Sam."

"Excuse me?"

"They're calling it nepotism."

The news had spread as fast as the encroaching wildfire. There were two main problems with running a family business: family and business. It was hard to switch gears from personal to professional relationships and vice versa. Longtime employees, like Jed Barnes, felt like family and, because of this, they sometimes acted like actual family members instead of employees in personnel matters, particularly if an instance smacked at all of favoritism. I couldn't blame them. I had my own ax to grind when it came to working in a family business. As both a female and family member, I felt like I had to work twice as hard to prove I was worthy of any advancement I made and that I'd earned it fair and square.

Jed read my pained expression accurately. "Look, I know we've been over this many times before. I'm not the one objecting. It's my workers. They've been grumbling about it."

"Who exactly? Is it Matt Ortega? He's the only one I know who's expressed interest in transferring into our landscape design division recently."

Jed glanced up and then away again. That look implied it must be Matt. I felt like telling Jed to tell Matt, and anyone else who got their noses out of joint over Sam's hiring, to mind their own beeswax, but instead I mustered some self-restraint.

"Wow, news travels fast. I just offered the job to him officially today. How'd they find out so fast? Please tell your workers it's a temporary position only, for the length of our new project. He's still in high school, for goodness sake. And please convey, politely, of course, to your employees to not jump to conclusions and to remember the context. This poor boy just lost his birth mother. I'm trying to keep him busy and be here for him if he needs someone to confide in since, unfortunately, I can relate all too well to his situation. I urge you all to have a little empathy."

Jed's face reddened. "I see what you're saying. But several of my employees see it differently, is all. And I don't want to lose them over something like this, something that can be easily avoided. Especially with the holiday season getting into gear."

The nursery made most of its money during Christmas, and we'd definitely be in trouble if key personnel left us in the lurch at this time of year.

I couldn't tell whether Jed was embarrassed to be bearing bad news or whether he was threatening me. Feeling defensive, I raised my voice. "You think they'd quit over me hiring Sam?"

"Hey, calm down. Don't kill the messenger. All I'm saying is they're unhappy and they wanted me to let you know."

I took a deep breath and tried to diffuse the heated emotions in our conversation. Switching subjects, I forced a smile. "Is that a new watch?"

Jed broke into a prideful grin and scooped up the pocket watch attached to a chain on his belt loop. "The opposite. It's practically an antique. It was my grandfather's." The gold watch was engraved with the initials "TK."

"How nice to have a family heirloom like that." I sighed. "Sorry, Jed, if I came off as defensive. Please tell your guys message received."

After a peaceful parting, I went back to my office, where Sam sat quietly looking at his phone. He smiled when he looked up. "Finished everything."

I bumped his fist. "Good for you. You're way ahead of me. I haven't even received all the paperwork from the Hotel Santa Sofia Corporation yet. Say, that's a nice phone you got there. Is it new?"

His phone looked about four models newer than mine.

The smile left his face. "Yeah. Esmeralda gave it to me for my birthday."

"How nice. Sorry." *Awkward.* "She must have cared greatly for you, and I'm sure you must miss her."

He shifted his eyes from side to side, as if uneasy talking about Jo. "When do I start?"

"I have a conference call set up with the prime architects on Wednesday. In the meantime, they'll try to send me their timeline. Our design concept usually comes in toward the end of the project, after the buildings' construction costs and design are calculated. Then we'll work with the remaining budget. But we'll consult with the architecture team and the other subconsultants throughout the process to make sure everything is in line and goes as planned. I'll need to make another site visit soon to take some measurements and photos. Maybe you can come with me?"

"A road trip? Cool!"

I smiled. "It's only about ten miles away but, yeah, we can call it a road trip. Hopefully this time we won't be run off the road. We'll have to schedule it so we can stop for a late lunch along the way too. Make sure you leave me your schedule."

He handed me a sheet of paper. "Here it is. I'm off at one on Fridays."

"Good to know. Thanks."

He excused himself and crossed the hall to stop by his father's office. After he left Uncle Bob's office, I dropped by myself. Uncle Bob glanced at me. The creases around his eyes softened his expression, and I saw the warmth that had replaced the more distant look he had lately.

"Your son is officially my new assistant."

Bob beamed. "So I've heard. Thanks, Tory. Just what the doctor ordered to get his mind off things."

"That's what I'm hoping, but apparently the nursery workers have already gotten their panties in a twist. The claim of nepotism has once again reared its ugly head."

Bob sighed. "Oh, no, really? Who is it this time?"

"Jed told me about the griping but wouldn't name names. I suspect Matt Ortega. Jed made it sound like Matt might quit over it. I'm not sure if he's being dramatic or stirring the pot because he's bored or if the nepotism rumors are, in fact, true."

Uncle Bob made a clicking sound with his teeth. "Matt's one of our best guys. Can't imagine him being that petty. I'd hate to see him leave. Okay, let me poke around and see if I can find out what's going on. Told you running a business can be a pain in the butt. Don't worry. We'll figure it out."

My neck aching from tension, I went back to my office a bit demoralized. The euphoria of winning the bid had been diminished by the stress of disgruntled employees. Plus, I also worried about the effect winning the bid would have on Chandler Architects' attempt to acquire Benning Brothers, if any. Ugh. I remembered something my therapist had once told me. When problems weigh you down, make sure you take care of yourself first. Pamper yourself to relieve the stress. To me, of course, this meant yummy food and a hair appointment with my Philip.

I fiddled with my hair. I could use a haircut. I texted Philip and asked him if he had any availability. He was usually booked well in advance, but I lucked out—he had a cancellation for later in the afternoon. Perfect. I'd swing by the police station to give Adrian the note then reward myself at Clementine's, Santa Sofia's premier bakery, with a cup of tea and one of their melt-in-your-mouth gingersnaps on my way.

CHAPTER 17

Philip worked in the Hotel Santa Sofia's Zoe Stella Salon, a satellite location of the celebrity-favorite main salon headquartered in Los Angeles's Brentwood area. From the hotel lobby, I ambled down the wide corridor until I came to the glass storefront with the salon's name in white Helvetica letters painted on a small dark green rectangle. One of the double glass doors was wide open. I entered and immediately became more relaxed. Its interior design was minimalist, with clean lines and modern fixtures and furniture. The scent of gardenias hung in the air. The soothing ambience extended to the stylists and customers, who spoke in hushed voices as if cued by the soft strains of piped-in classical music.

The Zoe Stella Salon attracted Santa Sofia locals as well as hotel guests. Loyal customers flocked to the salon for its hip stylists and calm atmosphere. Hairdressers and their clients, in various stages of hairstyling, occupied all the stations. The knots in my neck and shoulders magically disappeared the moment I spotted Philip at his station. He was blow-drying a pretty woman's hair that had light blond highlights similar to mine. He rolled a lock of her hair deftly around a round brush, pulling it taut like taffy, then straightened it into slick submission with a hot blast from the handheld dryer he twirled with the finesse of a TV cowboy spinning his six-shooter.

Philip burst into a smile when he saw me. "I'll be with you in a minute. Nearly done."

I grabbed the latest issue of *People* magazine from the coffee table before seating myself on the black leather sofa. I paged through it idly for a couple of minutes. Finding nothing new to hold my attention, I checked my phone for messages. Another missed call from Ernie Gomez. If he was anything, he was persistent. I flipped to my Notes app and jotted down some questions to structure my time with Philip. I wanted to make sure I remembered to ask him everything I'd wanted to ever since he revealed on the night of Jo's murder that she'd been one of his clients.

"Tory, darling!" Philip threw open his arms and pecked my cheek.

"How's it going, Philip?"

"The bigger question is how's it going with you, my dear. So sorry again for what happened to your aunt. And not knowing she was your aunt—what a mess!"

"I'm hanging in there. Thanks."

He steered me to his station and unfurled a black smock for me. "What are you having done today, my love?"

"Just a trim and blowout, with a side of gossip."

He doubled over with a loud guffaw and grabbed my arm to steady himself as other customers and stylists looked at us. He muffled his giggles with his hand and his eyes danced with glee in the mirror.

"A side of gossip. Good one. What can I help you with?"

"Everything you know about my aunt. Whatever you can tell me will be helpful because I knew nothing about her."

He straightened out my smock. "She was a very nice lady. She'd been coming to me for about seven years. I met her and her sister-in-law when I was volunteering to cut hair at a halfway house on Thanksgiving. They were residents there for about a year, I think. She loved the way I did her hair and when she left, she started coming to me here a few times a year for her highlights."

"Hold up! Her sister-in-law? You don't mean my Aunt Veronica, do you?" My head nearly exploded conjuring up my sweet, sedate Aunt Veronica having substance-abuse issues.

"What? No, no, no. Not Veronica Benning. Goodness no." Philip clutched his chest.

"Thank God for that."

"No. This woman was supposedly related to her ex-husband's side of the family."

"Oh, so actually her former sister-in-law. Why 'supposedly'?"

"I guess. They used to be related by marriage somehow. Jo had a habit of calling everyone family, so I didn't bother getting the exact connection."

I was still trying to process the possibility that Aunt Jo and I might have crossed paths while getting our hair done. "Did she ever mention her own family?"

"If you're asking me whether I knew she was your aunt, definitely no."

"What about her ex-husband? Did Jo or her sister-in-law ever mention him?"

"No, not really. Follow me to the sink, love, so I can get you shampooed."

He threw a small white towel around my neck while I reclined back in the chair. The warmth of the water on my head was soothing, purging all my worries down the drain, even if only temporarily. The scent of the coconut shampoo wafted up my nostrils and Philip's fingers massaged my scalp with almost too much pressure, but it was effective as my tension melted away. He rinsed away the shampoo with the sprayer and warm water trickled down my neck, despite the towel. I closed my eyes as he applied a conditioner that smelled like citrus. He worked the conditioner into my hair, swirling it around with his hands, and then followed with a final deep rinse that caused more water to soak through the towel to my neckline. He wrapped my hair in a towel and marched me back to his station.

"Oh my goodness. Your back is wet. I'm so sorry." Philip replaced the wet towel with a dry one and blotted the small damp area around my neckline before I sat down. "Jo told me she was married twice. I think she outlived both of her husbands, but I really can't remember for sure. But it was after she'd split with them." He removed the towel from my head and sprayed my hair with a vanilla-scented product.

I squinted to protect my eyes from the spray. "Did she ever mention having any kids?"

"She mentioned a son and a stepson. And that her son had recently contacted her since her family had raised him. But I had no idea she was referring to your family and that your cousin, Sam, was her son. But reconnecting with him made her really happy, and I was happy for her. Like I said, she was a sweet lady with a gentle soul." Philip placed the spray bottle on the counter and blessed himself. "May she rest in peace."

I was touched by his gesture. But that was pure Philip. I was sure part of his popularity with his clientele went beyond his skill as a hairdresser. He was such a kind, decent human being that going to get your hair done felt like less of a chore and more like a visit with a good friend.

He trimmed about a half inch from my hair, reminding me to keep my head straight as he did so. His concentration bubble was so strong while he cut my hair that I dared not disturb him and risk an uneven haircut. Once we'd passed that critical phase of my appointment, it was safe to resume questioning him about Jo.

"Can you remember anything else significant about my aunt?"

He cranked up the blow-dryer and grabbed a round brush. "Not really. She loved her work at charity events, and she was grateful to her friend Paloma, one of the other fortune-tellers at the fundraiser, for getting her all the bookings. What started as an occasional gig had turned into a steady income. She told me she also was involved with some online readings. She really felt she had a special power."

"Yeah, I guess. But if she was such a good fortune-teller, why didn't she predict her own murder and prevent her own death?"

Philip let out a hoot and bent over in laughter. "Tory, you're so naughty. 'Why didn't she prevent her own death?'" He could barely catch his breath he was laughing so hard. "Oh, my God."

As I giggled along with him, for the first time during my visit I noticed what he was wearing—a hipster plaid shirt and tight jeans. When I cast my eyes downward, I saw what he had on his feet—Wallington boots. *Not Philip too.* But Philip was with me during the time when Milo disappeared at the wedding. I needed to get a grip. I was beginning to suspect everyone. But then I remembered I didn't know Philip's whereabouts at the firefighter fundraiser between when I first saw him and afterward, when I'd found Jo in the maze.

"Philip, did you talk to Jo at the fundraiser?"

"Me? No. I saw her walking to her booth and we waved at each other. But that was it."

"Was she alone?"

"No."

"Well, did you see who she was with?"

"Yes."

"Do you know who it was?"

"Yes."

I was flabbergasted and ready to bust a gusset. "Well, who was it?"

"It was her sister-in-law."

Something was up with normally effusive and loose-lipped Philip. Prying this information out of him felt like he'd been instructed by a lawyer to only answer the question and not volunteer any additional information. Clearly, there was more to this than he was telling me. "Do you know her name?"

He stared into space. I figured he was either making up a story (very uncharacteristic—he might be a gossip but he wasn't normally a liar) or trying to retrieve her name from his memory. "Cathy maybe? No, got it—Katie! You know her, the lady who takes care of Iris."

My shock at receiving this news was palpable. My head spun into a woozy unbalance, thoughts sloshing around in my head like loose items on a ship's deck in a storm. Luckily, I was sitting down or I might have stumbled. "What! You're just now telling me that my neighbor and dog sitter, the person I entrust with my beloved Iris, spoke to Jo the night of her murder? I hope you mentioned this to the police."

He kept his eyes down and his guilty silence told me he hadn't.

"Philip, you've got to tell the police the connection between Jo and Katie. I'm going to call them right now."

After I hung up from leaving Adrian a brief message, I turned back to Philip. "Hmm. I wonder if it was Katie who peeked through the curtain of Esmeralda's booth while I was having my reading? Did she seem okay when she waved to you? Did she look angry or scared?"

"Honestly, Tory, I didn't notice anything different about her. Except . . . Oops, I just remembered something else."

"What?"

"Oh, nothing related to that night."

Philip was zoned out again, totally concentrating on my hair.

"What were you going to say about Esmeralda? She looked different?"

He held up a hand mirror for me to admire my glossy hair. "No, I just remembered I think I double-booked appointments for tomorrow and need to call my clients."

Whatever he'd remembered, it wasn't a booking conflict. But he wasn't going to tell me now.

"Wow. It looks great as usual, Philip. Thank you so much. You always make me look so glamorous."

"It's not hard when you're as gorgeous as you. With your hair, it's easy. It's so thick and has great body."

Philip knew how to make me feel special, and I loved it. We hugged after I paid him. He refused any tip, as he did from time to time. This time I suspected it was because he had a guilty conscience for not being totally forthcoming about something.

"Fine. Have it your way. But now you're obligated to meet me for a drink sometime soon, my treat. Deal?"

Philip held my hand. "Deal."

"I'll call you soon to set it up." I'd get him liquored up and find out more then. Loose-lipped Philip couldn't be repressed after a couple glasses of Chardonnay.

As I drove home, I was still blown away about Katie. I

remembered how she'd denied that Iris had acted up as Milo's text had implied. So, Milo hadn't lied when he texted he was taking Iris home? Had Iris been acting up? This made a lot of sense, given Iris's hyperactive nature. Was it Katie who'd lied about Iris being well behaved and that she hadn't spoken to Milo? Why would she lie? If only Iris could talk! I was totally overwhelmed and could hardly think straight enough to drive, let alone fathom what this new development meant in terms of Milo's and my aunt Jo's murders.

By the time I pulled into my driveway, I'd decided I was going to confront Katie about her relationship to Jo. Well, maybe not confront, maybe more hem and haw around the topic to see how she reacted. But first I was going to check on Iris. It was times like this that made me realize she and I were in pretty much a codependent relationship, but in a good way. I was so desperate to make sure she was okay, I almost forgot to turn off my ignition. I hurried out of my car and rushed to my front door. Hearing her bark hysterically from inside brought a smile to my lips and a wave of relief to every tense muscle in my body. "Iris! Hi! I'm back! Hold on. I'm coming."

Of course, as I knew it would, my shouting through the closed door only amplified her frenzy. I think the correct term for us in psychology was *folie à deux*.

At last, after a nervous fumbling of my keys, I got the door open and Iris and I were reunited. I squatted down and scooped her into my lap, holding her tight as she frantically licked me. I walked outside with her in the backyard before scooping her up and heading over to talk to Katie. I lingered in my doorway for a second. I'd always had a good feeling about Katie, but discovering she never mentioned her relationship with Jo now cast her in a shadier light. I texted both Ashley and Adrian about what Philip had told me and told them I was going to pay Katie a visit.

It was starting to get dark, and I turned on some lights inside and the outdoor front entry light. I took a deep breath and locked the door. I crossed over my driveway to her front lawn, nuzzling

Iris along the way. Katie had a couple of pumpkins in her entryway that made me feel reassured for some reason. There was a note taped on her front door. On it was written: *I was called away unexpectedly for a family emergency. Sorry no time to contact everyone individually. Be back in a few days. Katie.*

I was stunned. Based on the content alone, it was an odd coincidence that just when I needed to talk to her she'd left town unexpectedly. But what jolted me was the note itself. The paper and the printing were identical to the menacing note left on my windshield.

CHAPTER 18

I stared at the note in a daze, as if glued to the ground, not knowing what to do. Iris started to lick my face, sensing my tension. Should I rip the note off the door as evidence? On second thought, I realized it was Adrian's call to make. I took about five shots of the note with my phone from different angles and then jogged home to contact Adrian and Ashley again.

Adrian picked up after the first ring. "Hey, Tory. I got your text. Sorry I didn't respond earlier. So, your neighbor, Katie, is related to Jo through marriage?"

"Yeah, but wait till you hear this." I told him about her note. "And get this—the note was written on a yellow legal pad and all in caps, just like the one that was left on my car."

"Wow. Okay. I was just about to leave the station. How about I swing by your place on the way home and take a look?"

"That would be great, Adrian. Thanks."

Back at home, Otis circled my legs upon my return, and once I placed Iris down she started to hound me every step I made.

"Okay, guys. I get it. You're hungry."

I scooped Otis some kitty kibble, fed Iris her doggie kibble sprinkled with shredded cheese, and made myself dinner, a.k.a. opened a box of soup. After the filling lobster roll from Sadie's, I wasn't very hungry. I was, apparently, still on a lobster kick, so I chose lobster bisque for dinner. After we finished eating, Iris and I took a stroll in the backyard. The six-foot wooden fence separating my property from Katie's gave me some reassurance of security and safety. On our second lap around the yard, I heard a clink of metal from Katie's yard. I froze in place, trying to be quiet. Iris jolted into attack mode, ears erect and eyes alert.

Then she let out a shrill bark that punctured the stillness like an ice pick—so much for stealth. She then began to yap loudly, dashing back and forth along the fence like an old-fashioned electric typewriter's automatic carriage return stuck on repeat. A garage door thudded shut, followed by more clanking and clanging. I whispered to Iris in breathless shouts, begging her with wild pointing gestures to come to me. She acted as if she'd suddenly gone blind and deaf. Every time I caught up to her, she sidestepped my attempts to grab her and scampered away again. Finally, I managed to block her, scoop her up, and run inside.

Once we were safely locked inside, I ventured a peek out the front living room window. A white car was pulling away just as I heard a rap at the front door. The knock set off Iris again. She circled the entryway, barking hysterically.

"Who is it?" My trembling voice cued me in to how freaked out I was.

"It's me, Tory, Adrian. Are you okay?"

I cracked open the door while keeping it chained to make sure an impersonator wasn't pretending to sound like Adrian. Affirming that it indeed was Adrian, I feverishly slid off the chain, making a mental note to dial back on watching the Hallmark Channel's mystery movie marathons for a while.

I flung open the door. "I am now. I'm so glad you're here. I heard a noise coming from Katie's backyard and then a white car drove off."

"Yeah, I saw a white car speeding off. I think it was a male driver, but it went by so fast I can't be sure. Was it the same one that's been following you?"

"I'm not sure. I've never gotten a good look."

"I got a partial on the plate. I'll run it through the database tomorrow to see if we can come up with anything."

I put Iris's lead on and we all walked over to Katie's house to view the note. It was gone.

"It was right here. See? The tape left a mark."

Iris tugged at her lead. Walking on a lead had never been one of her strengths. So many scents, so little time. She pulled me toward the bushes near Katie's door.

"Iris, no. Whatever is in there won't be good." Cat? Squirrel? Rat? OMG, what if it was a skunk?

Iris emerged from the bushes with a trophy—the note.

"Give it to me, Iris. Good girl."

For once, she listened. It was a little damp but intact.

I handed the note to Adrian. "Here it is. Whoever was here tore it down for some reason."

Adrian inspected it and then took a few photos of it with his phone. "What kind of car does Katie drive?"

"A white sedan. I think it's a Kia."

We both locked eyes in an "aha" moment.

I gripped the railing bordering the two steps leading to her front door. "You think it was Katie who tore down her own sign? But why?"

"I don't know. I was wondering whether she was the one in the white car who's been following you."

Adrian made a quick check on Katie's property as I traipsed after him with Iris in my arms. The house appeared to be locked up and undisturbed, and other than a metal ladder lying on her driveway, her yard looked normal. After his inspection, we all strolled back to my house.

He scratched his head. "Have you tried contacting Katie?"

"No. I wouldn't know what to say, knowing she might have lied about talking to Milo after the ceremony. I'm so confused and have such mixed emotions about her right now. She's always been good with Iris, and Iris loves Katie and, believe me, I know when Iris doesn't like someone. I don't know what to think."

We stood on my doorstep. Adrian crossed his arms. "Do me a favor and text her. Tell her you saw her note and offer to collect her mail if she hasn't made other arrangements. Let's see if she responds."

I texted Katie as Adrian had suggested. He waited around for about five minutes to see whether she'd respond. When she didn't, he instructed me to lock up and to turn on my security system.

"I'll let you know if the license plate gets a hit. We'll dust the note for prints too. And I'll have the lab compare the two notes. Please don't hesitate to call me if something comes up—day or night. Okay?"

"Got it. And thank you so much, Adrian, for coming over."

"Don't worry. We'll put the perp behind bars, sooner or later. I appreciate all your tips. They've been very helpful. But remember, we're dealing with a violent person who's probably beginning to feel cornered. So, take care. I'd much rather you call me than risk endangering yourself or others in your impatience to catch the culprit."

"I definitely will." I laughed lightly to assure him I was fine. But my laugh sounded hollow because it was. I wasn't fine. I was scared. Scared of the killer and scared Ernie would settle on me as the prime suspect.

• • •

Three days later I sat at my office desk feeling satisfied with my accomplishments over the past few days. I'd received the building drawings and tentative construction schedule from Chandler Architects. Our initial landscape detail plans needed to be drawn up, even though the actual planting wouldn't be executed for at least another twelve months.

I had several other projects I was working on, a handful of proposals already submitted, and more proposals in the works. If half came through, our landscape design division would be busy for the next couple of years and financially flush. In the meantime, we'd have to lean more heavily on our nursery business to succeed in dodging the bankruptcy bullet in the event we didn't recover the embezzled money. But to do that, first we had to identify the embezzler and, so far, Uncle Bob hadn't made any progress on that front.

I pushed back in my chair, pleased that my productivity was paying off, plus, staying busy had kept morbid thoughts and fears at bay. My moment of satisfaction was interrupted by my phone's vibration. Without looking, I knew it was Ernie Gomez again. He left messages a couple times a day like clockwork. Adrian told me he was running interference for me, but Ernie was relentless. I couldn't keep putting him off forever.

I grabbed my phone, swiped to voicemail, and reluctantly played his message. He sighed heavily before he spoke. *"Tory, it's Ernie again. You can't hide behind Adrian forever. We will meet and you will answer my questions. Call me."* He'd dispensed with the formality of his title and spoke more slowly than usual, as if he were resigned to leaving me messages I'd never answer. He still seemed menacing, but it also seemed our one-sided phone tag had worn him down a bit. I took this as a good sign. It bought me more time, which I desperately needed.

Ernie wanted his promotion and I was his ticket, even though all his evidence against me was circumstantial. All he had was my relation and proximity to the victims. My plan to propose other viable suspects to him, so he'd have to think twice before continuing to pursue me, remained just that, a plan. The clues pointing to other suspects needed to be presented in a methodical fashion to persuade him. Once charges were officially filed, wheels would be set in motion that would take a great deal of effort to reverse. I refused to sit back and become a victim because an overzealous cop was incapable of conducting a thorough investigation—the Innocence Project was created for a reason. It was time to get seriously organized. Ernie's energy might be lagging right now but I couldn't count on him staying that way. It might be only a matter of time before he'd be recharged and come after me again at full speed.

Scooting my chair in closer to my desk, I clicked on the project management software we used to organize multiple projects. It would be perfect for arranging my clues and suspects. A new blank grid opened on my screen and I titled the rows "Suspects." I decided to make it all-inclusive to start with and to eliminate suspects one by one as I gathered more evidence.

For a moment, my fingers paused in suspended animation on the keypad. Writing it all down made it very real. I shook my head to clear away my apprehension and made my list: Katie, Uncle Bob, Aunt Veronica, Sam, Jed, Matt, Philip, Jake, and Paloma. Nine suspects—wow! I didn't add Ashley because she was with me when Milo went missing, not to mention I trusted her with my life.

I hated that the list mainly included my family and friends, with the only strangers being Jake and Paloma, who I still needed to interview. I checked myself for referring to Jake as a stranger —hardly true anymore since I'd had lunch with him earlier and gotten to know him a little better. But my head told me not to let his baby blues lull me into a besotted gullibility. I still didn't know much about him and a Google search to find out more was way overdue.

I was tempted to add Ernie Gomez to my list of suspects. His eagerness to solve the case quickly, even if it meant arresting the wrong person, struck me as shady. But I didn't add him. Bad cops existed, but I couldn't imagine him stooping so low that he'd commit two murders and arrest the wrong person just to get promoted. I wasn't that paranoid. Plus, I was pretty sure Ernie didn't even know Milo and Jo existed before they became murder victims.

Next, I labeled the columns with all of the clues I could think of. I typed in "Wallington Boots," "Windshield Note," "Katie's Door Note," "White Car," "Truck," "Rock," "Knife," and "Hoodie." That added up to a total of eight clues.

I started to put checkmarks in the grids next to the suspects who had connections to each clue. So far, I'd found out that five out of my eight suspects owned Wallington boots. All were males: Uncle Bob, Sam, Jed, Matt, and Philip. The windshield note could have been put on my car by anyone. So, all nine suspects got a check. The same was true of the note left on Katie's door.

Jake and Katie both had white cars, so each got a check under that column. Jed and Matt had pickup trucks and I gave each a check for that. Pretty much everyone had access to the rock, except Philip, who was with me, and Paloma, who I assumed wasn't at the hotel the day of the wedding. The knife and hoodie —any and all had access to items like these.

I pushed back my chair and surveyed the screen. *Well, crap.* The pattern of suspicion I'd hoped would magically appear to persuade Ernie failed to materialize. Instead, a mishmash of random checks all over the place.

I stood and stretched my arms over my head to relieve the increased tension I was feeling. I grasped my hands diagonally behind my back, first with my left hand behind my back, then with my right, and felt the stretch. I turned my head gently to the right and to the left then looked up and down. Finally, holding on to my desk, I lifted one leg in the air as I tipped downward and then switched legs. Stretching made me feel more limber and relaxed, as if I'd hit a reset button. I sat back down. Maybe I needed a different approach.

I pulled up a blank grid. Again, I listed the suspects in the rows, but this time in the columns I typed in the headings of "Clues," "Means," "Motive," and "Opportunity." I leaned back with pride—all those hours spent watching TV police procedurals had finally paid off.

In the "Means" column, all my suspects were capable of grabbing a rock from the Hidden Garden and using it as a weapon. Except Philip, of course, who was with me during the time Milo was presumably murdered. The same was true for Jo's murder weapon. Anyone could have hidden a knife in a handbag or under a coat thrown over an arm.

"Motive" was the most interesting category. If I could figure out what linked Milo and Jo's murders, I was sure I'd find the motive. My head swam with competing thoughts. No one was immune from having a dark side. Whether it was greed, envy, jealousy, fear, or revenge, someone must have had a motive strong enough to kill for. Yet, even as I pondered this, I thought just because someone had a dark secret didn't make them a ruthless murderer willing to kill to keep it secret, especially when they were my family and friends. Another troubling fact was that, as far as I knew, most of my suspects barely knew the two victims. I suspected everyone. I suspected no one. At this rate, I'd be chasing my tail forever.

Milo was the stickler regarding motive. I knew I was biased, but he was the nicest guy. He was selfless, really. Always willing to help people. I couldn't imagine anyone wanting to hurt him . . . unless somehow he was in the way. What if he was helping someone who the murderer didn't want him to help? I bet that was it. Milo wasn't murdered because someone didn't like him, I bet he was killed because he was helping someone in trouble, and the person in trouble was the target. Could Milo have known Jo? Was he helping her in some way? And why would someone want to murder Jo? She had a shady past. It must be related to that. The person who could fill me in on that best was probably her friend Paloma.

I Google searched Josephine Benning and several hits came up for companies that required a fee to get to the good stuff. And by good stuff, I meant arrest records, especially recent arrests that hadn't yet wound their way into the public domain.

I did, however, hit the lottery in terms of public information. I got the address of the apartment building where Paloma and Jo lived. It listed her as Josephine Benning, also known as Esmeralda Benning and Josephine Keaton, her former married name, I presumed. Another site even listed residents of the building with their phone numbers. I shook my head, marveling at how easy it was to obtain personal information online. I gave Ashley a call.

"Hi, what's up? Is everything okay?"

"Yeah, thanks. I'm okay. I'm going to visit Jo's friend Paloma. Remember her?"

"Sure. The other fortune-teller, right?"

"Yep.

"Feel like an adventure?"

"That sounds like a trick question. What do you want?"

I chuckled. "No biggie. I just wanted to know if you wanted to go with me to talk to Paloma about Jo. If after work is okay with you, I'll see if that works for her."

"It would have to be before eight. So, if we can be done by seven thirty, count me in."

"Great. Thanks. I'll let you know."

I called Paloma. She remembered me and quickly agreed to meet with me. We picked a coffee shop not far from her apartment. I let Ashley know and then turned back to my suspect grid.

For the "Opportunity" column, Philip was out for Milo's murder. I wanted to count him out for Jo's too, given his description of how much he liked her. I trusted Philip. But keeping in mind that, under the right circumstances, anyone could commit murder, Philip remained a suspect. To indicate his low ranking as a suspect, I put a question mark after his name.

All the other suspects had opportunity. My whole family was at the wedding and the fundraiser, and the same was true for all of our employees. Everyone got a double check next to their name for opportunity, except for Sam, who hadn't attended the fundraiser, and for Paloma and Jake, who hadn't attended the wedding.

I sat back and surveyed my grid. My family members had the fewest number of entries next to their names in terms of hard evidence. Yet they, more than the other suspects, were more involved with both murder victims and, hence, more likely to have had a motive for murder. Was I being objective? I had no idea. If the way my head throbbed was any indication, I had certainly tried. Once again, my visual display had yielded nothing but a random display of checks and entries. No definitive pattern of guilt jumped out at me as I'd hoped. Trying to process everything and make sense out of nonsense had knotted my brain to a halt. I was stumped. Something was missing.

CHAPTER 19

After calling Sam to arrange our site visit for the next afternoon, I got a call from the insurance company. Their investigator would be dropping by in the morning to interview me. I hastily went through the last of my father's files—nothing out of order, as far as I could tell. My neck and shoulders tensed up as I wondered about the insurance company's reaction when they discovered our company was on the brink of insolvency. Hopefully by now Uncle Bob had narrowed down the explanations for the irregularities and it wouldn't be an issue for the insurance company. But what if he hadn't? Would they try to connect our unexplained embezzlement to my father's death, claiming he committed suicide because he'd embezzled?

As if besmirching his character wasn't bad enough, would they also renege on their end of the deal? He'd paid the premium payments and now they'd deny the claim? I realized that working myself up into a frenzy of anxiety served no good use. I tried to calm myself down by taking a few deep breaths and looking on the bright side. I reminded myself that Benning Brothers was poised to receive a lot of business. Although, granted, nothing was a done deal. All I could do at the moment was cross my fingers and hope the insurance company would pay the claim so that even if the world turned to manure, the insurance payout would save Benning Brothers. I chuckled to myself, appreciating my own gardening reference as I headed across the hall to warn Uncle Bob about the insurance investigator's visit.

His door was ajar and I stuck my head in. "Hi, do you have a minute?"

Before I could say another word, he got a call. As I started to leave, Uncle Bob waved at me and pointed to a chair. "Stick around. This'll only take a minute."

I sat across from him as he winked at me. I checked my phone idly while waiting for him to finish his call. I'd received a text from Jake telling me something had come up and asking if we could meet up for dinner tonight instead of tomorrow night. Although I was still heartbroken over Milo, I surprised myself with my reaction to this change in plans. Friday had made it seem more like a date. I didn't know how I felt being moved up to Thursday and relegated to a weeknight.

I sighed and texted back, *Fine with me. Where and when?*

Lazarro's at eight?

That actually worked out perfectly since Ashley and I had planned to not stay any later than seven thirty for our meeting with Paloma. I texted back, *See you then.*

Uncle Bob ended his call and set his phone on his desk. "Sorry, Tory, that was Matt Ortega." Uncle Bob winked at me again. "Since his nose is apparently pushed out of joint over your hiring Sam, I thought it important to take his call so he didn't think I was being standoffish. I asked Matt to meet me after work for a beer and he just confirmed."

"Thanks. That sounds great."

"I've always had a good relationship with Matt so, hopefully, he'll feel like telling me what's going on. He seemed pleasant enough right now."

I crossed my arms. "Well, if he's fine with you, then maybe it's me he's mad at. I wonder why?"

I had a hunch. A lot of men still had trouble with a female boss, especially when she was the boss's daughter. I'd grappled with the female role, trying to reconcile my professional personality and my personal traits to be at once assertive and friendly. Architecture and landscape architecture had both made great progress in terms of women going into the profession, but generally the power positions were still dominated by men.

"Please remind Matt one of the reasons I hired Sam was to help him deal with the death of his birth mother because I just experienced the death of my own father too." My voice unexpectedly caught. "And that he's still in high school, for goodness sake. It's not like I'm making him the president of the company or—"

The ringing of Uncle Bob's phone cut me off. Thankfully, because I realized where my thoughts were going. I was the one who had been made president of the company because I was the boss's daughter. While it had always been the plan for me to take over in a few years when my father eventually retired, his death had accelerated the process. Did the workers resent me as their boss?

Uncle Bob scowled at his phone. "It's Ernesto Gomez. Probably wants to ask me the same friggin' questions again. I'm a busy man. I don't have time to waste." Uncle Bob declined the call. "I'll let it go to voice mail."

This was my opening. "Why do you think he wants to ask you the same questions? He wants to talk to me, too, because I was one of the last people to talk to Jo before she died, but why you? I wonder what it could be he thinks you can tell him."

Uncle Bob's eyes skittered from side to side, but his lips remained sealed.

I figured I'd let that percolate for a while. "Okay, new topic. What I wanted to tell you is that I got a call from the insurance company and they're sending someone to interview me. I told them tomorrow at eleven. Will you be around in case I need backup?"

He sighed in annoyance. "About what?"

"They said it's routine."

He checked his calendar on his phone. "I guess." He sighed again.

"You seem annoyed."

"I don't need strangers sticking their noses in our business. We both know your dad would never have committed suicide. We don't need someone coming here and dredging everything up. I'm positive his death had nothing to do with the state of our current finances."

"Then why the big deal? It's not as if he had an offshore account where he was squirreling money away from the company."

Uncle Bob squirmed in his chair.

I leaned in closer. "Wait. He didn't have an offshore account, did he?"

"No, of course not. It's just that we have some unusual withdrawals from the company account that might be perceived in the wrong way." He'd avoided eye contact with me, except for a quick glance.

"Unusual withdrawals? Like what?"

He kicked back in his rolling chair and whistled. "There are some withdrawals I haven't been able to explain. Until I figure out why they were made, I don't want to talk to the police, the insurance company, or anyone else."

"Who made the withdrawals? Not Dad, right?"

"No, not your father."

I took in a deep breath and exhaled slowly. "Thank God for that. I knew he would never embezzle."

Uncle Bob stared at me with a pained expression.

"What? It wasn't you, was it?"

"Of course it wasn't me."

"Then who?" And then it clicked. There was only one person Uncle Bob would be this upset over, his wife. "It's Aunt Veronica, isn't it?"

Uncle Bob got up and closed his office door. When he turned around to face me, his eyes were welled up with tears. He jutted out his jaw in an attempt to prevent tears from flowing down his cheeks and wiped away the few that trickled down with his sleeve.

"I hope not, but it's a possibility. When I first noticed an irregularity with our books and that someone had transferred out large sums of money, I thought of how she'd made a series of loans before. I checked. She paid them all back, and I asked her about the larger amounts. She insists the only loans she took were the small ones that got repaid. She'd made a few loans to Jo, or Esmeralda, or whatever she was calling herself at the time, after Jo had left the halfway house to help her with all the costs of renting her own place, security deposit, first and last month's rent, utility deposits, stuff like that. But she'd told both your dad and me about those loans and we'd authorized them."

"My father knew Jo had moved back?"

Uncle Bob nodded. "He probably would have told you eventually, once he was sure Jo wasn't up to no good again."

"So you think Aunt Veronica took out more loans and didn't pay those back? And that's why we're in a financial fix?"

"She claims she didn't, but who else could have made the withdrawals?"

"But you said she kept a record of all the loans she'd made before. And who else would be asking her for a loan? Your brother, George?" I got up and paced around the office. "I don't know, Uncle Bob. I'd believe her if she says she didn't take the money. Aunt Veronica always has been a straight shooter. If she says it wasn't her, why wouldn't you believe her?"

"That's just it. I do believe her. As you pointed out, she kept records, even when she made personal loans from the company. But it's the way it looks. She's our main financial person. I've asked her assistant, Sheila Bledsoe, if she knew about any loans, and she claims ignorance."

I rested my hand on his shoulder. "Look, I'm glad we're both on the same page about Aunt Veronica. She wouldn't look anyone in the eye and outright lie if she didn't have a good reason. So, either she didn't take the money or she's covering for someone who did, just like you've been doing. Loyalty obviously runs in the family."

He fought a smile but didn't win. "You're right about that."

"I understand better now where you're coming from and why you haven't been totally straightforward with Adrian, but honesty is always the best policy when it comes to cops you trust. Ernie, on the other hand, keep avoiding him until we get to the root of the embezzlement, okay?"

I knew how he must have felt. I felt the same way when Milo first went missing, before it was clear he'd met with foul play. Your world turned upside down when you considered the fact that someone you'd trusted might have been lying to you all along. You're overwhelmed with mixed emotions—sucker punched for feeling betrayed yet also defensive, denying their wrongdoing. Whether your denial stemmed from your desire to protect their reputation or your own gullibility was irrelevant.

I paced some more until a thought occurred. "On the other hand, our account could have been hacked and the transfers made remotely."

"Hacked?"

"Or maybe it was an inside job. Maybe someone broke into her office to use her computer to make the transfers. Aunt Veronica is pretty old school. I've seen her refer to a list of passwords locked in her desk drawer. Anyone could have popped open the drawer with a credit card or something. Those locks aren't that strong. Then all they would have needed to do was get the bank password and make the transfer. We could probably see where the money was transferred to if we looked right now."

"You think I haven't thought of that? I already tried to trace it. There were multiple transfers to an account that is now closed. Only the cops would have the authority to delve deeper."

"Okay. Let me think about how we should broach the subject with Adrian."

As if on cue, my phone rang and it was Adrian.

"Hi, Adrian. My uncle and I were just talking about you."

"Hey, this is an official call." His somber tone got my attention.

I startled to tremble all over, positive he was going to tell me I was under arrest.

"We just got a preview of your father's autopsy report back. Death resulted from blunt force trauma to his head."

"So that's consistent with what we already theorized, right? Caused from him falling off of the pier?"

Uncle Bob perked up and moved closer and whispered, "About your father?"

I nodded.

"Yes and no. The coroner found evidence of multiple blows. Since there are blows to both the front and the back of his head, they can't tell whether cause of death was from a blow or from a fall. The medical examiner told me some of the contusions and head injuries appear to have happened before he hit the water."

"What are you saying?"

"I'm not saying anything until the full report is concluded. I just wanted to alert you that the coroner's completed analysis is imminent. Theoretically, multiple possible scenarios could be responsible for those injuries. Hopefully the coroner will be able to pin down the sequencing of injuries in terms of time and be able to conclude which one was the actual cause of death. I'm not drawing any conclusions until the tox report is finished, which should be tomorrow morning. That'll give us more info to piece together the puzzle."

"Well, what are the other possible scenarios? Can you at least tell me that?"

"I don't want to jump the gun."

"It's not suicide then?"

"We're not ruling out anything until the full report is in. Accidental death, suicide, and homicide are all on the table. Look, Tory, I've gotta run. You'll hear from me as soon as I get the report on my desk, hopefully by noon tomorrow."

• • •

Homicide? I was stunned to hear the word stated aloud in reference to my father. It rang in my ears, echoed in my brain, and invaded every square inch of my conscious being. Thoughts swirled around, struggling to connect with other thoughts, thoughts I'd repressed ever since my father's death. I'd been afraid if I allowed homicide to rise into my consciousness, I might be overcome by the horror of it all. Better to keep such thoughts out of sight and out of mind, like a submerged submarine, undetectable. I'd always thought my father's death was odd, suspicious even. When Milo disappeared, I tried hard to downplay the chilling thought that the two were related. Jo's murder was the third mysterious death in my family within a matter of weeks. I could no longer deny the obvious. How could they *not* all be related? I'd been denying my own suspicions because they were too horrible to believe and I didn't want them to be true. If they were true, it meant someone violent was at large, hurting those near and dear to me. I gulped hard, struggling to catch my breath and not hyperventilate as the frightening realization surfaced into my consciousness, surging up through of the depths of my mind, like a deep sea diver rushing to the surface for air, to reveal its harsh reality. Whoever was responsible for these murders was probably someone I knew, someone who knew me. My whole body started to shake as the chill of evil closed in on me.

CHAPTER 20

After filling in Uncle Bob on the autopsy results, I drove home on autopilot. My worst fears were starting to materialize, and I didn't know what to do. Once at home I fed Iris and Otis, and afterward alternately held each of them on my lap, taking comfort in the cuddles of the fluffy white pompom of a dog first and then the purring black fur ball of a cat. Each nuzzled gently into me, seeming to sense their momma was in need of a strong dose of TLC. My nerves calmed and feeling better, I changed into the outfit I'd planned for dinner. All black, low V-neck top, skinny-fit pants, and heels. I brushed off Iris's hair, which clung to everything I wore, touched up my makeup, and brushed my hair, swinging my head down and up to give it volume. I gave Iris a tickle under her chin and Otis a little pat on his head and promised them I'd be back in a couple hours or so.

When I arrived at the Mugs & Teacups Café, a coffee shop near Paloma's apartment in a quiet neighborhood off of the Avenue, Ashley had already bagged us an indoor table. Two cups of steaming tea served in fine English china greeted me at the round table.

Her chair pushed back from the table, Ashley stretched out her long legs, wrapped in indigo skinny jeans. New black suede booties hugged her crossed ankles. As soon as our eyes met, she straightened up.

"Something happen? You look upset."

This girlfriend knew me so well.

I pulled up a chair. "Adrian called and said my dad's autopsy results are nearly complete."

"And?"

"They're not ruling out homicide."

She whistled a long breath. "Whoa, really? That's unsettling, to say the least. When will you know for sure?"

"Tomorrow." My put-togetherness started to unravel. "Look, Ash, could we not talk about it right this minute, please, because I might cry and I don't want to freak out Paloma when she gets here. I want to maximize our time with her and focus on my aunt. I'll tell you more about what Adrian said later."

"Of course. Are you sure you're okay to talk to her?"

"I'll be fine. Thanks for the tea. Exactly what I need. Love the boots, by the way—super cute."

"Aren't they? Got 'em on sale at Banana Republic." Her faux leather jacket was open to reveal a low-cut black top.

"Someone's fancy tonight. You have a hot date?"

"As a matter of fact, I do." She tilted her head and smiled coyly.

"Do tell."

"Well, it's not a date, really, at least I don't think it is. We're just meeting for a drink."

I swished a spoon around in my tea. "So, come on, tell me, who is it?"

"I'd rather not say."

"Seriously? Must everything be a mystery? Please, can't something in my life, for once, be transparent and straightforward?"

"Calm down. Everything isn't about you, miss. It's just that I really like him and I don't want to jinx it."

"Adrian?"

Her jaw dropped. "How did you know?"

I laughed. "Oh, come on. You two are always on-again off-again. I don't have to be a detective, or a fortune-teller, for that matter, to spot chemistry when I see it. Plus, you guys are like two peas in a pod when it comes to justice."

Ashley sank back and crossed her legs. "Yeah, we are. But also, I want to keep it on the down low because you're my client."

"Is that unethical?"

"Not really. You're not an official suspect yet."

"Yet?"

"If I date Ernie, start to worry."

I nearly spit out my tea. "That would be wrong on so many levels." I pursed my lips and made a zipping gesture. "Okay, my lips are sealed. I haven't heard a thing, and I'll try not to jinx your nondate with Adrian."

"Thanks. Now, can you tell me what else Adrian said about your father's autopsy before she gets here, or would you still prefer to wait until later?"

I deadpanned, "Who's Adrian?"

"You're a funny girl. Hurry up. Fill me in."

I fished the teabag out of my cup and added a bit of milk. "Just that the toxicological results aren't completed yet, probably will be in tomorrow, but he wanted to warn me that so far they know my father died from blunt force trauma to the head. They found blows to both the front and back of his head. Once they determine the timing sequence of the blows, we'll know more about which one killed him. He said the medical examiner told him some of the contusions and head injury happened before he hit the water."

Ashley stared at me as if she was processing her thoughts. "So, someone punched him in the face and he fell and hit his head?"

"Yeah, sounds like something like that."

"Hmm. Putting on my defense attorney hat for a minute, if I had a client charged with murder and those were the results, I'd be thrilled."

"Thrilled? Why?"

"Because I'd argue that they got into an altercation and my client didn't anticipate the deceased would fall and hit his head because of it."

"But that wouldn't get your client off the hook, would it?"

"Not necessarily, but it would definitely work in their favor if the case went to a jury trial. It would make it possible for the jury to find them guilty of a lesser charge than first-degree murder, due to lack of intent to kill."

"Well, at least it proves he didn't commit suicide, right?"

"It certainly wouldn't help the suicide theory. From a legal standpoint, your dad's death always struck me as suspicious, and a possible homicide, even before Milo disappeared. I always consider homicide in situations where I look at what behavior I'd expect against what behavior actually occurred and it doesn't add up. I couldn't imagine your dad, runner and fitness enthusiast, as a likely candidate for a fatal stumble. Equally implausible to me was that he took his own life. I mean, the man embodied optimism, right?"

"Totally. That always bothered me too, the incongruity of the accidental fall. As people get older, they have a greater tendency to fall, but he wasn't a frail older person. He was exactly the opposite—he averaged about twenty thousand steps a day on his Fitbit watch. His competitive nature resulted in him leading our Fitbit leader board more times than not. He was obsessive about keeping fit."

Ashley jokingly said under her breath, "The apple didn't fall far from that tree."

"You're not trash-talking my boyfriend Gym again, are you?"

We both giggled.

Ashley reached over and squeezed my hand. "After Milo's disappearance, it struck me as even more shady. That's why I was so protective of your assets when Milo disappeared. I couldn't rule out, at that point, that Milo might have been involved. Sorry, Tor, but I can't *not* think like a lawyer."

I nodded. "I think I knew my father might have been murdered all along, but the thought of someone killing him was so abhorrent to me that I kind of repressed it all."

She leaned over and rubbed my arm. "Aw, sorry, sweetie. But, that being said, I am also well aware that almost everyone has secrets and that people aren't necessarily who they appear to be. That's what makes law so complicated. If everyone told the truth, no problem, but people lie from time to time. Sometimes, for dumb reasons, having nothing to do with the crime. But nevertheless, by doing so they risk incriminating themselves or others."

"Well, that's good then in terms of the insurance company, right?"

Ashley sipped her tea. "I honestly have no idea how your insurance company will view it. If they're on the up and up, I would guess they'd view it like me and rule out suicide. But if they're the type of company who'll go to the mat rather than pay a penny for a claim, they'll probably try to twist the report to support their position."

"At least Adrian thinks homicide's a possibility too. I'm assuming he's waiting for the toxicological panel results before he rules anything out. If the toxicological results show my father had drugs or alcohol in his system, a case could be made that he fell and stumbled off the pier accidentally or he jumped off the pier intentionally and hit his head."

"Right. And if the autopsy results find he had nothing in his system, then the case for murder is stronger."

We both nodded, then sipped our tea in silence for a minute, lost in our thoughts as we mindlessly checked our phones. Paloma entered Mugs & Teacups a few minutes later. I almost didn't recognize her. Instead of the dramatic style she'd displayed at the firefighters fundraiser, flowing garments replete with layered shawls and scarves, she appeared wearing a more mundane outfit consisting of loose-fitting white slacks and a flowered tunic. The only remnants from the other night were her bangle bracelets, although she wore half the number she'd worn at the fundraiser.

I stood up and pulled a chair out for her. She smiled and told me she was going to place her order first.

Ashley's gaze tracked Paloma to the counter. "Oh, she's the palm reader, right? She read my palm the other night. Said she sees a lot of love in my future."

"Lucky you."

"I thought we were meeting with the other one, the fortune-teller."

"Yeah, that's Blanche, and she's a medium, but they're all fortune-tellers pretty much. I need to talk to her, too, but Paloma was the one I Googled first."

Paloma returned, setting down her teacup and saucer on the table. She smelled faintly of patchouli and cigarette smoke.

She held out her hand, first to me, then Ashley. "Hi, nice to meet you formally."

She had a deep voice and a theatrical manner that commanded attention. I wondered if she had been an actress at one time.

Ashley shook her hand. "Actually, you read my palm at the fundraiser the other night."

Paloma held on to Ashley's hand and flipped it over in a dramatic manner to study her palm. Ashley rolled her eyes at me.

After a moment, Paloma's eyes crinkled and her lips stretched into a wide smile. "Yes, I see it right here. There's a lot of love in your future. In fact, I see it happening very soon."

Ashley shot me a wide-eyed glance and I responded in kind.

Paloma settled into her chair and sampled her tea. "So, what can I do you for? You want dirt on Jo? Like what?"

"Yes, I'm trying to piece together my aunt Jo's life, specifically during the years between my memory of her as the nice lady who brought me ginormous lollipops to the fortune-teller who had the misfortune of being stabbed to death."

"Well, I'll try my best. I first met her at a halfway house when we both were bouncing back from some low periods in our lives. We kind of bonded over our struggle to stay on the straight and narrow."

"By halfway house, you mean a place where women with past substance-abuse issues can get back on their feet?"

"Yep. Some landed there as part of a plea bargain for illegal drug possession arrests or other victimless crimes instead of going to jail. Others were there after being in hard-core rehab, where they were monitored twenty-four seven. The halfway house was a transition period for them to learn how to be totally on their own again, without drugs or alcohol. I'd started drinking too much after I split from husband number two. Guess I felt sorry for myself for getting divorced a second time, and drinking made me forget about it. Then I crashed my car into a tree one night—hit it pretty hard, totaled it. I'm lucky I didn't kill myself or anybody else. You can always replace a car. I had a great judge who told me I'd come to a fork in the road and it was my choice whether I wanted to continue the way I'd been heading, which was down, or switch course and do something uplifting with my life."

"Good for you. How did Jo wind up there?"

Paloma fiddled with her bangles. "I knew her as Jo Benning back then. She didn't call herself Esmeralda until she started working with Blanche. We bonded almost immediately when we found out we'd both had two lousy marriages. Well, to be fair, I don't think she ever actually married number two. But both were deadbeats, by her telling. Good riddance to bad rubbish is what I told her."

"Did she ever mention having any children?"

"Blanche would know about that more because she had kids too. I never had any—no regrets, hard enough taking care of myself. If I recall correctly, I think she had one with each of her guys. What happened to them she never said and I didn't ask. Don't like to pry. Eyes front, mind my own business. Keep my head clear for my palm reading."

"So, you didn't know Sam Benning, the teenager that helped you with your booth moving and setup, was her son?"

"I do now. But no, I didn't. She told me she got him from a local high school. I never knew his last name. Only knew him as Sam. But I liked him. Good kid, if a little troubled."

"Troubled? Why do you say that?"

"His aura. He's a good person but vulnerable—that often attracts predators of all sorts. Not necessarily sexual predators. I got the vibe that people could use him for their own goals, that sort of thing. Like he was trapped."

"Really?"

She bobbed her head in agreement. "I read his palm once to confirm it. I told him to learn to stand up straighter to ward off others looking for weak people to suck into their own agenda."

"What did he say when you told him that."

"He went white as a sheet. So, I knew I'd touched a nerve."

"And when was this?"

"Just a few days before Jo got killed. I just feel awful because I told Jo about his reading. I felt her being in close proximity to this troubled boy might put her in danger."

"How did she react?"

"All she did was laugh. She told me to save it for my paying customers."

"So, you knew she was going to be murdered?"

"Jeez Louise, no. If I knew how to predict specifics like that, I'd be a very rich woman. No, I just pick up on people's auras and vibes, their light. Jo's aura had a dark shadow over it."

I shivered, making the teacup and saucer in my hand rattle. "Is there anything you can think of to shed light on her murder? Do you have any ideas of who might have killed her or why? Any enemies?"

"Jo was a person who had faced her demons and finally beat them. She was in a good place. No financial problems I knew of. She was happy being single and working and having friends. And now I see finding her son brought her joy. I'm happy about that. I can't think of anyone having a motive to kill her, to be perfectly frank."

"Well, thank you for your time."

"Oh, wait a minute. Jo was a big animal and nature lover. I guess you could call her an animal rights and environmental activist. Save the world, save wildlife. The fires we've been having upset her a lot. She was concerned for the wildlife and feared human lives might also be lost if the weather turned hot and windy. She often mentioned going to local protest meetings. She was anti-development too. Protesting when developers wanted to disrupt the bird sanctuary to build condos. Stuff like that."

I shook my head. "I had no idea she was into that."

I wondered what she'd think of our condo project for the Hotel Santa Sofia. Part of our site contained an old vacant strip mall, but the other part was undeveloped land. Most development disrupted some natural habitats. But I had peace of mind knowing I'd made the right decision making the community garden our design concept.

We'd all finished our tea.

Ashley checked her phone. "Gosh, where'd the time go? I have to meet someone in fifteen minutes. I better leave now."

I looked at my phone. Jake had texted me he was on his way to Lazarro's. "Me too. I have dinner plans."

Ashley cocked her head. "You do? Who with, Gym?"

"As a matter of fact, no. Someone new."

Paloma grasped my hands to say goodbye. Her smile melted into a frown.

I gasped. "What is it?"

Her eyelids fluttered shut for a few moments. When she opened her eyes, her gaze was steady and somber. "Be careful, princess. Your mission is beset with landmines. Beware of false friends and you will succeed at finding the truth."

Ashley and I bustled out of Mugs & Teacups side by side. As soon as we were out of Paloma's earshot, Ashley spoke. "What the heck was that all about? Sounded like dialog out of a *Star Wars* movie."

Cold overtook me and I started to shiver. "I don't know. It felt like she was inducting me into a Marvel superhero team. 'Mission' and 'false friends'? What's that about?"

"Well, she knows you're interested in finding Jo's killer. She just wants you to be prudent and careful, like we all do."

"Maybe."

"Are you going to tell me who you're having dinner with, or do you want me to guess?"

"Guess."

"Well, unless you're leading a secret life, the only cute guy you've seemed interested in is Jake."

"I'm not really interested in him like that." I frowned as I considered my own behavior—going out with another man when Milo's body hadn't even been found.

Ashley read my expression well. "Nothing wrong with going out to dinner. It will be good for you to relax and have a little fun."

"I just feel guilty, because of Milo. Plus, I hardly know this guy."

"I thought you had lunch together. And you Googled him."

"Yeah. He was fine for lunch. And I only Googled enough to ascertain that he was who he claimed to be, a PI. But I didn't do my level-two extensive Google search, like for arrest records."

"I'm sure he's fine. He wouldn't have a PI license if he had any arrests."

CHAPTER 21

Details of my parting conversation with Ashley reverberated in my head as I drove to Lazarro's. How had I given her the impression I was interested in Jake? Was it that obvious? How could I go on a date when my husband was still missing? Milo had been gone barely a month. Granted, he was presumed dead, but hello, grief period? And how could I possibly be interested in anyone romantically for whom I hadn't conducted a thorough Google screening? I was slipping. I felt at once like a heartless shrew and a sloppy researcher. My emotional distress had taken a toll.

Yes, Jake was good-looking and he had the best blue eyes I'd ever seen, but I was a hot mess, grief and guilt mixed with anxiety, cloaked in suspicion. Ever since Adrian had mentioned the word *homicide* in relation to my father's death, my churning stomach and knotted neck and shoulder muscles told me fear had started to tighten its grip on me. Who could I trust? How did I know Jake was who he said he was? What if he was a killer? Had he been following me? He had a white car, and I'd noticed a white car had been following me since my father's death. Why was he always showing up everywhere I went? Was he stalking me? Was I his next victim? Why on earth had I accepted a dinner invitation from a possible murderer at a secluded restaurant? Was I out of my friggin' mind? He'd even called it a date. Was he referring to a romantic date or a date with danger? I really didn't want to go. Maybe I should have texted him and canceled.

I drove with my head in the clouds, vacillating between continuing on to Lazarro's and turning around and going home to Iris. I missed Iris. All I wanted to do was hold my warm little fluff ball in my arms.

Before I knew it, I was pulling up to the valet parking at Lazarro's. The next moment, Jake pulled up behind me. There was no turning back now.

I bolted out of my car like a skittish deer and flinched when someone behind me touched my elbow.

"Excuse me, miss. Could you leave the fob please?"

"Wha-at? Oh, the key, the fob, of course. So sorry."

I spent the next two minutes wresting the fob from my key ring. I glanced up and the eyes of two valets, Jake, and another customer still in their car were all on me, patiently waiting as I fumbled to pry apart the key ring. Every time I managed to pry it apart it snapped back before I could slide the fob around and off. My thumbnail pulled apart a little more from my nail bed with each attempt, a special form of torture, but finally I managed to keep it open long enough to slide it off.

Jake strolled over to me with a smile on his face. "Success."

Heat flushed my face. "It just now dawned on me that I should have dismantled the plastic fob from the metal part and given it to the valet, leaving the metal part on the key ring. I don't know what I was thinking." *I know very well what I was thinking. I might have arranged a date with death.*

"Shall we?" He started up the steps to the entrance of the restaurant.

Lazarro's was a little bungalow that had been transformed into a renowned farm-to-table restaurant, noted for its owner chef who had the ability to turn organic produce and sustainably selected fish and fowl into delectable works of art. It had ivy and twinkle lights and the ocean could be heard in the background.

"Any more nasty notes on your windshield lately?"

"No, thank goodness. But there was a note my neighbor left on her door that looked similar to that note. Adrian and I want to ask her about it. The note on her door wasn't menacing, though. It just said she was called away due to a family emergency. It's somewhat disturbing to think that my sweet neighbor, who's demonstrated such kind behavior to me and to my dog, might have left me a menacing note. She's also the one who contradicted Milo's last text to me about my dog. It's like she has a split personality. She finally responded to a text I sent her and said she'll get back in town tomorrow. I plan on confronting her when she returns."

"Confront is a strong word. You're not one to beat around the bush, I see."

"Well, you know, ask her to explain why the two notes look alike."

"Or perhaps were made to appear that way. I'd reserve judgment about your neighbor until she has the chance to explain everything. What my job has taught me more than anything else is that things aren't always as they appear. In my line of work, I've found if things don't add up, there's usually an error somewhere, either in the evidence observed or what goes unobserved. It boils down to basic logic."

"You sound just like a PI I know." I was glad to see he talked the talk.

"Oh? Who? Maybe I know them."

Well, this was embarrassing. The PI I was referring to, and the only PI I knew "personally," was Kinsey Milhone, a fictional PI created by my favorite author, Sue Grafton, in her alphabet murder mystery series set in a Santa Barbara look-alike town called Santa Teresa.

"You probably wouldn't know her."

"A woman? Then you're probably right." He blushed and chuckled. "The only female PI I know from around these parts is a fictional character in one of my favorite mystery series. Have you read any of Sue Grafton's books?"

Best blue eyes and loves Sue Grafton? What's not to like?

After bonding over books, our conversation turned to favorite movies and TV shows. We were a lot alike, both being fans of the same independent films (*Sideways* and *Little Miss Sunshine*), TV dramas (*Scandal* and *How to Get Away With Murder*), crime procedurals (*Major Crimes* and *Law and Order: SVU*), and sitcoms (*Mom* and *Modern Family*). Plus, we both loved

Larry David. We also both shared a passion for fitness.

We dined on delicious ribbons of handmade handkerchief pasta with pesto, fillet of sole with shelled English peas and baby artichokes, and organic field greens and goat cheese salad. All was paired with an excellent Jorian Hill Syrah, from a local boutique winery in Santa Ynez.

When the server asked if we were interested in dessert, we simultaneously asked each other, "Do you want to split something?"

My giggling response was interrupted by the buzz of a text from Adrian. "Autopsy results are in—no drugs or alcohol in system, fatal blow likely from an instrument, not a fall. Homicide confirmed. Keep it to yourself while we investigate. We don't want details made public."

Everything ground to a halt. I had to muster all my will to text back my thanks and read Adrian's response that he'd call me in the morning.

Jake's smile had turned to a look of concern. "Everything okay?"

"Huh? Yeah. That was Adrian. They just completed the autopsy report on my father."

Jake turned to the server. "Can you give us a few more minutes? Thanks."

Jake's phone buzzed. He glanced at the screen. "Hey, I need to take this. It's a work call. I'll be right back."

I tried to focus on the dessert menu, forcing myself to hang on and not let the confirmation of my father's murder spin my emotions out of control.

Jake returned and reached over and took my hand. "I'm sorry. Are you sure you're okay? Finding out your father's death was a homicide must be devastating."

I nodded. I appreciated Jake's sensitivity and caring. Jake definitely was the whole package.

"Do you think your father's murder was related to your husband's and your aunt's? Do you have any idea what the link might be?"

"Unfortunately, no. Other than they were all related to me." My face must have portrayed abject glumness, my chin quivered, and my eyes welled with tears. "Everyone I love gets murdered."

Jake scooted his chair around to be closer to me. He put his arm around me. "Look, Tory, there's something I've wanted to tell you."

Really? Jake was perfect in every way, except timing. This was not when I wanted to hear the "I'd like to get to know you better" spiel. I tried to subtly wiggle out from under his arm, but it was firmly planted there.

His eyelids fluttered quickly over his baby blues. "Over the last couple of weeks, I have to admit, I've been obsessed. That's the type of person I am. I can't be distracted once I'm after something."

Whoa! Where is this coming from?

"Sorry, Jake. I need to use the restroom. Be right back."

I hightailed it to the restroom to think. What on earth had triggered Jake's sudden stalker-like behavior? Did my own neediness upon hearing the autopsy news somehow convey too much vulnerability? Did that elicit obsessive possessiveness on his part? We'd been fine up until Adrian's phone call. As I replayed our last few minutes of conversation after the call in my head I suddenly realized something was off. Wait. One. Minute. All I'd told him was that my father's autopsy results were in. I'd said nothing about cause of death being homicide. I was positive, because Adrian had told me not to reveal the results to anyone. Jake was the one who brought up the word *homicide,* not me. How would he know it was murder unless he was somehow involved? And then he proceeded to declare his obsession with me. Uh-oh. I needed to get out of here—and fast.

The problem was, I couldn't slip out of the restroom without Jake seeing me. I needed to lure him away from our table so I could escape by the front door. I dug around in my handbag for my phone. My quivering hands made it difficult to type, so I kept it brief and to the point. Let's see, what would make him leave the table?

I texted the first thing that popped into my head. "Hi, I'm sick and in the alley behind the restaurant."

I peeked out the door as he read the text. He jumped up and headed toward the rear door.

As soon as he was gone I dashed toward the front door and gave my ticket to the valet. Of course, this was the weak link. It took forever. Jake appeared at the front door and spotted me.

His face reflected utter confusion—big eyes roaming around for answers and mouth open in stunned surprise. "Hey, what's wrong? I thought you were in the alley."

I cleared my throat and crossed my arms defensively. "Um, I was. But I felt better and decided it's best I go home and rest up." *So feeble.*

"Uh-huh. And you were going to convey that to me when?"

I couldn't look him in the eye. "After I got home and I could report I was safe and sound."

"I thought we were having a great time getting to know each other better. I was, at least." His drooped eyelids matched his downturned mouth.

But I wasn't falling for it. I couldn't believe that now he was trying to guilt me into feeling bad to make me look like the bad guy.

"Yeah, it was fun but—"

He rushed over to me and steered me back toward the restaurant. "Look, Tory, I really need to talk to you. I've been trying to tell you something all night. Every time I try we keep getting interrupted. I just want you to understand where I'm coming from."

Oy. I was so not into his intensity. "Look, Jake, you seem like a good person, but we hardly know each other."

That confused look appeared on his face again. Did he really think the wounded puppy dog expression was going to fly?

The valet yelled. A second valet drove up in my car. I pressed a twenty into the first valet's hand, hoping the extra tip would enlist his help in my getaway. I trotted to my car, where the second valet held open the door. I grabbed another bill from my wallet, hoping to come up with a five. In my frenzy to leave ASAP I plucked another twenty instead, but it was no time to split hairs at this point, I needed a team to back me up—that my team was comprised of two valets was irrelevant. Good enough, a backup team was a backup team. I jumped in my car and the second valet accommodated by shutting the door promptly while the first valet waved me on, blocking any interference by Jake. At this point, our server emerged from the restaurant, anxiously attempting to settle our dinner tab with a very agitated Jake. The last I saw of Jake as I peeled off was our server taking his credit card from him. Timing was everything. I didn't feel one bit guilty over someone who was trying to suck me into who-knows-what type of sleazy song and dance about wanting to talk. Everyone who knows anything about criminals knows that was code for "hold still while I kill you."

I flew along the highway, at once exhilarated and terrified. I called Ashley and brought her up to speed in a voice-mail message. Jake called and left me a voice mail urging me to call him immediately because he really needed to tell me something. He even had the gall to suggest meeting for a nightcap.

Yeah, right. Like that's gonna happen, buddy. I blocked his number.

Once I pulled into my driveway, I took a long, careful look around to make sure no one was waiting to ambush me. Confirming that the coast was clear, I quickly exited my car. I looked over at Katie's house and her bedroom light was on. She was back. I'd deal with her in the morning.

Iris was delighted to see me, evidenced by her minutes-long prancing routine around my ankles. Ashley called me back and invited herself over to spend the night. A true friend, she'd read my mind.

I was so relieved when I heard the doorbell. I ran to the door, and even though I knew it was Ashley, I still checked. When I looked through the peephole, it was Jake. I froze for a good thirty seconds, trying to figure out what to do.

He knocked on the door. "Tory, I know you're in there. Please let me explain."

Ashley's voice rang out. "If you don't leave this private property right this minute, I'm calling nine-one-one."

"But . . ."

"Now or I'm hitting the call button."

Jake walked away reluctantly, calling over his shoulder, "You've got it all wrong."

Ashley held up her phone. "That's it. I'm calling the cops right now."

The sound of a car starting up broke through the silence of the night.

Ashley yelled through the door. "Tory, let me in. He's gone."

Through the front window I spied the lights of a car driving away, confirming her statement, and I opened the door.

We hugged quickly, once she was inside and the door was locked and security system turned on.

"That was a brazen move, coming over here when he knows you don't want to talk to him. Why didn't he just call or text like a normal person?"

"Um, maybe because I blocked his number."

"That would do it."

"I liked Jake up until you told me on your message that you were about to share dessert. Reminds me of my narcissistic ex. Always wanting to share dessert. You know what I finally figured out? He wasn't being romantic. He knew I was counting calories and would only eat a bite or two. More for him. Selfish dudes do that, all I'm saying."

"OMG, Ashley, I think Jake's a murderer, and that was your big takeaway after all this? Be careful of guys who want to share desserts?"

"No, there's more. Then they want to split the bill. Don't let them get away with any of that crap. He eats twice as much as me and then we split the bill? I don't think so. How is that fair? If he really wanted to be fair, he'd pay for what he ate, not pretend to be a feminist when really you're paying for more than your fair share. I'm on to that one. You're lucky to have gotten off of that train before it left the station."

Her rant had left my jaw hanging in disbelief. "What about him knowing my father was murdered before it was made public? And his persistent 'we need to talk' behavior to get me alone on our friggin' first date? That didn't raise any red flags for you?"

Ashley's eyes glinted with amusement. "Oh, and that too."

We both doubled up with laughter and hugged each other, with Iris barking and dancing wildly in excitement. Ashley called Adrian and left him a voice mail to fill him in.

After she hung up, I went to sit at my kitchen counter and patted the stool next to me for Ashley to join me. "So, how was your date? Better than mine, I hope."

"It wasn't a date, just drinks. It was fun."

At that moment, her phone buzzed with a text. Ashley smiled and turned to me. "Speak of the devil."

After a couple of minutes of texting, she looked up. "He wanted to make sure we were both okay and locked in for the night. He's having a car patrol every hour tonight to make sure Jake doesn't bother us anymore."

"That's so nice of him. Please thank him for me."

Her fingers typed out a quick reply. "Done. I told him thanks and we're snug as bugs in a rug."

I bobbed my head in agreement and displayed a wide smile, hoping to convey a confident outlook, knowing cops would patrol every hour. Behind my carefree mask, however, was hidden a whole heap of worry about everything, but mainly about the other fifty-nine minutes between each patrol.

CHAPTER 22

Iris woke me up by climbing all over my body. When I pretended to still be asleep, she upped her game by sneezing near my head, quickly followed by impatient jumps from side to side, each ending with a playful butt-in-the-air stance and a short, soft bark. I lifted my head to spot Otis sitting sphinxlike in the doorway, patiently waiting for his minion Iris to rouse me.

Ashley, the early bird, was, once again, clanking around in my kitchen. The aroma of eggs and bacon wafted into my room, with an overlay scent of fresh coffee. I swung my legs off the bed and stuck on a pair of flip-flops. I grabbed a comfy knee-length gray hoodie as I passed by my dresser and quickly threw it over my long-sleeved top and jogger-style PJ bottoms as I followed Iris's lead down the hallway in quest of breakfast, with Otis trailing behind the mini-procession.

Ashley was already dressed for work, in trim charcoal gray pants and a speckled light gray Everlane cashmere pullover, a brand she'd introduced me to after liking it on a certain American princess we both obsessed over.

She swung the carafe off the coffee maker and topped off her mug. "Scrambled eggs and turkey bacon are ready. Do you want any toast?"

I grabbed a mug and poured myself half a cup of coffee and filled the rest with nonfat milk. "I think eggs and bacon will be enough. Thanks, Ash. You're the best."

"My pleasure." She slid the eggs on a plate and added three slices of bacon before setting it down on the counter with a smile.

I zapped my coffee in the microwave and then joined her at

the counter to dig in.

After we finished our meal and Iris and Otis were fed and watered, Ashley and I shared our last cups of coffee together before we went off to work.

"Is it too early to pay Katie a visit and ask her about the notes?"

Ashley gulped the last of her coffee. "Go for it. I'll join you if you like."

"Thanks. Let's bring Iris along too."

The three of us strode across my front lawn and driveway to Katie's house next door. I rang her doorbell.

Katie peeked through a window and quickly came to the door. "Hi, Iris!"

I scooped up Iris, who had been jumping and licking Katie's hands in greeting. "Hi. I just wanted to check on you. Your note had me a little concerned, so I wanted to make sure you were all right."

Katie's smile dissolved into an expression of bewilderment. "I'm sorry, Tory. What note?"

Ashley and I exchanged a meaningful eye roll.

"The one you left on your door about going away for a family emergency."

She frowned and cocked her head to the side. "Sorry. I have no idea what you're talking about. I didn't leave a note on my door. And thankfully, there's no family emergency I know of, but now you have me worried there might be."

"Where were you then?" Ashley asked.

"Oh, I took a little drive down to LA to visit a friend for a few days."

I pulled up a photo of the note on my phone to show her.

Her eyes flickered and she spoke quickly. "No. I didn't write that."

"Huh. Well, I'm glad you and your family are well. Seems like this might just be a childish prank. Have a good day."

"Bye, Iris. See you later." Katie watched us cross the driveway and lawn then waved and went inside.

Ashley wrapped her arm around mine. "Whoa. That was weird. She might not have written that note, but I bet she knows who did. Did you see her blush when she saw the note?"

"Yeah. I know. Something is off with her today. She seemed surprised but also like she knew something. She couldn't look me in the eye. And she only had direct eye contact with Iris."

• • •

An hour later I was at my desk at Benning Brothers, checking my schedule for the day.

Uncle Bob strolled in holding a mug. "I wanted to tell you about my meeting with Matt Ortega."

"Oh, yeah. I've been wondering how that went."

"I'll cut to the chase. Matt claims he never complained about you hiring Sam. In fact, he was touched that you hired Sam—thought it was 'very kind of you,' to quote his exact words."

I swiveled in my seat to face him. "You're kidding. What about the other nursery employees?"

"He said he hasn't heard anyone even mention Sam or you."

"Wow. I wonder why Jed told me they were complaining. Obviously, one of them is lying. I wonder if it's Jed or Matt?"

"I'd put my money on Jed, mainly because of his drinking issues. I honestly think his brain is a little pickled and he gets some perverse satisfaction out of stirring stuff up."

"Yep. I've noticed that. Tends to have a dramatic streak, definitely. But why start something with me? And why target poor Sam?"

"Jealousy? That's the only thing I can think of."

"You'd totally vouch for Matt?"

"Yes, I can, both before and after a couple of beers, but Jed, not so much. I've had to pull him aside now and again at social functions and tell him he's reached his limit."

"He seemed fine at the firefighters fundraiser. He drove Aunt Veronica home."

"That was unusual. He seemed fine then. Otherwise I

wouldn't have let him drive her home. Probably on good behavior because I really laid into him at your wedding."

"You did? Why didn't you tell me?"

"It was your big day. I didn't want to ruin it by running to you with details of a drunken brawl during the cocktail reception."

"Thank you for that. That prize went to Milo's disappearance." I wistfully remembered our perfect wedding ceremony. My stomach churned thinking about the horrible aftermath. "Do you know who he fought with?"

"He didn't say, but he was a little bruised up."

I shook my head in disgust. "Hopefully he's on the wagon now. Do you think that's why he's starting trouble? Maybe he's irritable from alcohol withdrawal."

Uncle Bob's face lit up. "You might be right. Now that you mention it, I haven't seen him drink since your wedding. I can relate. I get grumpy every time your aunt puts me on a diet."

We both laughed.

"What time is your insurance person coming?"

"Let me double check. I think it's eleven. I have a couple of hours before that to get organized and figure out how best to explain the embezzling. I know you don't want it to go public, but I really think we should tell the police too. This is what they do. They might figure out who did it right off the bat. As long as we know it wasn't my dad or any of us, I don't think being victims of embezzlement will hurt our business. I mean, we're victims. It's not like we cheated our clients."

"I'll think about it. How about that? That's the best I can say right now."

I was about to twist his arm a little bit more when there was a tap at my door. Standing in the doorway was Jake. I gasped in utter shock, while reaching for my phone.

My voice quivered. "What are you doing here? How did you get in?"

Jake took a step inside my office. "I'm sorry—"

"Stop right there or I'm calling the cops. Leave, now."

"I need to talk to you. I feel so badly about last night. I tried to call or text to explain . . . but it appears you've blocked me."

Uncle Bob strode in front of me and turned his head from me to Jake. "What's going on here? Who are you?"

I unlocked my phone. "He's supposedly a PI."

Jake reached into his pocket and Uncle Bob and I both flinched.

Uncle Bob shielded me. "Whoa!"

Jake had dug a business card from his pocket. "I can assure you, I am a PI. I work for Sloan Mutual. Actually, we met the night of your sister Jo's murder."

Uncle Bob relaxed his guard dog stance.

I swiped the card from Jake's fingers, glanced at it, and waved it in the air. "Humph. A likely story. Anyone can print up phony business cards."

"It's real. I'm the PI your father's life insurance company hired to investigate his death. We have an appointment today at eleven."

I froze in place as I absorbed his words and reread his card.

"I know it's a lot to take in. That's why I tried to tell you last night over dinner. I thought it might be easier in a more relaxed atmosphere."

My face was on fire, and my heart's pounding reverberated in my ears. "Get out. How could you trick me into thinking you were somebody else? Your other business card didn't have Sloan Mutual on it. It just said Private Investigator."

"I didn't trick you. I only use the Sloan Mutual card when I'm on official Sloan Mutual business. I have another one for Beachwood Mutual, too, when I represent them. I mentioned my biggest clients were insurance companies."

I thought back. He was right, he had. "But all the other opportunities you had."

"I was working the case. We thought your father's death was suspicious from the get-go. I wanted to see if my instincts were correct."

"Your instincts about what?"

"That you weren't involved. That's why I followed your

activities. I guess I better brush up on being unobtrusive."

"*You* were the white car following me."

Uncle Bob piped up. "You've been following my niece?"

Jake nodded. "Because I wanted to observe your spending habits, see who you met with, what you did with your time. To make sure you weren't buying Ferraris and paying off hit men."

My brain felt scrambled from trying to process the information overload. "Get out. How could you betray my trust? I thought you were trying to kill me. How did you know that my father's autopsy results confirmed his murder?"

"What? That call I got at dinner, that was my contact at the county coroner's office giving me a heads-up your father's death was declared a homicide." Jake's clouded face revealed his pain. "The last thing I wanted to do is cause you more distress after all you've been through. I'm on your side."

"Are you?" My default lately had been to fear the worst, but I had to admit he had a good answer.

He held up two fingers. "Scout's honor. Team Tory."

I smiled weakly.

"Technically, I never lied to you. I was just waiting for the right time to tell you I was working for Sloan Mutual. I always intended to tell you eventually."

"How about when we first met? That might've been a good idea."

"But I was on the job, and then your aunt got murdered, so it was hardly a good time to worry you about insurance investigations."

"Well, then, after that, and every other time we met 'accidentally.'"

"Again, all those times I either had a subject under surveillance or . . ."

"Or what?"

"Or we were having a good time and I didn't want to spoil it."

My face got even hotter, but this time not from anger. "Oh."

Uncle Bob cleared his throat and stuck out his hand to Jake. "Bob Benning. Nice to formally meet you, Jake."

Jake shook his hand warmly.

Uncle Bob smiled at Jake and threw a concerned look my way. "How about we all take a moment to regroup and rendezvous back here at eleven as originally scheduled. That way Tory and I can make sure we're all organized and ready to answer your questions without wasting any more of your time."

"Oh, don't worry. You're not wasting my time." Jake gave me a meaningful gaze.

Uncle Bob looked at Jake and then me and suppressed a smile. "You're welcome to hang out in our reception area, or there are a couple of places to get coffee down the street."

I shuffled back to my desk with my head down. "Um, okay. That sounds like a good plan."

Jake left. Uncle Bob, probably realizing I was on the verge of tears, acted as if nothing unusual had just happened. He said he was going to print out something for the meeting.

I texted Ashley, although it took me forever to type two sentences since the screen looked blurry through my tears. *OMG, Never guess what happened. Jake is PI assigned by ins. co. to investigate my father's death.*

My phone rang a few seconds later.

Ashley was energized. "Now it all makes sense. That's why he was following you. Probably following a lot of peeps for his investigation."

I burst out in sobs.

"Take a few deep breaths, hun. Why are you upset?"

I cried and my voice warbled. "I don't know. I thought we were becoming friends, then I thought he was a stalker, now it turns out he's my next appointment. I feel like I'm on a roller coaster and Jake is at the controls."

"Try to calm down. Breathe. I'd love to sit in on your meeting, but I have a court appearance I have to go to. Hang in there and I'll call you when I get out."

I sniffled. "Thanks, Ashley. Sorry for the meltdown. I'm taking Sam to see our Hotel Santa Sofia condo site this afternoon. So, if you don't hear from me, I'll catch up with you later."

I got a cup of coffee from our office kitchen and pulled myself together. I organized and reviewed my father's files and rehearsed my spiel to Jake to convince him my father's death wasn't a suicide. Wait a minute. Jake said he wanted to make sure I wasn't involved in my father's death, which meant he didn't think it was suicide.

Eleven rolled around and Jake tapped on my door. "Hi."

"Hi. I was just reflecting on what you said earlier. Sorry if I overreacted, but if you were ruling out my involvement, that assumes you don't think it was accidental or a suicide, right?"

"Correct. I never thought your father committed suicide. I suspected he was murdered. That's why I've been conducting an undercover investigation. Initially, my investigation centered on the supposed accident because of the unlikely scenario of tripping and falling into the ocean from the pier, especially given your father's fitness level indicated by the results of his last physical submitted to Sloan Mutual. In cases like this, we always look at the possibility of suicide. After speaking to people who knew him and digging around, there was nothing that suggested a suicidal profile. Then, when your aunt's murder followed on the heels of your husband's disappearance, both confirmed my suspicions that something nefarious occurred with your father too and fell in with the theory I was developing."

"Theory? You have a theory about his death?"

"I do."

Uncle Bob sauntered in. "What'd I miss?"

"I was about to tell Tory my theory of the case."

"Go on."

"Well, first of all, I think they're all related."

"All?" said Uncle Bob.

"John Benning's death, Milo Spinelli's disappearance and probable death, and Jo Benning's murder."

"That's what I've been thinking all along. I made a spreadsheet to list the possible suspects and clues."

"You did? Great."

I pulled up my grid and made some tweaks. "I'll delete you as a suspect now, given you're officially working with the insurance company."

Jake raised an eyebrow. "Thank you."

"And I'll delete you, Uncle Bob, since now I know why you weren't being totally straight with the cops." As soon as the words escaped my lips, I heard my mistake.

Uncle Bob winced and looked at me with dismay.

Jake perked up and addressed Uncle Bob. "What haven't you told the police?"

Uncle Bob hesitated for a moment and sighed heavily. "Someone's been embezzling from Benning Brothers. I discovered it a couple of weeks ago."

"Do you know who?"

"No, but I have my suspicions."

I snapped my head. "You do? Who?"

Uncle Bob clicked his teeth. "There are only so many people who have access to our computers."

I bobbed my head. "True, but nowadays computers can be hacked remotely."

Jake nodded. "She's right. But in the event we're not dealing with a computer whiz, who has access to your business bank accounts?"

Uncle Bob cleared his throat. "Well, if you mean access to our computers, there are several people. My wife, my son, my late brother, John, Tory, Milo, and me, of course. We all have access to our office computers. Also, our secretary, Raquel, and the receptionist, Claudette, have access. The two nursery managers, Jed Barnes and Matt Ortega, also have access to the office computers."

Jake, who'd been listening intently, raised his head. "Okay, that's access to your computers. What about actual access to your firm's bank accounts, either online or otherwise?"

"Only me, my wife, and John were authorized on our firm's bank accounts. Since John's passing, it's still my wife and I, and now Tory is authorized too. Our nursery managers, Jed and Matt, are authorized on the nursery business bank accounts, but not on the general Benning Brothers' accounts that include monies from both the nursery and landscape architecture divisions."

Jake gave a thumbs-up. "Got it. Thanks."

I grabbed the files off my desk. "Here are my father's financial files, including all his bank account information. I went over all of them. Nothing seems out of the ordinary to me, meaning no large, unexplained deposits or withdrawals."

"Good. I'll need to review these for my report to Sloan Mutual. Also, Bob, I urge you to report the embezzlement to the authorities pronto. Maybe your SSPD friend, Adrian, could make sure it's not made public. The police can get warrants to look at phone records, credit card info, bank accounts, all the stuff we as private citizens can't get readily. They'll look for recent big expenditures, stuff like that."

Uncle Bob turned to me. "Do you think Adrian can be discreet?"

"Definitely. He's great. They probably don't want to publicize it anyway. Why give the person who stole the money a heads-up?"

"I never thought of that. Okay. I'll give him a call right now." Uncle Bob left to make the call.

"Okay. Let me update my suspects and clues spreadsheet." I rounded my desk, plunked down in my chair, and typed "bank accounts access" and "company computers access" as headings for two new clue columns. "Should I delete Uncle Bob?"

"Leave him on for now, for the sake of argument." Jake leaned over me slightly to view the screen. "Hmm. Now, with the bank account and computer access stuff added, the suspects with the most checks next to their names are Bob, Jed, and Matt, followed closely by Sam and your aunt Veronica."

"Great. So that means the murderer is probably someone in my family or an employee."

Jake straightened up. "In most cases, family members are always the first suspects. All three victims are related by blood or marriage to you, your uncle Bob, your aunt Veronica, and your cousin Sam. Since I've ruled you out, we have to look at your other family members—your uncle, your aunt, and your cousin. Before you interrupt me, let me put it another way. By scrutinizing their behaviors, bank accounts, and credit card purchases, we'll be able to eliminate them as suspects as well. Hopefully."

I rubbed the back of my neck. "Hopefully? What does that mean? You think one of them is the killer?"

He leaned one arm on my desk. "Nothing surprises me anymore. But let's go with innocent until proven guilty for now. And the same goes for your employees, the two nursery managers, the secretary, and the receptionist."

When I turned to look at him, I felt a pulse of electricity emanating from his eyes.

I turned back to staring at my computer screen, conscious of his breath close to me. "Something's missing, but I don't know what."

Jake leaned in closer. "What's missing is a motive that unifies all the murders."

We turned and looked at each other as if the same lightbulb had gone off in our brains.

I sucked in air in excitement. "Are you thinking what I'm thinking?"

Jake nodded. "The embezzlement is behind the murders."

"Maybe my father confronted the embezzler and maybe Milo and Jo found out too."

"And then the embezzler killed your father and anyone else who knew about it."

"Okay. Well, I have a date to visit a project site right now with my cousin Sam. I'll see if I can find out whether he knows anything about the embezzlement. I get the impression he's hiding something, and Paloma thought he was troubled. So, I'll let you know what I find out."

"Sounds good. Meanwhile, I'll see if any of my contacts can help me with phone logs."

My phone buzzed. It was Adrian. "Hi, Tory. Just got off the phone with Bob. Thanks for encouraging him to talk to me. Helpful information. I think he felt better getting everything off his chest too. Don't worry. We'll get whoever's responsible. We'll try to keep our investigation on the down low as much as possible."

"Thanks, Adrian. I can't take full credit for convincing my uncle to come clean. Jake Logan, the PI, helped persuade him."

Jake's gaze pulsed through mine again as I turned to him and smiled when I mentioned his name.

"Yeah. He's a good guy. I took the liberty to run a thorough background check on him at the urging of Ashley. He's legit."

"Um, thanks?" My face heated up with embarrassment. Why the heck did Ashley ask Adrian to do that? Did she think I was an idiot who couldn't think for myself?

"Before you go off on Ashley, she did it from a good place, Tor. We all care about you. You've been through so much and have so much on your plate. Ash just wanted to make sure he was on the up and up."

"You read my mind." I laughed, and as I did, feelings of love and gratitude for my dear friends overwhelmed me and swept away all the negativity I'd felt seconds earlier.

"Also, Ashley told me your neighbor Katie claims she didn't leave the note on her door. We got surveillance tapes from around your neighborhood for the dates when both notes were found. We're in the process of going through them, and I'll let you know if we find anything."

"Yes. Please keep me in the loop."

"Last thing. FYI, Ernie is still hot to trot on nabbing a suspect ASAP. He's going for the usual suspects—in other words, the victims' family members, particularly you, now that your father's death has been officially declared a homicide, too, and it looks like Milo and Jo's murders might be related. Bob tells me you're the beneficiary of your dad's insurance policy too. Once Ernie gets wind of that, it will be hard to distract him from making an immediate arrest."

"So pretty much BOLO for Ernie."

Adrian guffawed. "Exactly. Look at you, a cop in the making."

A heady feeling of satisfaction overcame me despite just being warned I had a target on my back, making me smile as we said goodbye. I promised to keep in touch.

I relayed Adrian's update to Jake.

"Great. Let me know how your road trip goes."

I turned to walk Jake out of my office. Sam was at my doorway. How long he'd been there, I didn't know.

CHAPTER 23

The steel blue ocean sparkled in the noon sun as if diamonds had been scattered on its surface. Brilliant white cumulus clouds floated in an equally bright blue sky as we drove up the Pacific Coast Highway (PCH) to the condo site. I'd decided to take the scenic route, even though it added another ten minutes to our drive, since it was such a beautiful day. Sam turned toward me. I followed his gaze through the open window to the whitecaps dancing on the incoming tide. The therapeutic effects of viewing the ocean, hearing the waves, and breathing in the salty air never lost its magic.

I rolled up the window. "How's school going?"

"Okay."

"What's your favorite subject?"

"Math."

"Least favorite?"

"Psychology."

"Really? Why? I used to love my high school psych class. I loved reading social psychological studies about relationships. It was fun trying to apply the findings to myself and figure out why guys I liked didn't like me." I laughed and got a reluctant chortle out of Sam.

"I like learning about experimental design and methodology. It's all the touchy-feely stuff I don't like."

"Like what?"

"Like my psych teacher asking me if I want to share my feelings with her."

"In front of your class?"

"No, after class. With her or with one of the counselors."

"And that's a bad idea, why?"

"I don't know."

All righty then. New topic. "Are you still working part-time for Paloma and Blanche? I had tea with Paloma the other day. She seems nice."

Silence from Sam.

I decided to go for it, at the risk of having him totally clam up on me. That wouldn't be much worse than his taciturn manner thus far. "Paloma mentioned to me that she'd read your palm."

He snapped his head in my direction. "What else did she say?"

I paused, deciding between door number one, total honesty, and door number two, white lie. I decided to go with two. "Nothing much."

I cringed when I heard my own high-pitched, singsong response. I was sure he'd detect my attempt to feign ignorance and wouldn't speak to me for the rest of the trip. I resigned myself to silence, kicking myself for not choosing door number one. Some detective.

A few minutes passed and out of the corner of my eye I caught Sam's chest heave as he sighed.

Sam's voice quavered. "I think Esmeralda was murdered because of something I told her."

"What!" My heart skipped a beat and I hit the brakes abruptly out of shock, inflicting a mild whiplash on both of us. "Sorry 'bout that. That's quite a revelation. Why would you think that?"

"Because I think someone found out she knew. I should never have told her. She'd probably still be alive."

Stunned, I took a deep breath to maintain my composure. I resumed my normal speed while shooting him astonished glances. "What was it that you told her? Did it have anything to do with someone stealing money from Benning Brothers?"

"I can't tell you."

"Why can't you tell me?"

He suppressed a sob. "Because I don't want the same thing to happen to you."

I inhaled and exhaled audibly. "Well, we're in agreement on that point, for sure."

For better or worse, we'd arrived at our destination. I figured getting out of the car, breathing in some fresh air, and stretching our legs would alleviate the tension. The site was comprised of one-third old abandoned strip mall and two-thirds empty lot dotted with dry brush and tumbleweeds. The mall contained stores that marked it from a different era. A video store, a vacuum repair shop, and a diner called, fittingly, the Greasy Spoon. I pulled up in front of the deserted storefronts and parked.

I wracked my brain, trying to think of an angle to get Sam to confide in me. Milo and Sam had had a good relationship. They both could talk sports forever, particularly basketball. Like me, they both adored the Los Angeles Lakers.

"What do you think about the Lakers this season? Milo would have already planned out his life around their schedule."

His head was hung low and I barely heard his response of "Okay."

"Did you happen to tell anyone else what you told Esmeralda?"

When he raised his head, tears were welling up in Sam's eyes. He nodded his head and fought them back.

"Was it Milo?"

He nodded vigorously and finally let out a sob.

I sucked in a breath and felt lightheaded and clammy. I took a deep breath and then another. "Do you know who murdered your mother?"

Sam jumped out of the car and ran into the empty lot. I flung open my door and trotted behind him. He was half my age, in good shape, and faster than me. As I ran, an onslaught of emotions filled my head. This kid definitely knew something about Jo's murder, and probably Milo's too.

Huffing and puffing, I finally caught up to him, only because he'd slowed his pace, which was a good thing since I was ready to collapse. I jogged up behind him and grabbed onto his arm for balance. "I thought I was in good shape. No wonder you're so good at sports."

He spun around and violently shook off my touch.

I lurched back. "Sorry. I didn't mean to startle you."

Sam scowled. "I don't want to talk about any of this anymore."

"Okay. We won't. My intention wasn't to upset you and, for that, I'm sorry, but if you know anything that could help the police arrest the person responsible for your mother's death, it would be helpful for you to let them know."

He bowed his head, but when he raised his eyes to look at me, they were smoldering with anger. Okey-dokey. This line of questioning was going nowhere and emotions were thick for both of us.

I backed off and forced a smile. "Let me show you some features of the site."

I spent the next twenty minutes showing Sam around the site and taking photos. I took out a printed copy of preliminary plans from my tote. As we strolled along the strip mall's sidewalk, I reviewed the landscape design we'd proposed, pointing out where different design elements, like the community garden, would go on the site to give him a better sense of what we envisioned.

Once back in the car, I turned on the radio to lessen the pressure of making conversation, since I didn't want to risk upsetting him again. As I drove along listening to coverage of the wildfire and investigation in the background—so far this fire season had been the most destructive on record—I reflected on Paloma calling Sam troubled.

I shot a concerned glance over at him. His reddened face reflected a thunderous storm inside him. When he looked back at me, I could've sworn I saw fear in his eyes too.

The next second a flash of anger overrode the fear and he blurted out, "Can you change the station?"

"Sure." I pulled up the screen and clicked on an oldies station, hoping it was a safe choice that would calm him down.

"Thanks."

I wondered if Paloma was right or whether her talk of auras was just nonsense. I had to say, I agreed he seemed troubled. Had Sam fallen in with a bad crowd at school? Who had he gotten himself mixed up with? Or had the stress of his mother's death caused him mental distress to the point he was making stuff up to get attention? But Paloma had sensed his distress prior to Jo's death. One thing I did know was that adolescents were hormonal, and hormones were the devil when it came to mood swings.

I'd planned on taking the freeway home, but it was already three thirty. The time I'd spend in traffic made the PCH the quicker route this time of day. Besides, the sea beckoned.

Sam twisted in his seat a couple of times.

Now what?

I tried to leave the annoyance out of my voice. "Something wrong?"

When I took my eyes off the road to glance over at him, he was drained of color.

"What's the matter? Are you feeling sick?"

I started to pull over, concerned he might be carsick. Truth be told, I wanted to avoid having him vomit all over my car, caring cousin that I was.

"That car behind us. I think they're following us."

I squinted in my rearview mirror. We were alone on the road except for an older sedan several car lengths behind us. As I slowed to park on the shoulder, the car slowed down also. Sam became more agitated and I realized he wasn't sick—he was terrified. There were no other cars to be seen in either direction, and I suddenly freaked out too. I came to an abrupt stop and grabbed my phone out of my purse. I punched in Adrian's number. Of course, it went to voice mail. I told him our situation and then called Ashley. She answered and said she'd call SSPD.

"Take a photo of the license plate if you can," she said.

"Good call." I twisted around and took several pictures.

The driver must have figured out what I was doing. The car

made a U-turn and took off in the other direction.

I glanced at Sam as I sent the photos to Ashley. "Well, that was exciting."

Sam raised his eyebrows and shifted his gaze over at me. He looked at me like I was crazy.

Despite still feeling tense, I flashed him a smile. "Fun road trip, huh?"

We both chortled out our nervous energy in a brief moment of relief and lapsed into a comfortable silence for the rest of the trip back to the office.

I didn't know whether Sam had clammed up for good or just for today. While I drove, I cooked up a little reconnaissance plan of my own. I'd follow Sam for a couple of days to see if he led me anywhere interesting. If he couldn't tell me what he was hiding with his words, maybe I could figure out what it was by his actions.

Once back at the office, Sam wandered off across the hall to visit his father. I sighed loudly once he'd left, relieved I didn't have to walk on eggshells anymore. I wasn't going to lie—I was rethinking my decision to hire him. Maybe Jed or Matt, or whoever didn't want him here, had been doing me a favor. Last thing I needed was a testosterone-fueled kid on my hands. Let him spread his own brand of sunshine on my uncle.

I checked my messages. Adrian had called to thank me for the photos and told me he was going to run a check on the license plate. He said he'd call if they got a hit. I put in a call to Blanche, Jo's other fortune-teller friend. I wanted to find out more about Jo's personal life. We agreed to meet at Mugs & Teacups in an hour.

• • •

Blanche was waiting for me when I arrived at the café. She had a jolly air about her, aided by physical characteristics reminiscent of Mrs. Claus—generous build with a round face, full cheeks, a small bulbous nose, and eyes that twinkled when she smiled, which was often. And her white curly mane completed the similarity, tamed today by a paisley scarf. She stood to give me a hug when I joined her.

"Thanks for meeting me on such short notice."

She adjusted her silky gypsy blouse and voluminous skirt as she sat down. "My pleasure. How are you holding up? I'm still so upset about Jo."

"I'm hanging in there, thanks. Paloma said you would know more about Jo's past relationships."

"Sure do. I've been divorced twice and so was she. Well, the second one took off before they actually got married. But they were engaged. The jerk got her preggers and then up and left her. From what she told me about him, that was a good thing. He was a bad seed."

"In what way?"

"Mentally unstable. He couldn't keep a job or a dollar in his bank account, but most of his problems, far as I could tell, were rooted in his mental problems. Drugs and alcohol didn't help either. That baby was better off not being exposed to all that. His leaving was a blessing in disguise to Jo and her kid, I used to tell her."

She took out a Kleenex and blew her nose and dabbed at her eyes. "Sorry. I still can't believe she's gone."

I waited until she was more composed. "Do you remember her husband's and her fiancé's names?

"Sure do. Her husband's name was Tom Keaton. He had a kid from another marriage. What was his name now? It's on the tip of my tongue. Tad, no. Todd! In my humble opinion, that was the first bullet Jo dodged. Tom was a lot older than her and married Jo so she could take care of the kid is how it sounded to me. It'd be fair to say Tom wasn't much of a feminist. The kid was around ten when they got married. She was closer in age to the kid than she was to Tom."

I wrote down both names on my Notes app. "And her fiancé's name?"

"Let me think for a minute. Randy, Randy what now?

Tuttle! That's it. Crazy Randy Tuttle." She sipped her tea with satisfaction.

I added Randy to my list of Jo's formers. "Do you know what happened to Tom or his son or Randy?"

"Nope. Probably all in jail, from the sounds of them, or dead."

"Well, thanks so much." I put my phone down and drank some tea.

"You bet. How's Sam doing? I called him about a moving gig. He hasn't gotten back to me yet."

"I hope he's okay. Hard to tell with teenagers."

"Tell me about it. They're crazy enough without having a crazy father in the gene pool. But I'm a strong believer in love. Looks like he's been raised in a loving family. Love heals all, right?"

"Hopefully."

I drove home happy Blanche had remembered all the names. I couldn't wait to Google them. It was only five thirty, but I was ready to call it a night. I stopped and picked up takeout for dinner and headed home. Adrian called as I turned onto my street.

"Hi, what's up?"

"We got a hit on that license plate you sent me."

"No way! Whose is it? Anyone we know?"

"It's registered to George Benning."

"You've got to be kidding me!"

"Don't you have an Uncle George?"

"Apparently. I didn't even know he existed until the night Jo was murdered. I can't get over it. I wonder why he was following us?"

"I ran a check on him and he has a criminal record, but no arrests in the last seven years. Turns out, George is a white-collar criminal. He worked for an accountant several years ago and submitted some phony expense reports, bought himself a new TV, charged it to the company credit card, reimbursed himself twice for buying something, stuff like that over several years. It added up, to the tune of almost twenty thousand dollars. His boss pressed charges and he was sentenced to ten months in jail, with a fine and restitution, which apparently he is still in the process of paying back in monthly installments. The good news is that he's never hurt a fly."

"Wow. I can't believe it. I'm in shock."

A pregnant pause in our conversation told me we were both probably thinking the same thing.

"You don't think my uncle George had anything to do with Benning Brothers' embezzlement, do you?'

"That's exactly what I'm thinking."

I whistled. "I wonder why he followed us. Any news on the neighborhood surveillance tapes?"

"Not yet. We've got about four more to look at. I'll keep you posted."

CHAPTER 24

Iris's barks greeted me from inside the house even before I turned the key in the lock. When I opened the door, I was met with her usual dance and prance. Otis padded into the entryway and stretched nonchalantly.

"Hello, Otis! How are you?" He rubbed against my legs while Iris continued to jump on me, each time landing with an intentional body slam to Otis, to nudge him out of the way.

"Be nice, Iris. Who's hungry?"

I parked my purse on the hallway bench and headed to the kitchen in a commotion of a rustling Tender Greens takeout bag, a jumping dog, and a circling cat. I gave Iris and Otis fresh water and scooped their kibble into their respective bowls. Once the animals were happily fed and Iris was walked, I extracted the plastic container of grilled salmon and two side salads from the bag and opened my computer. In between bites, I Googled the names of Jo's exes and stepson.

Jo's first husband, Tom Keaton, still appeared to be a sketchy character, despite pushing seventy. His name turned up in a newspaper article from a few years back that described him as a suspect in an arson investigation. He'd been living in a homeless encampment near where a wildfire ignited, but there hadn't been enough evidence to charge him.

Jo's stepson, Todd Keaton, was a tougher nut to crack. There were about thirty people across the country named Todd Keaton and seven in California. I paused to estimate what his age would be now based on what Uncle Bob had said—around forty. Only one person named Todd Keaton fit in the correct age range. He'd been arrested for assault and domestic violence in Santa

Barbara and sentenced to jail almost two decades ago, when he was just twenty-one. Since Ashley used to work as a public defender in Santa Barbara, I texted her to see if she could use her connections to find out where he'd been jailed and if he'd been released since I didn't want to impose on Adrian for searches that weren't directly related to the murders.

I focused on my dinner for the next few minutes, savoring the succulent salmon, the lemony vinaigrette on the arugula salad, and the cabernet vinaigrette on the spinach and goat cheese salad. Randy Tuttle would have to wait. After eating every last crumb of the included slice of garlic bread, I was ready for another round of Googling.

Another newspaper article turned up, and this one revealed Randy Tuttle had died in a DUI motorcycle accident several years ago. He and the woman riding on the back were killed instantly. So, Sam's birth father was dead. Luckily, he had Uncle Bob as his adoptive father. I sat back and gazed at Iris curled up at my feet as my brain struggled to connect all the dots. I opened my spreadsheet and added new suspects: my uncle George, and Tom and Todd Keaton. I pondered a little more and then added Blanche to the list too. I counted up the suspects—currently, twelve.

Shaking my head, I added a thirteenth, Unknown Suspect. I hated to admit it, but the murderer might be someone not on my list who I didn't even know existed. Unlikely, for sure, but I wanted to be as thorough as possible.

I sat staring at the grid for several minutes, hoping for some insights, but felt defeated. I was supposed to be eliminating suspects, not adding more. I propped my chin on my hand. My head throbbed from information overload to the point I thought it was going to burst when my phone buzzed.

It was Jake. "Hey, what are you up to tonight?"

"I'm sitting here looking at the suspect spreadsheet."

"Anything new?"

"Only that I added five more suspects." I filled him in on Uncle George, Tom, and Todd Keaton.

"I was calling to ask if you ever took a look at your father's phone."

"We couldn't find it. We assumed it got washed away to sea. I checked out his emails on his computer and didn't find anything that looked incriminating."

"That was my next question. Assuming you checked his search history."

"Yep. Nothing suspicious." My phone vibrated. "Jake, my aunt Marian is calling. I should get this. Can I call you back?"

"Sure."

"Hi, Aunt Marian. Everything okay?"

"Yes, dear. Everything is fine. I ran into Blanche Hammerstein at the library a little while ago. She told me about seeing you today and asking about Jo."

"Yeah, I wanted to find out more about Jo's past relationships."

"Talking to Blanche brought back a recollection from several weeks ago at the library—about Jo. I don't know whether or not it's important, but I thought I'd better let you know anyway, just to play it safe."

"Okay. Shoot."

"Of course, I didn't know at that time she was your aunt and related to me through marriage, so I didn't think twice about it."

"Okay."

"And I didn't want to bother you. I know you've taken on additional responsibilities at the company—your mother would be so proud of you, sweetheart."

"Aw, thanks, Aunt Marian. She'd be proud of you too—her little sister, head librarian at Santa Sofia Library."

"I like to think she watches over us, like our guardian angel."

"So, what did you remember that you wanted to share?"

"Oh, right. I tend to get off on tangents when I'm not at work. I spend all day being precise and focused. When I'm not working, I let it all hang out." She chuckled.

We'd been on the phone for five minutes. *Please get to the point.*

"You remembered something about Jo?"

"Why, yes, she was at the library and she was arguing—the other voice was a male's, or possibly a deep-voiced female."

"So you never saw who it was?"

"No, I'm afraid not. I was at my desk and they were between the stacks. The only reason I knew it was Jo was when I saw her walk out of the stacks. Her face was thunder. Remember, I didn't know it was Jo at that time, and I had never met her when she was younger, only heard about her from your dad. I knew her as Esmeralda. She'd always been sweet and pleasant to me. Always returned her books on time. That's why I noticed her that day. It was uncharacteristic for her to be angry."

"Then what? You said you didn't see who she was fighting with."

"Unfortunately, no. The desk got busy and I got so caught up with kids asking me questions that it slipped my mind to watch and see. I did see your cousin Sam that day, though."

My throat tightened. "You don't think it was Sam she was arguing with, do you?"

"Honestly, I don't know. I haven't spoken to him lately. Does he have a deep voice?"

"Kind of. Just lately his voice has been getting deeper."

"Oh. Then maybe it was."

"And I take it you didn't hear what the argument was about?"

"No, just the raised voices. Couldn't hear what they were saying." Our conversation segued into chitchat about the wildfires.

"That last one came very close to my house, one of the drawbacks of living in the foothills, I guess."

"Glad they were on it and got it contained quickly this time."

"You and me both. Especially since it was arson. Makes me so angry, endangering human and animal life, let alone all the trees. Our whole neighborhood nearly had to evacuate."

"How did they know it was arson?"

"That's what I asked the firefighter who let us know we didn't have to evacuate. He said they found the same incendiary device that was found at other recent fires. Plus, there were footprints this time."

"Oh? At least that gives them a lead to follow."

"Not really. More confirms that it's arson because it was a standard-issue work boot that is very common."

"Not a Wallington?"

"Why, yes! Did they mention that in the news?"

"No, just a hunch."

"Oh, I almost forgot, don't think it matters though."

"What?"

"I saw Milo that day too."

The thickness in my throat was growing. "You did?"

"Now that I think about it, maybe it was Milo who Jo was arguing with. He had a deep voice too."

"Are you sure it was Milo?"

"I'm positive, dear. He even waved to me as he walked out the door."

We said goodbye and hung up. So many thoughts collided in my head, threatening to blow up my brain.

I called Jake back and told him about the boot print near Aunt Marian's fire and that Tom Keaton, Jo's ex-husband, had been a previous arson suspect. I also told him that, apparently, Jo and Milo held a heated meet-and-greet at the library only days before their murders. And Sam was there too.

CHAPTER 25

Otis jumped on the bed with a light thump. His heavy purrs sounded like an idling car engine. I lay still, hoping he'd curl up at my feet. Instead, the bed vibrated from his paws kneading my legs through the covers, like a soothing massage. That lasted for all of twenty seconds before Iris lunged at him while simultaneously barking in my ear—so much for sleeping in on a Saturday morning.

By the time I'd fed them and walked Iris, it was still only seven forty-five. I poured myself a second cup of coffee and sipped it while plotting my day.

At eight I called Uncle Bob. "Tell me more about Uncle George."

After Aunt Veronica heard him greet me by name, she yelled out in the background, "Tell Tory to come over for breakfast if she's not busy. I'm making blueberry muffins."

Uncle Bob cleared his throat. "You hear that?"

"I'm on my way."

Low clouds blanketed the sky that my weather app predicted would burn off by late morning, a typical October day in Santa Sofia. There were several runners enjoying the sea breeze along the beach sidewalk as I drove along the Promenade. Soon I'd passed through the Ryder Ranch gate and was pulling up in my aunt and uncle's driveway—less than a ten-minute trip on a traffic-free Saturday morning.

Aunt Veronica greeted me at the door. She was wearing a beige Williams Sonoma apron over jeans and a black top with three-quarter-length sleeves. I handed her a brown paper bag full of lemons from my backyard tree.

"Aw, thank you, Tory."

I followed her into the kitchen and adjoining breakfast room. The aroma of coffee, eggs, and toast filled the air, along with the fruity sweetness of her glorious blueberry muffins, cooling on racks on the tile counter.

"Help yourself to coffee and muffins. There are scrambled eggs with mushrooms and spinach on the stove." She buttered several slices of sour dough toast as she rattled off the menu.

"Thanks." I picked up a plate and served myself a chunk of eggs from a red copper frying pan. I set my plate down on the table, grabbed a mug of coffee and reached for a muffin. I pulled in my chair and dug in.

Uncle Bob was a few mouthfuls ahead of me across the table. Sam sauntered in barefoot, in shorts and a T-shirt. Aunt Veronica pulled up a chair next to me.

I broke a muffin in half to reveal a center bursting with warm blueberries. I popped a chunk in my mouth. The tart sweetness of the berries and the sweet buttery muffin were a perfect blend. "These are divine!"

Aunt Veronica beamed. "Thanks."

Sam popped half a muffin into his mouth and hugged his mother as he sat down next to her. "She makes the best blueberry muffins in the world."

Aunt Veronica tittered. "Well, I don't know about that."

"I totally agree." I sipped my coffee and turned to Uncle Bob. "Hey, can I talk to you about Uncle George?"

"Sure. What do you want to know about him?"

"When was the last time you saw him?"

"Why do you ask?"

"Because he was following Sam and me yesterday at the condo site."

"Funny. Sam didn't mention it."

Sam squirmed in his chair. "Yeah, maybe because I didn't know. So, Adrian tracked his plates?"

I nodded to Sam. "We were both pretty freaked out since we didn't know who it was at the time. Adrian ran the plates and the car belongs to Uncle George."

Uncle Bob clicked his teeth. "I heard he'd moved back to the area. I haven't had any contact with him for a while, though, two, three years, maybe. I wonder why he was following you."

"That's what I'd like to know."

Uncle Bob checked his watch. "Uh-oh. I told a potential new client I'd meet them for coffee this morning. Referred to us by the Hotel Santa Sofia folks. Don't want to create a bad first impression and show up late. I'll fill you in on the details later."

"That's great. Good luck."

Uncle Bob bustled off, leaving the three of us to finish our breakfast.

Sam headed to his room, grabbing another muffin as he did. "I'm going to get ready. Paloma asked me to help her out today at another fundraiser."

Aunt Veronica winked at me. "Glad we can talk privately now. I didn't want to burden Bob, but I'd be remiss if I didn't tell you. Sam told me the other day he had a meeting with your father the night he died."

I jolted to attention and gasped, "What? How come he never mentioned this before?"

"I don't know. I think it slipped out by accident. But since you're spending time with him now, I thought maybe you can coax more information out of him."

"I'll try. But frankly, he was so moody yesterday he made me reconsider whether it was a good idea to have him work on the Hotel Santa Sofia condo project. He was great at first, then he got temperamental."

"For what it's worth, he said he's already learned a lot about landscape design by spending time with you. I think he truly likes working for you."

"Well, he sure has an odd way of showing it."

We both laughed and resumed our munching.

• • •

On my way home, I decided to revisit the pier because the only time I'd been back since my father's death was when I dined with Jake at Sadie's Seafood Restaurant, and I'd found it difficult to be in true sleuth mode while his mesmerizing gaze held me under its spell.

I parked in one of the diagonal slots that ran along the Promenade near the pier.

The beach steeply sloped down from the road for about fifty feet and then flattened. It was low tide, so the beach was visible for two hundred and fifty feet or so. The pier spanned the beach before it extended over the ocean for about another thousand feet. No one was on the beach around the pier, but a few surfers were in the water. A smattering of people were strolling or riding their bikes on the pier. I ventured about a quarter of the way out on the decking, where my father had supposedly fallen into the water. I peered over the railing, first at the sand, then the water. The distance was about twenty feet down from the pier to the water.

Next, I headed underneath the pier. Because the tide was out, I could walk between the pylons. I took off my sandals and padded around barefoot, the damp sand massaging my toes as I left footprints. The cool sand had a soothing effect on my psyche as I considered the dozens of tides that had risen and receded here since my father's death. I wasn't expecting to find anything of significance. I just wanted to see if I could imagine how it all transpired. Barnacles clung to the seaweed-wrapped pylons. A few beer bottles buried deep in the sand peeped out like tombstones. Plastic bags, the bane of local environmentalists, wove in plaits with the seaweed.

I climbed the boulders piled high up against the sandy slope, almost touching the underside of the pier's decking. A rat scurried between the rocks a few yards away.

I flinched. "Yikes!" A few choice words followed while I debated whether my quest was really worth the risk of getting bitten by a rabid rodent. I shuddered and slipped my sandals back on. Any protection was better than none.

I pressed on and found more plastic bags and an athletic shoe. At the top of the pile, a plank was wedged between two rocks that someone had clearly used as a shelf. On it were the remains of a joint, cigarette butts, and a few burnt wooden matches. It was above the barnacle line, high enough to be protected from high tide. Next to the rock pile, something black, half-buried in the silt, stuck out. I bent down and dug it out. Was it a phone? My second of hope was dashed as I dug away the sand, only to find a cell phone cover, the exact same kind my father had had on his phone, except a bit worse for wear. I looked at the planks above me and thought the phone could have easily slipped between the cracks and separated from its cover when it hit the rocks. I furiously searched every nook and cranny around the rocks, rats be damned. After twenty minutes and an aching back, I came up empty—no phone. I had to assume either it'd been washed out to sea or someone had beaten me to it. Was it Sam? He seemed a likely suspect. If it was true he met with my father, as Aunt Veronica had told me, what happened before and after? Dejected, I made my way back to the car, my only prize my father's cell phone cover.

• • •

I spent Sunday catching up on various household chores I'd neglected, went grocery shopping, and did several loads of laundry. As my reward, I spent an hour at the gym, mainly jogging on the treadmill and listening to music. I picked up Tender Greens again and spent the evening paying bills then retired early, hoping to get a good night's sleep. But Otis barfed on my bed around one and Iris went on a barking jag an hour later that put me on edge for the rest of the night.

• • •

On Monday afternoon Sam came to my office after he was done with school. He tapped lightly at my door and asked politely if there was anything I needed him for today.

"Actually, I do. Come on in and have a seat."

He smiled and settled his lanky frame in a side chair. He looked around my office. He fixed his gaze on a *People* magazine peeking out from a pile of folders on my desk and his amber eyes twinkled with mirth as he slid it out and flipped through it briefly before setting it down again. His playful demeanor suggested he was back to being the cousin I knew and loved.

We sat facing each other across my desk.

I got up and shut the door. "I have some questions for you."

The smile left his face and he became wary. "Okay."

"But they're not related to the condo project. They're related to my father's death."

Startled, he sat up straighter and his eyes grew wide.

"Why didn't you ever tell me you met with him the night of his death?"

Sam hung his head and mumbled his response. "Because I didn't want to get in trouble."

"Why did you think you'd get in trouble?"

He raised his head. His face was flushed. "Because I was there when it happened."

"When what happened?"

"When he was killed."

I took a deep breath as the pinpricks of light in my eyes signaled lightheadedness, as it seemed all the oxygen had been sucked from the room. I reached for a bottle of water and took a few long gulps. "You saw who murdered my father and you haven't said anything? Who was it?"

He swallowed. "That's not what I said. I heard it. I was under the pier. I couldn't see anything."

"What were you doing under the pier?"

"Swear you won't tell my dad?"

Whatever it was, it couldn't be worse than withholding evidence in a murder investigation. "I won't tell him—promise."

"Uncle John had told me he wanted to talk to me in private, on the pier. I was supposed to meet him but lost track of time because I was under the pier with a friend, smoking weed. I remembered the time when I heard steps on the pier. My friend took off, and I was getting ready to go up on the pier to meet your dad when I heard another set of footsteps. Then there was a scuffle and the phone dropped."

His story matched the joint remnants I'd found under the pier.

"Did the phone drop on the sand or in the water?"

"It hit the rocks. I picked it up."

"What did you do with it?"

He hung his head lower. "I threw it away."

"Why did you throw it away?"

He shrugged.

"Where did you throw it away?"

"Into the water."

"Did anyone see you pick up the phone?"

"I don't think so."

"Then what happened?"

"Then someone threw Uncle John's body into the ocean."

"You're sure he was dead before he was tossed over?"

"I'm positive. I heard his body fall on the pier after the scuffle. It fell hard, and he never got up."

I felt like screaming "Why didn't you do something?" But he was getting more and more agitated. I backed off, fearing a meltdown like the other day. I needed to keep our communication channel open since he'd just revealed he witnessed my father's murder.

"And you're sure you didn't recognize who the other person was?"

He started to sob. "Tory, it all happened so quickly. I didn't really know what was happening till after the fact. Someone approached Uncle John, they argued, his body hit the boardwalk, the phone dropped down, and then the splash of your father's body."

"Then what did you do?"

"I called nine-one-one."

I took a couple of deep breaths. No use wondering whether or not my father might have still been alive when he hit the water and whether anything could have been done to save him. I was sure this was the exact thought that was torturing Sam, if he was telling the truth. Right now, that was a big "if."

"Okay, you've got to tell the police."

His eyes flashed in anger. "My parents can't find out."

"Look, Sam. Your parents are the least of your worries right now. What if the person who killed my father thinks you saw him?"

He looked toward the floor and mumbled, "No one saw me."

"How can you be sure?"

His eyes smoldered as he jutted out his chin and pursed his lips in defiance. He'd officially clammed up.

"Okay, how about we call it a day. We're both upset. Let's cool down. Come back tomorrow afternoon and I'll have an assignment related to the condo project ready for you to start."

He slunk out of my office.

My head was swimming with questions. Why didn't he speak up right away? Smoking weed paled in comparison to witnessing a murder. His parents would have understood. And why would he throw my father's phone away, unless something on the phone incriminated Sam? And why had my father wanted to meet with Sam in a private location? That sounded so melodramatic. And then it hit me why so much of what Sam had told me didn't make sense. Sam must be lying. And why would he be lying? The one logical explanation that answered all my questions—Sam lied to protect himself. Either he knew who killed my father or Sam himself must be murderer.

I called Jake and Ashley and told them I needed to talk to them about something important and private. "Because it's important, let's meet at my house."

Jake sensed the urgency in my voice. "I can bring dinner if pizza is okay."

"Sounds great, thanks. See you soon."

Jake and Ashley arrived at the same time. Jake carried

two medium-sized pizza boxes from Santini's on the Avenue, *the* pizza joint in Santa Sofia, raising my estimation of him several notches. When he lifted the first lid, my senses swooned at a mouthwatering array of Italian sausage, pepperoni, and mushrooms. He opened the second box to reveal a margherita pizza, with the fragrant aroma of basil intermixed with tomato and cheese.

Pizza was exactly what I needed. "Thank you so much. And salads too!"

Santini's chopped salads were packed with chunks of mozzarella and provolone cheese, salami, and garbanzo beans. I beamed at Jake approvingly as I arranged bottles of Pellegrino sparkling water on the kitchen counter. Ashley and Jake dug in while I explained to them what Sam had told me.

Ashley quickly swallowed her mouthful of salad. "We've got to tell Adrian. We can't wait around hoping Sam will tell him."

Jake wiped his hands with a napkin. "Totally agree. Whether or not he's being totally truthful, it looks like he was witness to a murder."

I took a swig of water for courage. "Do you think he could actually be the murderer?"

Jake leaned in. "If you look at your father's murder in isolation, possibly. But remember, you have gone to a great deal of effort analyzing the clues and, I think Ashley and I agree with you on this, your father's murder looks like it's related to Milo's and Jo's."

Ashley looked up from her phone. "I just texted Adrian and he's on his way over."

I sighed in relief. "Yeah. I'll feel better knowing he's aware of this."

Jake helped himself to another piece of pizza. "Sam was at your wedding, right? But was he at the fundraiser? I don't remember seeing him there."

"I'm pretty sure he wasn't, since my aunt wanted to go home to tell him about Jo's death."

The doorbell announced Adrian's arrival. He followed me to

the kitchen and his eyes lit up. Whether it was because of Ashley or the pizza, I couldn't be sure.

Adrian grabbed some salad and pizza and sat next to Ashley. "Ashley gave me the short version. Sam says he was under the pier when your father was murdered. He heard a scuffle, saw the body thrown into the ocean, but didn't actually see who it was. Correct?"

I nodded. "Yes."

"Okay. I'll have someone watch him."

"Good. I've wanted to follow him ever since he acted so weirdly on our site visit but haven't had the chance yet."

Jake shook his head. Ashley looked at me in disbelief.

Adrian was fuming, indicated by the bulging vein in his reddened forehead, but he struggled to control his temper. "Look, Tory, I know you're impatient about getting to the bottom of this. It's your family. I get it. But we're dealing with a desperate person. My best guess is your father's death wasn't necessarily intentional. Guys fight all the time, sometimes with unintended consequences. The fact that he had contusions on his face and jaw and an injury on the back of his head suggest he might have hit his head after someone decked him. Nevertheless, a decent person would have called nine-one-one to get medical care. This person didn't. I'm thinking maybe Milo figured this out. Maybe Jo did too. And now the perp is in damage control mode. Silences anyone who becomes a threat. That puts a big bull's-eye on you if the wrong person catches wind of you snooping around on them. Therefore, do not follow any suspects. Understand?"

"I'm always careful."

Ashley grabbed my forearm. "I know you are. But still, if someone feels cornered, and they already have killed, what's to stop them now?"

Adrian's gaze bored into me. "Ashley's right. Under duress, people do strange things. Case in point—every car pursuit ever televised. These guys get hopped up on drugs, booze, and adrenaline and lead cops on wild-goose chases—everyone knows it's going to end badly for them except them. The mind-set of someone who kills repeatedly to cover up a crime is similar. Each crime just gives us more to go on. But they think by eliminating witnesses they'll get away with it."

"Is Sam in danger?"

"If he is in fact a witness and not the killer, then I'd say yes. And that's another reason why you should let professional law enforcement officers follow him. We can arrest him if warranted or we can protect him if necessary."

I bowed my head, partly in shame, partly to hide my fear.

Jake stepped in. "Last thing you want to do, Tory, is interfere with their investigation."

Ashley agreed. "Definitely. From a legal standpoint, you don't want to prevent the cops from lining up all their ducks in a row. You could possibly inadvertently weaken their case by interfering, by compromising important evidence. Let them do their job unencumbered so that no evidence is disallowed once it goes to trial."

"All right. Enough. I got it. Message received."

Ashley rubbed my back.

"But can I point out Sam was with me when we were followed and when our car was run off the road."

Jake nodded. "You're right."

I gobbled a few bites of pizza to fuel my brain. "Maybe he had an accomplice."

Adrian pushed back from the table. "Or he was the accomplice to the murderer."

Along with the remnants of pizza and salad, the four of us chewed on these possibilities in silence.

We all agreed to sleep on it and see if we had any insights in the morning. My three friends left together, with Adrian reassuring me he was keeping the hourly patrol on my property for the time being.

After an eventful day, I was happy to be cozy in bed with my crew: Iris, Otis, and my Netflix account. I randomly clicked through the lineups in various genres, from mysteries and thrillers to romantic comedies, but didn't have an attention span long enough to watch the shows I typically adored. My mind drifted back to our evening conversation about Sam. The more I thought about it, I was convinced Sam was lying. He must know who murdered my father if he was under the pier when my father was killed. And I bet he figured out that same person killed Milo and Jo. That must be what he was lying about. Otherwise, why would he seem so afraid?

CHAPTER 26

I went about my morning routines with Iris and Otis on autopilot and it wasn't until my second cup of coffee that my brain began to function fully. Walking in my backyard with Iris, I wondered about Sam, rolling out the conclusion I'd arrived at last night—Sam was lying about not knowing who killed my father. There was no other plausible explanation for his reluctance to be forthcoming. He was clearly hiding something important and afraid that telling me would put me, him, or both of us in danger.

I got ready for work and was on the road when Ashley called.

Excitement burst from her breathless voice. "I took the liberty of leaning on some of my buds at the public defender's office, and I tracked down your uncle George."

"No, you didn't! Thanks, Ash. That's great. Text me his address and I'll go pay my long-lost uncle a visit."

"Oh no you won't! Not without me as backup. You heard Adrian last night. We are dealing with a murderer. Let's not get ourselves killed in catching him."

"So you think the murderer is a male for sure?"

"Don't try to distract me, girl. I see what you're doing. That was just a manner of speech. The key word I hope you heard was 'killed.' As in us, we don't want that."

"Fine. When can you go with me?"

"My morning is pretty flexible. How about yours?"

I stopped for a red light. "Nothing more urgent than solving a murder."

"I'm at home still. Why don't you swing by and pick me up?"

The light changed and I turned around to go back in Ashley's direction. "Done. See you in five."

Ashley lived not far from me on a cute cul-de-sac. Her house had a similar look to mine—the Mediterranean white stucco exterior and red tile roof. I'd designed her front yard with its alternating squares of lawn and longer grasses bordered with stone pavers, with big terra-cotta planters of flowering succulents for colorful accents. As I parked, I noticed one of the lawn squares wasn't doing too well.

She opened her fire engine red door as I walked up the path.

"Have you been watering your lawn regularly?"

Ashley closed her door and locked it. "Don't need to. It's drought-resistant."

"Yes, you do. It still needs water. It's drought-resistant, not bionic. Program your drip sprinkler to water twice a week or everything will die. Which seems to be the theme in Santa Sofia lately."

"Very funny. Okay, I'll do it tonight after work."

We got in my car and she showed me Uncle George's address: Ocean Breeze Trailer Park. I knew where it was. Actually, Sam and I had passed it on our way up to the condo site.

We spent the ten minutes it took to get to the trailer park devising a strategy for interrogating Uncle George that wouldn't backfire.

Ashley turned in my direction. "We can start talking about family history and roots. Make it sound like you're just curious and reconnecting with family, or something like that."

"Did you let Adrian know we're going to see him?"

"Duh. I don't have a death wish like some people I know. I believe in full disclosure and police backup at all times."

"Good. I don't think my uncle will buy the ancestry stuff. From what Uncle Bob said, he's a con man, so he probably projects his own deceptive nature onto everyone he encounters. I think we should be straightforward and tell him we know he followed me. Then see what he says."

"Okay. But don't say I didn't warn you."

We pulled up to the gravel clearing on the bluff that

overlooked the ocean. There were eight trailers arranged around the clearing in a semicircle. A seagull perched on an old sedan parked in the adjacent lot.

I tipped my head. "That looks like the car that followed Sam and me the other day."

We got out and crunched across the gravel to the closest trailer.

"Does his address specify a particular parking spot?"

"No. But that man over there, sitting on the lawn chair in front of his trailer, resembles your father and your uncle Bob. I bet that's George."

I squinted in his direction. "He does look like a younger version of them."

Low fog clung to the shoreline, as it did most mornings. My hair absorbed the moisture like a sponge. "Great, so much for the sleek, well-groomed look today."

Ashley gave me the side-eye.

My face twisted into a wistful frown. "I know, I should've gotten the Brazilian straightening treatment like you did when you wanted me to go with you last week."

Ashley turned and swung her head, flaunting her smooth hair.

"I'll go with you next time, when there's a lull in the murder rate."

We'd reached the man who looked like he was my uncle. "Hi there. My name is Tory Benning—"

The man snapped his head to attention before I could introduce Ashley. Bingo.

Ashley took over. "From your reaction, I'd say you're George Benning. Hi, I'm Ashley Payne."

"That's right." He thrust his hand out to Ashley and then to me. His vigorous handshake struck me as contrived to give the impression of a straight-up guy, the opposite of the profile his police record had revealed.

He looked us both up and down and smirked. "To what do I owe this pleasure? I've been back in Santa Sofia for a couple of years now. Way overdue for the Welcome Wagon ladies to pay me a visit."

Game on. He was purposely egging us on. The air bristled with the electric reaction Ashley and I had to his comment. By the grimace on Ashley's face, I assumed both of us were making a concerted effort to control our tempers.

"No. We're here to ask you why you were following me the other day."

"You got your facts wrong, girlie. I've never followed you. Why would I?"

"I was hoping you'd tell me."

"This related to Jo's murder by any chance? Cuz I have some information you might be interested in knowing, seeing we're family and all." His slimy smile, spread from ear to ear, revealed a gold tooth, and he projected the guile of a Dickensian villain.

Ashley shifted her weight. "What information? I'm sure the police would be interested in anything that would help their murder investigation."

"Wouldn't they, though. But my information can only be had for a price."

Ashley and I exchanged glances.

Ashley stood straighter and pushed her shoulders back. "In the legal world, that's bordering on extortion."

He snorted. "I'm not threatening anyone. Just offering a business proposition."

My curiosity couldn't be stifled any longer. "If someone were willing to pay for your information, how much money are we talking about? Hypothetically, of course."

He didn't hesitate. "Ten grand."

I took a deep breath. That was a lot of money for information I wasn't even sure would be helpful. Not to mention, if he had an ounce of decency in him, he'd volunteer it freely. "I'd hate to have to report your following me as a stalking incident."

"Cupcake, you do what you want. I swear I didn't follow you. But I don't ever lock my car, so anyone could have borrowed it and followed you. In fact, I leave the keys inside, hoping someone steals it and I can get a new one, compliments of my insurance company." He smirked. "Go see for yourself, if you don't believe me."

Ashley heaved a deep breath of annoyance. "Okay. Well, I guess we're at an impasse. Let's go, Tory."

He called out when we reached our car. "I'll be here if you change your mind about the information."

My phone pinged as we walked back to my car. I had a voice mail from Ernie. He said if I didn't make an appointment with him today, he was going to draw up a warrant for my arrest and submit it to a judge tomorrow. I let Ashley listen to his message.

Suddenly, I was sweating. "He can't do that, can he?"

"He can if he has sufficient evidence to make you a suspect. And a judge who agrees with him. Call Adrian and ask him what he recommends you do."

I called Adrian and left him a detailed message.

I opened my car door. "Do you think Uncle George was telling the truth?"

Ashley slid into her seat. "Hard to tell."

• • •

After I dropped Ashley off at her house for her car, I headed to my office. I dove into work as a welcome escape from all of the new developments. After an hour that saw many things crossed off my to-do list, I stood and stretched. Maybe I'd take a walk around the block before the next round of assignments. I reached for my phone and a notification popped up that the Find My iPhone app was now up to date. I hadn't looked at the app since Milo had gone missing and his phone was smashed. Actually, it had been my father who suggested to me we use the family feature shortly before he died. When Milo heard about it, he joined too. They both felt better being able to track me if I worked late, so my father claimed at the time. But in light of now knowing my father's death wasn't an accident but murder, I wondered whether my father had feared for my safety for a particular reason.

After he died I'd concluded his iPhone had been lost for good when it was marked as offline. It now occurred to me that conclusion corroborated Sam's story about throwing it into the ocean. I opened the app out of curiosity to see if the update had changed anything and almost dropped my phone. My father's phone was online now. And it was updating with new locations, which meant someone had it and they were in transit. I watched the updates in real time as his phone moved along the Promenade, passing where it intersected the Avenue, and continued along the coast heading south, then turned on the drive at the Hotel Santa Sofia. I made the map bigger to better see where on the property the person traveled. It passed the main building until it stopped—in the Secret Maze.

I called Ashley but she was in a client meeting. I called Jake and it went to voice mail. Finally, remembering his stern lecture from the other night, I called Adrian, but he didn't pick up. I left messages for all three and jumped in my car.

I drove down the Avenue to the Promenade. Turning left, I made myself focus on the road since the whirlpool of emotions swirling in my head was teetering out of control. I was pretty sure it must be Sam who'd had my dad's phone the whole time. It'd seemed like a lame story he'd told me about finding it and throwing it away, but then I had sprung it on him so I guess it was the best he could muster at the time.

I parked in the little parking lot nearest the maze. I started up the path and stopped as I heard a rustling in the hedges. My heart was pounding so hard I could hardly hear myself think. The maze was tall, deep, and isolated. Especially on a weekday, there weren't many people around. I got out my phone, ready to dial 911 if necessary. I rounded a corner and ran into Octavio, the groundskeeper.

"Hello, ma'am. Funny I should meet you again right now. I'm positive I just heard the same voice in the maze I heard in the maze the day of your wedding."

"You did?"

"Yes, ma'am. Just moments ago."

My heart pounded hard and adrenaline pumped me up. I headed toward the rustling noise, trying to be quiet. The element of surprise was all I had, plus an unsurpassable knowledge of the intricate pathways of the maze, in case I needed to run away. I crept around the next corner, only to come face-to-face with none other than my nemesis, Ernie Gomez. *Crap.*

"Well, what do you know? The elusive Tory Benning. Finally."

"Hi, Ernie. What are you doing here?"

"I'll ask the questions. And I'll start by asking you the same."

"Hello! I'm the person who designed this maze, and I happen to be here working. I check it out periodically to make sure the hedges are healthy and being properly maintained by the groundskeepers."

Ernie's smug smile froze on his face. He was clearly surprised that I'd offered up a somewhat plausible explanation for my presence. Frankly, so was I. Sometimes I amazed myself.

After an awkward pause, his smile disappeared. "Fair enough. You haven't happened to see your cousin, Sam, around, have you? You wouldn't be here to meet him, would you?"

"Nope. Why?"

Ernie repressed a snicker as he reached into his coat pocket. "Because I have a warrant here for his arrest. I called him, but he didn't return my calls. Seems to be a trait that runs in your family."

"Yeah, well, we're a busy bunch. What's the arrest warrant for?"

"The triple murders of your father, husband, and aunt."

I raised my eyebrows. "What! Based on what?"

"Let's just say circumstantial evidence."

"So your message about a warrant for me—"

Ernie snorted and his eyes glistened with triumph. "Oh, yeah. You were next in case the judge didn't grant Sam's warrant. You can disregard that. I have enough evidence to arrest your cousin now. I've pretty much got the case all wrapped up."

I wouldn't be honest if I didn't admit this news filled me with mixed emotions. Shock about hearing my suspicions about Sam shared by Ernie, and relief that I no longer was in Ernie's sights.

There was a rustling on the other side of the hedge and we both snapped our heads up. Ernie took off down the pathway. Car doors slammed, voices yelled, and then the sound of cars driving away.

I pulled out my phone and tapped Find iPhone. The icon for my father's phone was still in the Secret Maze. Sam must have either dropped it or hidden it. I was betting on hidden, since what other purpose would have brought him here. I followed the icon, but then the signal stopped updating, just giving me its old location. I looked again and noticed its battery icon indicated it was low, practically dead. I headed to the center of the maze, where the icon seemed to direct me, past the spot where Milo had found the hummingbird nest in one of the little carved- out sections of the hedge. I searched all around the area, not finding anything, wildly going around in circles throughout the maze. I was stumped until I saw a hummingbird hover in front of me, like a magic sprite trying to tell me something. I went back to the nook where Milo found the hummingbird nest. I got on my tiptoes and looked all around, poking in the branches with my hands, until I found something. There it was, stuck snuggly in the dense foliage, my father's phone. It had a red line of juice left in the battery icon. I punched in the password, my mother's birthday. I clicked on Messages. The screen lit momentarily to flash the names of people he'd been texting. Milo's name was at the top of the list. And then the phone went black.

My father's phone used a different charger than mine. I still had an older model charger at home from my previous phone, the upside of having a slight hoarding problem. I stuck his phone into one of my handbag's zippered compartments and trotted back to my car. As I headed home to get the old charger, Sam called me. He sounded desperate. Ernie was after him but he managed to shake him for the time being. Sam said he needed to show me something that would prove his innocence. He wanted me to meet him at the condo site right now.

CHAPTER 27

The urgency in Sam's voice weighed on me as I considered the delay I'd incur if I went all the way home for my old phone charger. Then I remembered my father kept a phone charger in his car. We'd kept his car parked at the office, so I swung by our office lot and grabbed his car charger before heading north on the freeway to the condo site.

About halfway there, Ashley called me. "Got your message about your father's phone. That's wild."

"Yeah, I'm charging it right now. I'm on my way to meet Sam. He called and said he has something to show me to prove his innocence."

"Like what?"

"He wouldn't say."

"I don't like the sound of that one bit. Did you tell Adrian?"

"Left a message about the phone, not the meet-up. But I did run into Ernie and he has a warrant for Sam's arrest for all three murders."

"No way. Well, at least you and your uncle are off the hook."

"I know. Exactly what I thought."

"Well, I have news too. My public defender colleagues did more digging on George. Years ago his cellmate was Todd Keaton, a.k.a. Jo's former stepson, who was in jail for assault, armed robbery, and arson."

"Hmm. I wonder what they talked about."

"Exactly. How each of them came this close to the Benning fortune."

"Hardly a fortune now after someone stole a big chunk of it. Luckily my father and uncle Bob were smart enough not to put all their eggs in one basket."

"Anyway, I have them digging on Todd Keaton right now. I'll let you know if they find anything else."

After we hung up, I reflected on Todd Keaton, which triggered something in my mind, but I couldn't put my finger on what.

Before I knew it, I'd arrived at the site. Sam wasn't there yet, so I parked, happy I finally had a chance to take a look at my father's phone. I was so excited and anxious to finally read the texts that I didn't bother to turn off my engine. My father had text messages from Sam, Milo, Uncle Bob, Aunt Veronica, Jed Barnes, and myself. He also had some with no name attached, just a number.

As I started to read the texts between my father and Sam, my heart revved up with each passing word. I swallowed hard as I learned my father had set up the meeting with Sam that night to discuss Sam's involvement in the area fires and the logistics of turning himself in to the authorities.

Oh, my God! I paused for a second to consider the new revelation and stared blankly out the window in a daze. Wow! No wonder Sam had seemed terrified. He was facing heavy-duty criminal charges for arson.

The text also cautioned Sam not to let "him," whoever that was, know they were meeting. A wave of nausea rippled through my stomach, and my whole body felt sick in an instant. Clamminess, lightheadedness, and heart pounding took over. The thought of my father and Sam plotting to avoid the ire of someone nefarious was chilling in light of my father's fate. But I told myself to stay angry, not afraid, and to breathe deeply to regain my strength.

Next I read the texts from Milo. It was surreal to read texts between the two men I'd loved so much. They revealed that my father and Milo had also planned to meet on the pier the night my father died. They wanted to discuss "the money issue" and how to keep Sam safe. My dad and Milo were both being good guys, trying to help Sam out of some fix. Again a wave of weakness threatened my consciousness, and deep breathing banished the feeling as I braced myself and squeezed the edge of my bucket seat. Why didn't my father want "him" to know? Was he afraid the mystery man would tell others about Sam's arson? Or was the mystery man involved in some way?

I looked at a text from a phone number without an ID. It was threatening and I felt fearful just reading the menacing words. My father accused the person of embezzling. *So my dad knew!* My father suggested a meeting to settle the debt or he'd go to the police. The person texted back, *Over my dead body. You owe me this money. I'm family.* The anonymous texter told my father to back off or he'd tell the cops about the "kid's" involvement in the fires or worse. It went on to say, *You've got such a smart, beautiful daughter. I'd hate to see her lose her dad, or something happen to her and her boyfriend.*

A loud breath escaped my lips as I leaned back in my seat in shock. The sound of a car pulling up interrupted my daze. It parked facing me head-on.

Sam was driving Uncle George's old sedan. That totally threw me. How did Uncle George figure into this?

As soon as I saw Sam's face, I knew something was wrong. In that same instant, I realized I'd been lured here as a trap. *How could I have been so naïve?* It all made sense now. George had spent time in prison for embezzlement.

A head popped up in the backseat, and an arm reached from the back to the driver's seat and fumbled behind Sam's back. Then the arm unlatched the driver's door and Sam stepped out, with his hands handcuffed behind his back. The person in the backseat emerged. It wasn't Uncle George—it was Jed Barnes. He was holding a gun.

I watched Jed and Sam as if they were on a screen in a drive-in movie. When my phone rang through my car's Bluetooth, I hit the green telephone icon on my steering wheel.

Ashley's voice came through breathless with excitement. "I think Todd Keaton and Jed Barnes are one in the same person."

"I was just in the process of figuring that out. Jed's here with

Sam right now and—"

Jed barked at me as he pointed the gun at Sam's head. "Shut off your car and give me your phone."

Jed was at my door, trying my locked door handle. I didn't have a plan other than to stall for time, hoping I'd come up with one or help would arrive.

I shouted through my closed window, "Move away so I can open the door."

I was shaking as I dug my phone out of my purse and held it up for him to see. Petrified, I hoped Ashley was still on the Bluetooth connection, hearing my interactions with Jed since I'd never hung up. I prayed she'd figure out what was going on and get help. I feared I'd lose our call if I shut off my car, so I opened my window after Jed had stepped back a few feet and lobbed my phone like a baseball toward Jed.

Still seated in my car, I hid my father's phone under my thigh. As Jed scrambled for the phone I'd thrown at him, I reached for my father's phone to call 911 and somehow hit the call button of the open text from the unknown number I'd been reading. Jed's phone rang. My face flashed with the heat of recognition as I realized the unknown number was Jed's number.

He ignored his ringing phone and, thankfully, didn't realize it came from me on my father's phone. "Get out of the car!"

I reluctantly shut off my engine. As I opened my car door, I grasped the full meaning of Jed's phone being the unknown number. Jed was the menacing "him" who'd threatened my father and was the killer we'd been searching for. I tried to stand up, but my knees buckled. The wave of nausea returned. This time it delivered the contents of my stomach and I puked right outside my car door. Clammy, I draped myself against my car like a wet washcloth.

Jed relaxed, seeming to assume I was no longer a threat, and ordered Sam to stand next to my car so he could keep an eye on both of us. Sam and I exchanged panicked glances across my car's hood.

Jed waved the gun at me and told me not to move or he'd

shoot Sam. Then Jed rested his gun on top of Uncle George's car as he opened the trunk and hauled out a gasoline can. He started to sprinkle gasoline around the vacant strip mall and surrounding brush. It didn't take a rocket scientist to figure out what he was plotting. It was clear he planned to kill Sam and me and cover up our murders with a fire.

I felt better after I threw up, even energized. It was a now-or-never moment. With Jed's back to me, I picked up a rock and hurled it at Jed's head, at the same time yelling at Sam to get in my car. The good news was the rock hit its target. The bad news was the rock hit its target—with an effect akin to poking a hornets' nest. Jed bellowed cusswords. I ducked into my car and opened the passenger door for Sam, since he was still in handcuffs. Sam rolled into the passenger seat and I locked the doors. Jed caught up to the car as I turned over the engine, glaring at me as a thin rivulet of blood dribbled down his neck from the wound on the back of his head. He pounded the driver's side window with the gasoline can, instantly causing a web of cracks. He moved in front of my car and pounded my hood. I flinched, flooring the accelerator. We jerked forward. He jumped back out of the way and hurled the can at the windshield. It landed with a heavy thump, causing the glass to craze. I could relate. I was feeling pretty crazed myself right now. I automatically hit the brake from the impact, pausing long enough for Jed to lunge at the hood. I swore and stepped on the accelerator pedal so hard I thought my foot would push through the floor. Jed tumbled back and we sped away as I heard the sound of sirens in the distance get increasingly louder—the most glorious sound I'd ever heard. Jed dashed back to Uncle George's car and grabbed his gun, but it was too late. The next second, in a blur of lights and sirens, four cop cars whizzed into the lot and cornered Jed.

I parked, trembling, and cast a look at Sam. "It's over."

He nodded, tears streaming down his face in relief.

Jake pulled up in his car and parked next to me. Adrian ran over to make sure we were okay.

I gingerly opened my door, afraid my cracked window would cave in. "How'd you get here so fast?"

Adrian flashed me a smile. "Your aunt Veronica called because she sensed something was wrong with Sam when she called him. She said he sounded terrified. She was concerned for his safety. We tracked his phone to the condo site. We were nearly here when Ashley called to let me know you were in trouble." He opened Sam's door and went to work getting him out of the handcuffs.

Jake ran over to me as I stumbled out of my car.

He threw an arm over my shoulders. "Are you okay?"

I nodded, still trembling. "I am now. Thank goodness for my family and friends and the guardian angels watching over me."

CHAPTER 28

I'd insisted to Adrian and Jake I was fine to drive back to Santa Sofia alone in my battered car. I really wasn't alone on the road because Jake followed closely behind me in his car. I was grateful to have some time alone to decompress. A million thoughts swirled around in my head and a host of emotions filled my heart. More than anything, I was still trembling from the shock that someone I'd known and trusted for years had murdered my father, my husband, and my aunt. The enormity of violence still stunned me. I also felt a tremendous relief that Jed Barnes, or Todd Keaton, or whatever name the poor excuse for a human being called himself today, would now be behind bars, no longer able to hurt anyone else.

Back in Santa Sofia, we all regrouped inside the police station, taking turns giving our statements to various officers and waiting for a debriefing. Sam followed Adrian down a hallway to be interviewed while the rest of us, Jake, Ashley, Uncle Bob, Aunt Veronica, and me, all sat around a large meeting room's oval conference table, speaking in hushed tones.

A few minutes later, Adrian joined us and pulled up a chair. "Sam rode back to the station with me and he shared some of what had been going on with him recently."

Uncle Bob cleared his throat. "Can we see him?"

Aunt Veronica, teary-eyed, asked, "Is he okay?"

Adrian smiled briefly. "You can talk to him after we've finished questioning him and he's signed a formal statement. Your lawyer is there with him. He's hanging in there. I think he's relieved to have it all over and out in the open."

A whimper emanated from Aunt Veronica. "He must be. I

can't imagine the stress he's been under. He must have been constantly living in fear, with Jed's threats of jail or hurting us. It breaks my heart he had to endure all that."

I reached across Ashley and patted my aunt's hand as Uncle Bob squeezed her shoulder.

Adrian offered her the box of tissues he grabbed from a small table behind him before he spoke. "I'll try to give you a chronological outline of events from what Sam told me. As most of you know, Sam went in search of his birth mother several months ago. Sam's parents had told him that his birth mother was Bob's sister, Jo. But Bob and Veronica had never given him many details about his adoption, other than his birth mother couldn't properly care for him because of her personal problems. Because of Jo's history of mental illness and addiction issues, they thought this was the best way to go."

My aunt and uncle, both with sad eyes and downturned mouths, nodded to confirm Adrian's explanation.

Adrian sat up straighter in his chair. "Sam didn't completely believe his parents' story that Jo Benning was his birth mother. He interpreted his parents' reticence to elaborate as meaning they'd concocted that story to make him feel like a blood relative. So he did one of those DNA tests to see if he could find conclusive evidence, one way or another, that Jo was his birth mother. As luck would have it, Jo had previously done a DNA test through the same company to trace her Benning family ancestral roots and made her results accessible to other database members. Sam's results came back showing he was related to Jo and he managed to find Jo through the site's database. He contacted her, without telling his parents. Sam and Jo met and started slowly to get to know each other. After a few meetings with Jo, Sam told his parents and they all got together and got along well for Sam's sake."

Uncle Bob chimed in. "I can provide the historical perspective about Jed Barnes, a.k.a. Todd Keaton, Jo's stepson. John hired Jed ten years ago."

I startled to attention. "I never knew it was my father who

hired him."

Uncle Bob turned to me. "Let me clarify that. It was our old nursery manager who hired Jed as a part-time nursery worker initially. Jed was a hard worker, came in early and stayed late. That got the attention of your father and why he then offered Jed a full-time job."

I sat back feeling slightly less guilty, by association, for my father hiring Jed and bringing him into our company.

Uncle Bob had a little coughing jag and took a sip of water from the bottle in front of him. "Anyway, Jed moved through the ranks of the nursery division quickly. All went well for several years and then things changed. He started to make a practice of going to happy hour after work and end up drunk off his ass. I witnessed this myself, but some of our other employees started to comment about it as well. Around the same time, Jed started asking for a raise, but the grief he'd cause at company events due to his drinking was affecting our employee morale. I told him he'd have to clean up his act first if he wanted a raise because I was getting complaints about his unprofessional behavior from other employees and their wives. About this time, he told me his wife had left him and he was taking it hard and drowning his sorrows. He claimed she wanted to take all he'd worked hard for, plus alimony. I felt sorry for him and warned him not to show up drunk at work or any company function. From that time on, he still worked hard, but he became moodier and complained about other employees, it seemed like, out of spite."

Adrian picked up the story again. "Sam told me that one day Jed saw Sam and Jo at a restaurant having lunch. Jed recognized Jo as his former stepmother. Jo told Sam that, after seeing them together, Jed had contacted her. Jed told her Sam was his long-lost brother, which, of course, is hogwash, since no relationship existed between them either through blood or marriage. Jo was divorced from Jed's father way before she was in a relationship with Randy Tuttle, Sam's late birth father.

"Jed's father, Tom Keaton, hadn't told Jed much about Jo's family. But when Jed was in jail for assault, he met George

Benning, the disowned Benning brother. George told Jed that the Bennings had disowned Jo, his former stepmother, too. George's only claim to fame was being from a rich family, but he was embittered and held a grudge about being disowned. He went so far as to accuse his older siblings, John and Bob, of intentionally swindling him and Jo out of their fair share of the family business."

Uncle Bob grumbled under his breath and started to cough again.

Adrian turned to Uncle Bob. "Again, this is hogwash since it was your father, Bob, who dictated that stipulation, correct?"

Uncle Bob responded to Adrian. "Yes, sir, you're totally correct. John and I had nothing to do with that. That was my father's doing, but, in his defense, he meant well. He was scared of, one, money ruining his two youngest children any further, and two, losing the hard-earned fortune he'd amassed over the years."

Adrian shook his head. "Regardless, when Jed found out Sam was Jo's son, he approached Sam and presented himself as his brother. Sam was young, impressionable, and an only child. Jed wooed Sam with his song and dance about being brothers. They hung out and did things like smoke weed and drink, and Sam was flattered by the attention, at first. But Jed was simply grooming Sam as his meal ticket, his bid for part of the Benning family fortune. He figured nurturing the adoration of a bona fide Benning would give him a leg up. Around this time, Jed's father, Tom Keaton, got up to his old shenanigans of starting arson fires and enlisted Jed's help. Jed brought Sam along, making Sam a witness to arson. But, despite not being directly involved, Jed told Sam he would tell the cops Sam started the fires if Sam told anyone and that Jed would hurt Sam's parents. When that fear tactic worked, Jed had Sam under his spell."

I interjected a thought. "I knew Todd Keaton and Tom Keaton sounded familiar. Their names triggered an association in my mind—Jed's pocket watch with TK engraved on it. I should have figured that out way sooner."

Ashley threw her arm over my shoulders. "You're much too hard on yourself. He goes by a different name now, making the connection even more obscure. How could you have possibly thought of the Keatons when you saw the watch since Blanche had just mentioned their names to you? Let alone make the connection between Jed Barnes and Todd Keaton?"

"But I'd Googled them. I should have remembered the initials on his watch." My voice sounded pathetically weak.

Ashley gave me a squeeze. "No time for thinking about that. Don't beat yourself up."

Adrian nodded. "Ashley's right. Great advice. Don't drive yourself crazy by second-guessing yourself now. You're not responsible for Jed's behavior."

I smiled. "Thanks, guys."

Adrian flashed me a grin. "Anyway, to continue, from what I can surmise, your father, John, discovered Jed had embezzled money. Jed had threatened Sam. If he didn't hand over his mother's password list, Jed would hurt his parents. Because of Sam's coercion, your father wanted to handle the delicate situation carefully. Apparently, your father shared this with Milo and, I'm assuming, based on Sam's comments, Milo offered to play a good big brother role to combat Jed's bad big brother role for Sam. John had an earlier meeting with Sam, telling him he might need to testify against Jed at one point, and if he cooperated with authorities, Sam wouldn't be in trouble. Jed followed Sam and overheard this. Milo was also going to meet John at the pier later that night. John confronted Jed about the embezzlement on the pier but still offered to settle it privately if Jed paid back the money he'd embezzled. Jed lost it when John added that he was firing him too. Jed punched John and John fell and hit his head. When Jed realized John had sustained a fatal injury, he panicked and dumped John's body over the railing into the ocean. Sam witnessed this all from beneath the pier and told Jo. Milo showed up for his meeting with John. He must have thought something was shady when he didn't see John but saw Jed leaving the pier."

I shuddered. "So Sam saw my father murdered. How awful."

Adrian grimaced. "It gets worse. Sam said Jed got drunk at your wedding and started to harass him, scaring Sam, who had kept your father's phone with him as collateral in case Jed hurt his folks. Sam thinks Jed must have been watching him and saw him give Milo your father's phone for safekeeping. Jed then lured Milo to the maze using Katie's phone with a made-up problem about Iris. Milo had probably become suspicious when he got Katie's text and hid your father's phone in the maze on the way to the meeting. Anyway, when Jed demanded your father's phone, Milo handed over his own phone. They argued and then Jed hit Milo with the rock he'd swiped from the Hidden Garden and then destroyed Milo's phone with it too. Sam had followed Milo into the maze, saw everything, and ended up becoming a witness to a second murder."

I was flabbergasted. "Oh my God, poor Sam!"

Ashley let out a whistle. "Holy cow! Poor Sam is right. But props for retrieving the phone."

I nodded. "But how on earth did Jed get Katie to give him her phone?"

Adrian slapped the table. "Because Jed's ex-wife was Katie's sister, Julie. Katie called me earlier today and told me Jed told her he'd hurt her sister if Katie told the police about him borrowing her phone. That's why she skipped town. She went to LA to talk to a lawyer and he advised her to contact us."

"Wow. Looks like Jed had issues with all his former in-laws, not just us."

Adrian nodded and turned to me. "Jed has also admitted that he made it seem like Milo took off and left you by planting Milo's boutonniere back at his town house, knowing it would look like Milo might still be alive. He also knew he could divert any suspicion from himself by leaving that note on Katie's door, implicating her as the author of both notes. Jed is just a bitter, bad seed and troublemaker, spreading his misery wherever he goes."

Jake rearranged himself in his seat. "If I may, I have some

other details from my own Sloan Mutual investigation that might be relevant, pieced together with some guesswork about what might have transpired. The altercation Tory heard in the maze the night of the firefighter fundraiser was Jed Barnes probably threatening his former stepmother, Jo, that he would report Sam as an arsonist if she dared to tell anyone about John's and Milo's murders, since he knew Sam had told Jo about them.

"When Tory went to Jo's fortune-teller booth, Jo saw it as an opportunity to give Tory the clue about going to the Secret Maze, hoping Tory would find John's phone there, not knowing Sam had already retrieved it."

An idea flashed in my mind. "So I bet it was Jed who peeked through the booth curtains when she was reading my fortune."

Jake nodded. "Probably. I'm sure he intimidated her by telling her he'd ruin her life and her son's by telling the police that her precious biological son, Sam, whom Jed had coerced into being an accessory and witness to arson, was actually the mastermind responsible for starting all of the recent wildfires. Jo also knew John's texts with Milo would let you know, Tory, that Milo was a good guy and was trying to help Sam, along with your father, out of the fix Jed had gotten him into with the arson, and exonerate Sam as being the main arsonist."

"Wow!" My mind was officially blown. "That's a lot to process. Do you really think that's how it all went down?"

Adrian stood up. "I think it's pretty close to accurate. I also have some more info on your uncle George. George saw his car in the breaking news stories on TV and hopped a bus out of town. We tracked him down. He'd rented his car to Jed. So, technically, he was telling the truth when he said it wasn't him following you and Sam that day, but he omitted to tell you he knew who it was, Jed Barnes. George has been arrested as an accessory."

I shook my head. "My own flesh and blood—once a weasel, always a weasel."

• • •

Many hours later, Ashley and I snaked our way along the streets of Santa Sofia in my car to Mariposa Drive, a.k.a. home sweet home. Aptly, it was Halloween night, and the day had certainly been full of tricks and treats. Jake volunteered to make another pizza run, joined by Adrian. Iris and Otis greeted Ashley and me at the door exuberantly, whether it was because they were happy to see me or hungry, it didn't matter, I was thrilled to cuddle with their warm little bodies again. I attended to their needs while Ashley uncorked a bottle of Fetzer Cabernet Sauvignon. She took out four of my favorite Crate and Barrel wineglasses and poured each of us a glass.

I took a long sip. "Ah. Do you think I should post an Instagram update about Milo? You know, like for closure?"

Adrian had told us Jed had confessed to all three murders, more or less. He claimed my father's death had been an accident. Milo's and Jo's deaths he called "provoked" because he said both told him they were going to call the police about my father's murder and, his words, "unfairly accuse him of murder." He had told Adrian where he had buried Milo—not far from the Hotel Santa Sofia condo site. A team had driven out earlier this evening and confirmed what appeared to be human remains.

Ashley clinked her glass against mine. "Honey, if it makes you happy, do it."

It only took me a few minutes to compose the short update. "How's this?"

> **Instagram Post** @ToryBenning: UPDATE: October 31. Milo Spinelli's remains have been found. His murderer has been apprehended. At this time this is all the information that is being released. Please respect our family as we go through this grieving process. Thank you all for your posts, shares, and kind words.

A playful knock on the door roused Iris from her bed to bark a noisy welcome. Ashley opened the door for Jake and Adrian, who not only bore pizzas and salads but also carried freezer bags, a clue predicting ice cream for dessert was in my future.

I ran my Instagram update by Adrian and he said it sounded fine. As soon as I posted it, a weight was lifted, and I could breathe easy again, although my heart still ached. As a close relative of all the victims, closure didn't bring back my loved ones, but knowing the motivations behind the actions that ended their lives and, more importantly, seeing justice prevail, offered me some solace.

We all encountered loss and change in our lives. They were part of life, but neither was ever easy. If we were lucky, we experienced love and hope in our lives too. Family and friends, new and old, helped us through painful times and transitions. I counted myself one of the fortunate ones. Despite profound loss, I had loving people who supported me as I navigated choppy waters. I had a wonderful job, whose mission was to promote nature and the therapeutic effects of exquisite flowers and plants. Benning Brothers would be saved from bankruptcy and a takeover, thanks to my father's insurance policy payout. I had a condo project to landscape, along with other prospects. I had a feeling those plantings weren't the only things that would grow and thrive in the future.

Tinkling sounds filled the air as Jake raised his wineglass to mine, Adrian pinged his glass with Ashley's, and we all clinked our glasses together with poignant smiles, toasting the end of one chapter and the beginning of another.

ABOUT THE AUTHOR

Judith Gonda is a mystery writer with a penchant for Pomeranians and puns, so it's no surprise they pop up in her amateur sleuth mysteries featuring landscape architect Tory Benning. As for the hot buttered lobster rolls, black tea, and California wine that also pepper her pages, they can be traced to her growing up in Connecticut, London, England, and the San Francisco Bay Area.

Trained as a Ph.D. psychologist, she taps the knowledge gained from her time spent conducting research at USC, heading a human resources department, and running focus groups as a jury consultant to inform her characters and plots.

Judith currently resides in Southern California with her architecture professor husband and her two rescue Poms/ surrogate daughters. Her two human daughters, a landscape architect and a TV writer, live nearby. All, along with crime stories in the news, have inspired her books.

To learn more about her upcoming releases, please visit her website at judithgonda.com.

www.ingramcontent.com/pod-product-compliance
Lightning Source LLC
LaVergne TN
LVHW100520110826
845146LV00002B/720
* 9 7 9 8 9 9 4 1 4 6 4 1 5 *